THE REVENGE PARADOX

To Meredith,
Enjoy !
Regina

Regina Buttner

Black Rose Writing | Texas

ISBN: 978-1-68513-496-9
PUBLISHED BY BLACK ROSE WRITING
www.blackrosewriting.com

Printed in the United States of America
Suggested Retail Price (SRP) $20.95

The Revenge Paradox is printed in Minion Pro

*As a planet-friendly publisher, Black Rose Writing does its best to eliminate unnecessary waste to reduce paper usage and energy costs, while never compromising the reading experience. As a result, the final word count vs. page count may not meet common expectations.

Praise for
The Revenge Paradox

"Be prepared for dark and turbulent suspense
in this gripping page-turner."
–A.J. McCarthy, bestselling author of
***the Charlie & Simm mystery* series**

"Inspired by real life events, *The Revenge Paradox* has the can't-look-away pull of the best true crime fiction. A fascinating story of retribution, redemption, and the long reach of mistakes made from hurt and anger. More than a tale of one family's unravelling, this is a story that sticks with you."
–Brooke L. French, author of
Inhuman Acts, The Carolina Variant,* and *Unnatural Intent

"Deception, family drama, and more secrets than I could count permeate the pages of this gritty portrait of an untapped slice of Americana. It definitely has me thinking twice about the people I invite into my life, and their true intentions."
–Dan McDowell, award-winning author of
When She Comes Knocking

THE REVENGE
PARADOX

"Revenge may be wicked, but it's natural."
–Becky Sharp in *Vanity Fair*

1

Rudy

The judge is smug and chinless in his shiny polyester robe, his comb-over plastered to his liver-spotted head. He removes his reading glasses and turns his gaze down to where I stand below him in front of the bench. "Young man, before we begin, I have one question for you. Are you certain you wish to represent yourself in this matter?"

I shoot virtual death rays back at him with my eyes. "Yes," I answer, then tack on a "Your Honor," to keep him happy. I've watched my share of *Hot Bench*, I know how a defendant is supposed to act. Mind your manners, answer the questions, drop the attitude.

"All right, then." Judge Hearn clears his phlegmy throat, replaces his glasses on his nose, and pops a Sucret from a small metal box that magically appears from within the folds of his robe. It's the evening session at my town's musty municipal courthouse, the place where they like to stash the pill-popping, alcoholic judges who just got out of detox. By the looks of Hearn's pasty complexion, he must've been sprung from the treatment center this morning.

The sky outside the narrow courtroom windows has faded to gray, and the fluorescent lights overhead are giving off an annoying buzz. Hearn peers at a document in his hand. "I see that your parents, Mitchell and Debra Bateman—"

"*Step*parents."

My interruption pisses the judge off, but he lets it slide because he's the one who screwed up. "Your stepparents," he continues, "over the course of the preceding year, have made repeated requests for you to either find gainful employment and begin contributing your fair share of the living expenses at 213 Crestview Drive, or move out of their home. Is that correct?"

The cherry Sucrets vapor wafts down to me, and I exhale through my nose to deflect the odor. "Yes, Your Honor."

"When this matter first came before me a few months ago, I instructed Mr. and Mrs. Bateman's attorney to draft an eviction order. You were given sixty days notice to leave, which is a reasonable timeframe, and in accordance with the law." Hearn pauses to allow my stepparents' sleazy lawyer to concur, then continues. "Despite the incentive of a considerable amount of cash from the Batemans, which was intended to aid you in your search for alternative living quarters, you still refused to leave."

Hearn slides his glasses down the bridge of his nose and stares down at me. "Mr. Hodgens, you are twenty-five years old, able-bodied and seemingly perfectly intelligent. Would you please explain to me why you refuse to find employment, and continue to test the limits of your stepparents' patience and goodwill? Do you not have any sense of gratitude or pride, young man?"

Finally, my chance to speak. I straighten my borrowed tie, mentally pumped for the speech I composed last night, with the help of an online thesaurus. "Your Honor, I *am* in fact employed, as an Amazon merchandise reseller. Or at least, I was until my car broke down and I couldn't get to the post office anymore. In the interim, I'm considering a sales position with a multi-national telemarketing company. It doesn't pay very well, but it's all I can find right now, the economy being what it is. My stepparents' hateful rhetoric and their constant threats of kicking me out of my home have caused me a great deal of angst, which has inhibited my ability to focus on my job search. The deadlines they've imposed have been far too stringent, and despite my earnest efforts, I've been unable to comply with their unreasonable demands."

Judge Hernia looks taken aback, no doubt surprised by my articulate defense. Over-educated men like him have an automatic prejudice against guys like me. My longish hair and scruffy chin strap beard may not convey the proper picture of courtroom decorum, but I do possess a brain.

Hernia rolls the stinky lozenge around in his mouth and regards me with curiosity. "That's a fine outfit you're wearing today, Rudolph," he says, trying for the intimidation factor by using my full first name. He observes the collared shirt and pants that I found on clearance at Target yesterday, along with a pair of dress shoes that are pinching the crap out of my toes. "I suggest you take advantage of your spiffy wardrobe, consult a bus schedule, and go out and apply for a job tomorrow, because I am issuing a warrant for your eviction."

I can hardly believe the words coming out of the judge's mouth. "You have fourteen days to comply with this order," he goes on, shifting his eyes back to the documents. "If you fail to vacate the Crestview Drive premises by noon on the tenth of August, you will be forcibly removed by local law enforcement."

You've got to be kidding me. I've been living with Mitchell and Debra since my mom died when I was in kindergarten. I grew up in the house on Crestview, it's the only home I can really remember. Two decades of manufactured family togetherness have been shot to hell now, all because my stepparents are too selfish and uncaring to cut me some slack and give me a little more time to get my shit together.

I turn and scan the courtroom until I spot them, seated in a middle row. Debra's dressed in her usual mousy getup of a plain blouse and shapeless slacks, and her hair looks like she's forgotten it's attached to her head. Mitchell's gripping her hand, a deepfake expression of concern on his face, and I can tell he's deliberately avoiding eye contact with me. He passes Debra a Kleenex, and I spy a glint of tears as she dips her head and quietly blows her nose. They've both been complete jerks to me lately, but Debra at least made an effort to stand up for me when Mitchell first started trying to kick me out of the house. *Get off your butt and get a job, Rudy!* he yelled at me every damn morning when he got home from his loser night job, pounding on my bedroom door, trying to roust me from my sleep. *Start paying your own way, or you're outta this house. Take a class, get some training. Do something, for godsakes!* Like it's so easy to just go out and do stuff like that when you've been an orphan your whole life, raised by people who aren't even related to you, being mocked by your schoolmates and marginalized by your teachers, and everyone else in the world. He has no idea what it's like to be me.

Hernia drones on about some legal technicality or other, but I completely block him out, lost in a seething cloud of disbelief. When my case is dismissed, I whirl around and scowl at Debra as she rises from her seat, clinging to Mitchell's arm. Her eyes meet mine for a second, then she averts her gaze. She picks her way along the row of chairs to the aisle, and as she and Mitchell exit the courtroom through the double doors at the back, he wraps a solicitous arm around his snowflake wife's waist. I know exactly what he'd say to me right now, if we were standing face-to-face: *It's for your own good, Rudy. Trust me, you'll see I'm right one day.* It's all I can do to keep myself from sprinting up behind him and smashing my fists into the back of his skull.

They deserve each other, those two. They're the perfect example of a co-dependent relationship—Mitchell the controlling caretaker who needs to be needed, Debra the wimpy little woman who can't think for herself. I have no patience whatsoever for that crap. Get a grip on yourselves already, people! Middle age is creeping up on them, but all they're doing is stagnating here in this dull suburb. I'd be out there making something of my life if I only could, but I've got too much baggage from my past to overcome. And now I'm homeless.

I storm out of the courtroom behind them, but a female police officer positioned outside the doors takes a quick sidestep and blocks my way. I back off—*no trouble here, lady*—and pretend I'm looking for someone else. My friend Fudgie is standing in the lobby, hands jammed into the pockets of his saggy cargo pants, a black knit hat holding down his cloud of frizzy hair. "Hey, man," he says as I stalk up to him. "Tough break."

I snort in response, and don't say anything as we head for the exit and go outside. Fudgie lags behind, talking to some girl he knows who's come to argue a traffic ticket. I make a beeline for his beater Nissan, which is parked under a tree in the far corner of the parking lot. The car's a rust bucket that failed its last state inspection because of the cracked windshield, so Fudgie had to buy a sticker from an obliging auto repair shop. I get in on the passenger's side and slam my door shut.

I can feel panic rising, my pulse thudding in my ears. Fudgie's vape pen is in the cupholder, so I take a couple hits to try and calm my jangling nerves. What am I supposed to do, now that the assholes have followed through on their endless threats and evicted me? I'll have to find a real job, some way, somehow. The telemarketing story I gave the judge was a fabrication, to make him think I'm an industrious and responsible person. I'd last about a minute as a telemarketer, since I can't stand talking to strangers. The part about my car was true, though. I'd been thinking about making the switch from Amazon reseller to DoorDash driver, so I could work less and make more money, but my vehicle had other ideas. A few weeks ago, the oil pump failed and the engine blew, so it's toast. Now I'm screwed.

Aaaaahhh! I'm shouting now, cursing Mitchell with every foul name I can think of. He's such an arrogant prick, thinks he's some sort of ultra-macho, ex-Army badass, when he's only a lowly security guard at the hospital. You'd think after all these years, he would've worked his way up to the day shift, so he could live like a normal person. Maybe he does it to avoid sleeping with Debra.

Fudgie yanks his door open and slides into the driver's seat. "Cute girl," he says with a quiet smile. "Got them digits." He doesn't seem to notice me sitting there seething. He fumbles with the keys and starts the car. The Nissan has a wonky clutch and we lurch out of the courthouse parking lot, Fudgie muttering a mechanical commentary under his breath.

An uneasy silence hangs over us as we swerve onto the main road. I stare through the windshield, feeling the tension building in my chest. My brain's on overload and my thoughts are jumping from one thing to the next. I've got to find a place to live. Then I need a car, a job, and a new life. Good luck with that last one. I was born a loser, and no matter where I go or what I do, I'm doomed to be a loser forever, just like my idiot stepfather. *FML.*

I slam my fist against the dashboard. I'm going to get back at Mitchell for what he's done to me. When I'm through with him and his dingbat wife, they'll both regret having been so hard-hearted. They'll wish they'd tried harder and been more understanding, and hadn't gone to such drastic lengths to humiliate me.

My anger flashes like a grease fire. I pound my fist over and over again, and Fudgie jerks his head toward me. "Whoa, man! Stop. You're gonna break my dash."

I can't stop. I keep slamming my fist into the dashboard until it starts to bow inward and a crack appears. *Fucking Mitchell. This is all his fault. He's going to be sorry for this—really, really sorry.*

Keeping one hand on the wheel, Fudgie reaches across and grabs my arm. "Quit it, Rudy! Calm down." The pressure of his fingers on my wrist hauls me back from the ledge I'm teetering on in my head. I yank my arm away from him and slouch down in my seat. The vape pen is still clutched in my other hand; I take another hit to compose myself, and rub my throbbing knuckles on my thigh. "I need to crash at your place again, bro," I say after a minute. "No way I'm going back to that hellhole with those fools tonight."

"No prob, man." Fudgie flicks me a sideways glance, making sure I've calmed down, then turns his eyes back to the road. "You can stay as long as you need to."

That's a huge relief to hear. Fudgie's a good friend, totally chill and non-judgmental. His apartment is a dump, but I don't have any other options at this point. I'll let a few days go by, then hit him up for the permanent use of his couch, since I don't have the means to rent a place of my own. I know he won't mind. Fudgie comes from a broken family himself, so he gets it. "You'll have to help me move out of the house, too," I tell him. "We should wait till the very last minute though, to piss Mitchell off."

"Sounds dope," Fudgie says with a grin. We've been friends for years, so he knows what my stepfather's like.

The weed kicks in and I begin to mellow out a little. More than anything, I need money to buy food and stuff, so I don't have to keep mooching off Fudgie. In my mind, I tick through the contents of my basement bedroom. The only thing I own of any value is my PlayStation, but that's my only form of entertainment, so selling it's out of the question.

I keep thinking hard, and then it hits me—the cellar closet! It's stuffed full of Mitchell's collection of guns and ammo, and these fancy knives he uses for hunting and camping. The closet door is padlocked, but I know where the key is hidden because I used to spy on Mitchell through a crack in my bedroom wall. As far as I know, he hasn't opened that closet in years, and he's so disorganized, I doubt he can even remember everything that's in there anymore. I could swipe a few items and sell them online, or take them to a pawn shop for quick cash, to tide me over till I find a job.

I'd rather not clue Fudgie in on my plan because he's a straight-arrow guy, and might not approve. "I'll give you some rent money," I tell him. "After I sell the stuff I don't feel like moving."

"Sweet," he says, wrestling with the sticky gearshift.

I agree—it *is* sweet. Easy money. And possibly an opportunity for some serious revenge.

2

Rudy

Fudgie borrows a pickup truck from one of his co-workers at Jiffy Lube, and we roll up to my stepparents' house at a quarter after eleven on the morning of August 10. They live in Centerport, a few miles outside the thriving metropolis of Syracuse, in central New York state. Centerport's an old Erie Canal town, about two hundred years past its prime. Mitchell and Debra's house is in Spruce Tree Knolls, a 1970s-era subdivision on the outskirts of town, filled with boxy split-levels and overgrown landscaping.

Crestview Drive is a curving, wooded loop that encircles the tract. As we round the bend by the house, I spot a police car parked down the street, partially hidden by the neighbors' scraggly bushes. The sight of it gets my back up. *Seriously?* Mitchell must have called them, in yet another show of force, meant to demonstrate his superiority over me. I roll my window down and give the cops a salty wave.

The house is an aging Colonial sitting at the top of a steep driveway that's a bitch to shovel in the winter. The roof's covered with scaly green mold, and the shingled siding has aged to a pukey greenish brown. A big picture window juts from the living room in the front, and as we pull in behind Mitchell's truck, I can see Debra peeking out at us from behind the curtains. It's Mitchell's weekend off, so I'm sure he's standing right there beside her, jumping with joy that he's finally getting rid of me.

I climb out of the pickup and stand waiting in the crumbling asphalt driveway until the storm door swings open and Debra appears on the front steps. She's got on a pair of pleated jeans and her fave Syracuse Orange basketball sweatshirt that's a million years old, and she looks like she's been crying. I want to punish her for the part she played in this debacle, so I don't even bother to greet her. I gesture impatiently, signaling for her to open the garage. She disappears back inside, and a moment later, one of the twin overhead doors begins to rise with a grinding squeal.

Fudgie follows me through the garage, squeezing between Mitchell's cluttered tool bench and Debra's Honda Civic. There's so much junk stored in here, there's no room for Mitch's truck. In the back of the garage is a musty staircase that leads to the basement. We clatter down the stairs and enter an unfinished room that's used for laundry and storage. Weaving our way around stacks of dusty plastic bins and cardboard boxes, we pass through another door into the finished side of the basement, where my bedroom is.

I used to have a real bedroom upstairs, across the hall from Debra and Mitchell's, but I moved into the cellar when I turned fifteen, so I could have more privacy. The space suited my needs. With an entire floor between us, my stepparents couldn't keep tabs on the music I listened to, or the TV shows I watched. Back then, I had a part-time foodservice job at the hospital, so I bought myself a used futon in fashionable basic black, and strung an old set of Christmas lights across the ceiling. When my Grampa died of a heart attack, I used the savings bond he left me to buy myself a brand-new TV and PlayStation, and passed my spare time playing *Grand Theft Auto* and *Call of Duty*, or bingeing episodes of *South Park* and *Family Guy*. A couple of guys I used to hang out with in high school would sometimes come over on the nights when Mitchell was working, and sneak beer in through the garage. Never had any girls over, though—I was way too nerdy and ugly for anyone to be interested in me. I don't think the guys even liked me that much, they were just using me for a place to get lit on the weekends.

But I did enjoy being able to come and go as I pleased, and wimpy Debra never bothered to check up on me.

It takes nearly an hour for Fudgie and me to pack my stuff and carry it outside. We have to go slow because Fudgie's got this disease that's deformed his legs. When we're done stowing everything in the bed of the pickup, I remember my mountain bike, a green Cannondale that my Grandma Nan gave me on my eighteenth birthday. I haven't ridden it in years, but it's probably still worth something, and I might need to sell it. I wheel the bike out of the garage and hoist it into the pickup by myself, then tell Fudgie to wait while I go back down cellar to make sure I didn't miss anything.

My real purpose is to get into the closet where Mitchell keeps his firearms. The key is hanging on a nail beneath the staircase that leads up to the kitchen. I take it from its hiding place, then slide a storage bin out of the way, insert the key into the padlock, and swing the closet door open. The shelves are crammed with all the he-man crap Mitchell's been hanging onto since his Army days: survival knives, boxes of cartridges, scopes, holsters, camo-patterned clothing. His handguns are on the middle shelf, lined up in a metal rack. The last time I snooped in here, I was too nervous to touch the guns; but in anticipation of this golden moment, I've been watching a YouTube channel hosted by an ass-kicking firearms expert from Tennessee, so I know what I'm doing this time. I reach for the biggest gun in the rack, hold it up to the light and examine it. From the videos I watched, I'm able to identify it as a 9-millimeter Glock 17, and I know how to check if it's loaded. Pulling the slide back, I verify that the chamber's empty.

The gun is cold and heavy in my hand. I curl my fingers around the grip and place the tip of my index finger on the trigger, enjoying the feeling of power it gives me. But my heart's slamming against my chest, and I don't dare linger down here much longer. From outside, I can faintly hear Mitchell calling to Fudgie, asking where I am. I push back the sleeve of my jacket to check the time on my watch, and old Timex that used to belong to Grampa. I've got to get out of here before Mitchell comes after me, telling me it's past noon and I'm trespassing.

I close the closet and replace the padlock and the key, then slip the Glock into the side pocket of my windbreaker, which I wore for this specific purpose. The gun barely fits in the pocket, so I shove my hand in to prevent it from falling out, then hustle up the basement stairs and go back out to the driveway. Mitchell's waiting beside the borrowed pickup. His crewcut looks fresh, as though he ran out earlier this morning and got it touched up for this momentous occasion. He scowls at my Nirvana t-shirt, then taps his fingers on his crossed arms. "Time for you to get going."

"*Jawohl!*" I say in German, giving him a heil Hitler salute with my free arm, to show him what a poser he is. From the corner of my eye, I see Debra coming at me, her arms outstretched. She plops a teary kiss on my cheek, tells me she loves me and she'll always be here for me, yadda yadda—the usual drippy stuff she's constantly spouting. I pull away from her, afraid she'll feel the gun in my pocket, and her face falls in disappointment. It makes me feel bad for a second, but I shrug it off.

My little brown cocker spaniel, Cocoa, is pawing at my shins, a gummy piece of rawhide drooping from her mouth. I can't take her with me because Fudgie's landlord doesn't allow dogs. She's the only member of this family that I'm going to miss. As I squat down to pet her, the Glock almost slips out of my pocket, and sweat prickles my forehead. I'm gripping the hidden gun tightly and rubbing my cheek against the top of Cocoa's silky head, when suddenly Mitchell's there, pulling the dog away from me. "Time to go, Rudy. *Now.*"

I stand up and glare at him. "You don't need to be a dick about it. I'm going, okay?"

Mitchell puffs up with self-righteous anger. Thrusting Cocoa into Debra's arms, he takes a threatening step toward me. "Get off my property right now, or I'm calling the police."

Hostility flames up in me. I'm not much of a fighter, but when someone sets me off, it's like I can't hear or see straight, and all I want to do is lash out. For a fleeting moment, I consider pulling the gun out and threatening Mitchell with it—but that would be a total bonehead move, especially since it's not even loaded. Instead, I raise my chin and ball my free fist. "The police are already here, asshole. You go right ahead and call them over."

Debra lets out a little cry. She puts the dog down and flutters her hands around. "No, Rudy! Please, just go. *Please.*"

Ignoring her, I make a move toward Mitchell, but Fudgie manages to deftly insert himself between us, despite his limp. In the background, I hear a car door slam—probably the cops, eager for an excuse to intervene. "Let it go, Rude," Fudgie says, splaying his hand on my chest. "We gotta roll."

Fudgie's right. The last thing I need is for the police to come walking up, when I've got a stolen handgun concealed in my jacket. Debra tugs on Mitchell's sleeve, and I can see his anger deflating. We both take a step back. Fudgie slams the tailgate closed and we climb into the pickup, but then Mitchell marches up to my open window and holds his hand out. "Give me your house key."

I'm one step ahead of the fool. I hide a smirk as I dig into my jeans pocket and hand the key over, because I had a copy made at Lowe's last week. Mitchell takes the key, then steps back to Debra's side and places his arm around her shoulders. She's crying again, but I don't care anymore. As Fudgie drives away, I raise my hand in fond farewell to my stepparents, then lower it and flip them the bird.

·　　·　　·　　·　　·

Fudgie lives in an older, industrial part of Syracuse where the Polish and Italian immigrants settled in droves, back in the early 1900s. He likes to tell people he moved here to skew the demographics with his mixed-race background, but the real draw was the cheap rent and the local electric company, which supposedly charges the lowest rates in the country.

I've known Fudgie since I was a teenager, when we both worked in the hospital kitchen. Like me, he had issues with his mother and father, so he ended up being raised by his grandparents. His granny badgers him to come over for dinner all the time, and always sends him home with buckets of homemade food; but for the most part, Fudgie's self-sufficient. He works full time, doing oil changes and state inspections at Jiffy Lube. He's trying to save up money so he can study business at Bryant & Stratton, and become a store manager one day.

Fudgie's got a tiny one-bedroom apartment on the ground floor of a multi-family house that's sandwiched between identical dilapidated two-and-a-half-story houses, each with a row of battered metal mailboxes nailed to the porch rail, and the original venetian blinds hanging crookedly in the windows. He backs the pickup down the narrow driveway, and stops in the paved parking area behind the house. The day has turned warmer and it looks like it might rain, which isn't unusual for Syracuse. Before we start unloading, I need to do something with the gun. Like I said, Fudgie's a good friend, and I don't want to implicate him in any of my misdeeds. He's a peacemaker who wouldn't hurt a mosquito, and if he finds out about the theft, he might make a stink about it. He'd insist on me returning the gun to Mitchell immediately—which simply isn't an option, because I need the money so bad.

Fudgie walks around to the back of the truck and lowers the tailgate. I can't lift the bike off without the Glock falling out of my pocket, so I carefully remove my windbreaker and ball it around the gun, then set the bundle on the passenger's seat. I leave the bike propped against the side of the truck while Fudgie and I make a quick job of unloading, carrying my belongings into the apartment, and dumping everything in the middle of the living room. The only thing left to bring inside is the metal futon frame and mattress. "I already got a couch," Fudgie says, eyeing it doubtfully. "It might not fit."

"Fudgeman," I say, "this futon is essential to our gaming needs. We'll each have our own couch to sit on while we play *Halo* and *Need for Speed*. It'll give us elbow room, y'know? Personal space. Plus, I need it to sleep on."

"Huh." Fudgie squints his eyes, considering the possibilities. "Okay, we can make it work." We haul the futon inside and position it at a right angle to Fudgie's lumpy couch. We'll have to squash ourselves against the wall every time we need to get up to use the bathroom, but my new roommate isn't concerned. "Cool," he says, as he admires the new setup, then he turns to me. "You hungry? We still got those leftovers from Papa Johns."

I polish off my share of last night's pizza in hurried gulps, because I'm getting worried about the gun sitting out in the truck. Between bites of cheese and pepperoni, Fudgie says he's got to return the pickup to his co-worker soon. "Guy lives only a block away, so you might as well stay here and get your stuff organized, and I'll walk back. Just gimme a few bucks to pay him for the gas we used."

I fork over some of my dwindling supply of cash, and we both go outside. I grab my bundled jacket from the truck and tuck it beneath my arm, then retrieve my bike from where I left it. "You can store it in the shed," Fudgie says, pointing his thumb at a falling-down wooden structure sagging against the back fence.

Perfect. I wheel the bike into the shed and lock it to an old lawnmower that won't be seeing any further use because the entire backyard's been paved over with asphalt. I pretend to fiddle with the bike until Fudgie drives off, then look around for someplace to stash the gun. Along the rear wall of the shed is a shelf holding containers of motor oil and engine coolant, and on the floor beneath it is a wooden crate filled with empty soda cans and greasy rags. I wrap the gun in a rag, place it at the bottom of the crate, and pile the cans on top of it. It's a good enough hiding place for the time being, until I figure out how I'm going to sell it.

My phone vibrates in the back pocket of my jeans. I pull it out and my stomach lurches when I see it's Mitchell calling. I have no desire to talk to him, but it's probably not a good idea to piss him off when I'm in possession of his stolen property. I swipe the screen and say a tentative hello.

"What is wrong with you, Rudy?" Mitchell shouts. "Did you think I'd be too blind to notice what you did?"

I'm instantly petrified—*he knows I stole the gun!* The cops are on their way, ready to drag me to the slammer. I blurt the first response that pops into my head: "I have no idea what you're talking about."

"You stole my drill, you stinking thief!"

His *drill?* Now I honestly don't know what he's talking about. "Your what?"

"You heard me! You took my brand-new cordless DeWalt when you moved your stuff out this morning. If you don't bring it back, and I mean *now*, you're going to be in serious trouble."

Screwdrivers challenge me, so what the heck would I want with one of his complicated power tools? "I did nothing of the sort. I'm afraid you are mistaken."

Mitchell sounds like he's spluttering all over his phone. "You're really a piece of work, Rudy. It was in a big black case, sitting on the tool bench in the garage. One of you guys grabbed it when I wasn't looking. I'll bet you got that punk friend of yours to do your dirty work for you, didn't you?"

Now, that makes me mad, hearing Fudgie's character maligned. "Listen carefully, *Mitchell*," I say, dragging his name out with disdain. "I did not take your drill, or anything else from the garage, besides my bike. You can drive over here right now and search my entire apartment. I guarantee you won't find anything that belongs to you." It's technically a true statement—the gun I stole from him is now *outside* the apartment. "Bring the police if you want, I don't care." That last statement is a tad risky, but I'm gambling he won't call my bluff.

He doesn't. Mitchell's silent for a moment, then says, "You swear you didn't take it."

It isn't a question, but I answer anyways. "No, I did not."

I hear him sigh. "I guess Debra must have put it away somewhere, and didn't tell me." No *sorry, my mistake*, or anything at all like an apology. God forbid the almighty Mitchell should ever admit he's wrong. Screw him, anyway. He's gonna get what he's got coming, and soon. "This conversation is over," I say, and hang up.

•   •   •   •   •

Fudgie returns a short while later, but then he has to leave again, to go give his grandparents a hand with something at their house. I spend the rest of the afternoon sorting through my things and planning my next steps. Despite the masterful way in which I handled the phone call from Mitchell, I have to admit I'm rattled. I need to sell that gun, asap, before he discovers it's missing and sends the cops over here. Selling it is going to be a challenge, though. After doing my research, I've learned that New York is really strict about gun sales, so I'll have to sell it to some hood on the street. But there's a hitch—I don't know too many of those kinds of people. None, in fact.

After racking my brain awhile, I think I've come up with a solid plan. There's this guy I used to know when I was a kid, who lived in the apartments on the other side of the woods behind my stepparents' house. He grew up to have what I'd politely describe as *unlawful tendencies*. If I can track him down, I think he just might be the sort of person who'd be in the market for a stolen Glock.

With the problem of the gun solved, I turn my thoughts in a more creative direction. Mitchell has no idea of the vengeance I'm going to unleash on him and Debra, when they least expect it. My mind buzzes with all kinds of wild ideas. I picture myself doing a drive-by shooting on their house, and I laugh out loud at the thought. Unfortunately, it's a foolish notion—I'd be the number one suspect, since my eviction is part of the public record, and my motive would be glaringly obvious. I've got to be more subtle than that.

I decide a prolonged campaign of domestic terrorism will be much more effective, not to mention more enjoyable. I can lie in wait for Mitchell, and sabotage his every move. Toying with Debra is going to be especially entertaining, since she's so easily frightened. With her home alone so often when Mitchell's at work, I can sneak back to the house and wreak all sorts of havoc late at night, and scare the living crap out of her. I laugh out loud again, imagining the range of possibilities. This is gonna be the most fun I've had in a long, long time.

3

Mitchell

Two days later

I'm a security guard at University Hospital, on the 6 p.m. to 6 a.m. shift, with alternating weekends. I pull a lot of overtime because my department's chronically understaffed. I've been sleep deprived for years, but it doesn't bother me much because when I sleep, I dream. I'm haunted by the things I experienced during my tour in Iraq, at the height of the Global War on Terror. That, and the death of my first wife. It's a wonder I ever sleep at all.

When I get home from my shift on Monday morning, I follow my usual routine—kick my boots off and hang my coat up in the mudroom, then call hello to Debra in the downstairs room she's been using as a home office since the pandemic. I grab a bottled water from the fridge, and head upstairs to jump in the shower. As I'm getting undressed, something out the bathroom window catches my eye, and I lean on the windowsill to get a better look.

Last night was clear and cool, so the grass out back is coated with a heavy layer of dew. There are two sets of footprints between the patio and the edge of the woods, one of them human, and the other one the dog's. It seems odd to me, since Debra never sets foot in the yard when she lets Cocoa out, so I go back downstairs to investigate. The vertical blinds on the sliding door are partially closed, so I pull them back all the way. My gaze is immediately drawn to two distinct handprints on the outside of the glass, right about eye level, and I feel the hair rise on the back of my neck. *Someone tried to get in last night.*

I holler for Debra, and she hurries from her office with her headset dangling. "What's wrong, Mitch?"

"Did you go outside with the dog this morning?"

"No, I haven't been outside at all. Why?"

"There are footprints in the backyard." I don't mention the handprints right away because I know Debra gets nervous when she's home alone, and I don't want to scare her. "Did you hear anything during the night? Any strange noises?"

Debra goes over to the slider and looks out at the yard, then her focus shifts to the glass in front of her, and she gasps when she sees the handprints. "Oh my gosh!" She turns back to me, her eyes round with alarm. "I was at my church meeting till nine. I heard a noise out back around midnight, but I thought it was just the wind. I guess I should have gotten up and turned the floodlight on, to scare them off. Who do you think it was?"

My money's on Rudy. I'm certain the little jerk lied about stealing my power drill, and skulking around in the middle of the night, trying to scare his poor stepmother, is exactly the sort of obnoxious thing he'd do. He wants to get back at us for kicking him out, and in his immature little mind, he must have thought this would be a good way to do it.

But I can't say that to my soft-hearted wife, who has always been quick to jump to Rudy's defense. "I heard there are some teenagers over at those low-rent apartments behind us, who've been causing trouble in the neighborhood," I say. "It was probably them."

Debra looks concerned. "Should we report it to the police?"

I'd way rather deal with Rudy myself, but I don't want to upset Debra. "Yeah, I'll report it, but I'll do it later. I gotta go to Lowe's first. I'm gonna put an extra lock on the slider, in case those hooligans come around again." I'm also going to pick up a set of deadbolts for the exterior doors, and a new power drill to replace the one that's gone missing. Even though Rudy gave me his house key back, I'd rather be safe than sorry. I had meant to change the locks after he moved out on

Saturday, but I got called into work that afternoon, to cover for someone who was out sick, and I didn't get around to it.

Debra twists her hands together and I feel bad for scaring her. I hate leaving her alone at night, but I don't have much choice. My supervisor's a control freak with an authority complex, and he's had it in for me ever since he turned down my request to switch to the day shift, and I accused him of playing favorites with the scheduling. He said it wasn't my place to question him, and he wrote me up for insubordination. I suppose it's just as well that I didn't switch to days, because I would've had a tough time adjusting. If I'm going to be awake all night anyway, I'd rather be working than at home, tossing and turning in bed, with my wife asking me what's wrong every five minutes.

I give Debra a quick hug. "Don't worry, hon. You know how teenagers are. I'm sure they were just out goofing around, and won't come back."

She sighs, still looking worried. "I hope you're right."

Before I leave for the store, I search my messy workbench one more time, but I still can't find my drill, which annoys the hell out of me. Rudy's got a lot of damned nerve, thinking he can steal from me, then deny it with a bald-faced lie. If he pulls any more of this childish nonsense, he's going to wish he'd thought twice about it.

•   •   •   •   •

After a quick trip to Lowe's, I install brand new deadbolts on all the doors, and put up a security bar on the slider in the kitchen, to prevent it from being jimmied from the outside. When I'm done, I put my tools away in the garage. I'm getting a headache because I've been awake far longer than I usually am after a shift, but I still need to double check that the casement windows in the laundry room and Rudy's former bedroom are securely latched. I carry my stepladder down to the basement, where everything appears to be in order. Time for me to go to bed.

As I'm carrying the stepladder back through the laundry room, a rectangle of light appears at the top of the staircase that leads up to the kitchen, and Debra calls to me. "What are you doing down there, Mitch?"

"Nothing, honey. Just making sure everything's locked up tight."

She starts down the stairs, a laundry basket balanced on her hip. "I wanted to put a load in the washer. I won't be in your way, will I?"

Typical Deb, always worried she's going to inconvenience someone. "No, you're fine. I'm all done here. Gonna head up to bed in a minute." She comes down the stairs and I watch as she stuffs an armload of towels into the washing machine and measures out detergent. Her movements are slow and deliberate, as though she's very tired. The noises she heard last night probably had her lying awake for hours, wondering if she should call the police, but afraid of raising a false alarm. She didn't even text me, said she didn't want to bother me at work.

Don't get me wrong here—Debra's timid nature can be aggravating at times, but I try to overlook it because I owe her so much. She closes the lid on the washer and twists the dial, and a lock of her brown hair falls over her face as she bends down for the laundry basket. I step closer and brush her hair behind her ear, and drop a quick kiss on her cheek. She dips her head with a shy smile, then looks up at me with a worried expression. "Are you sure those deadbolts are really necessary? I don't want Rudy to think we don't trust him, or to feel unwelcome when he comes over."

I don't trust him, and I'm certainly not expecting him to pop in for a family dinner with us any time soon, but that's a conversation for another day. "It's just a precaution," I say. "It's got nothing to do with Rudy."

"Have you contacted the police, like you said you would?"

"Not yet, but I will." This isn't entirely true. I've already made up my mind—I'm only getting the police involved if Rudy tries any more of his stupid stunts. I don't want the cops coming to the house and discussing my suspicions about him in front of Debra, when I know what a soft spot she has for him. Rudy treated her badly before he left, and I don't want her getting hurt anymore.

I should explain here that Debra and I aren't technically Rudy's stepparents, even though we've always referred to ourselves that way. It's a long story. I was married once before, about twenty years ago, to a bright and beautiful girl named Ann Marie. I know it's a cliché, but she was the one true love of my life. We dated for a short time in high school, until a fast-talking bad boy with a motorcycle stole her away from me. Our breakup was the main reason why I joined the Army right after graduation. Through letters from home, I heard the creep got her pregnant, then skipped town when she told him she wanted to keep the baby.

Ann Marie is Rudy's mother. She dropped out of school before he was born, and her parents helped her raise him for the first few years, until I was discharged from the service and we got back together. She'd grown up a lot by then, and was eager to settle down with me and become a family. We married after dating for only a few months, because we were crazy about each other, and didn't see any reason to wait. I felt like a man who'd been blessed. I had a loving new wife and an adorable little boy, and the dark cloud of my wartime memories slowly began to lift.

Then my world fell apart. On her way home from work one night, Ann Marie was killed in a car accident. In one instant, I went from happily married man to single father of a child who wasn't legally mine, and I was entirely unequipped for the role. Ann Marie's parents offered to take Rudy in, but they were both suffering from health problems, and I decided it was too much for them to handle. Besides, I felt it was my duty to continue caring for the child of the woman I loved, rather than slough him off onto someone else. It seemed like the right thing to do, so that's what I did.

In the months following Ann Marie's death, I was overwhelmed by my loss, and the strain of raising Rudy on my own. Debra saved my life when she married me a year later, and jumped right into becoming a mother to him. She had plenty of reasons to reject the child I brought into our marriage, but she found a way to get over my baggage, and embraced Rudy with her whole heart. She deserved far better from him than what she ended up getting. Frankly, so did I.

I did my darnedest to take good care of Rudy, and went out of my way to treat him like he was my own natural son. Debra and I had always intended to formally adopt him, but then his deadbeat father showed up after years of being gone, and refused to give up his parental rights. The schmuck got away with a bare minimum of effort. He made his child support payments every month and visited Rudy a few times a year, which was enough to satisfy Family Court that he was maintaining ties with his son. He'd show up on random Saturdays and take Rudy out for a hamburger or a trip to the science museum, then drop him off home and disappear again.

The lack of concern from his dad left a huge chip on Rudy's shoulder, and as he grew older, he blamed it all on me. I tried explaining to him that adoption wasn't legally possible as long as his father was still in the picture, but Rudy didn't want to hear it. I even petitioned the court for temporary legal guardianship during one of his father's prolonged disappearances, but that wasn't good enough for Rudy, who argued the "temporary" part of it was proof that I'd never really wanted him. He threw a fit and announced he didn't want anything to do with me and Debra anymore, then packed up all the things in his bedroom and moved himself into the basement, where he stayed for the next ten years.

Rudy's attitude grated on me, when I'd been trying so hard to be a good parent to him, and my resentment deepened as time went on. The kid had absolutely no respect or gratitude for anything we did for him. Through my contacts at work, I got him an after-school job in the hospital's foodservice department, which paid pretty well for a teenager with no experience. Rudy started out as a competent worker, but after a few months, he began showing up late and calling in sick whenever he felt like it. He eventually got fired, a consequence he somehow twisted around and pinned on me, as if I'd had something to do with it.

I made it clear that I expected him to find another job in a timely manner, but he dragged his feet about applying anywhere, saying no one would want to hire him because of the poor reference. His friend with the gimpy legs started coming over a lot, and the two of them would hole up for hours in the basement, playing their mindless video games. Other than that, Rudy didn't seem to have any friends, and he rarely stirred from home, except to go to school. He never lifted a finger to help out around the house either, but Debra insisted on paying him a weekly allowance anyway, "to boost his self-esteem." Something she read about in a magazine, I suppose. The very idea of giving Rudy money for nothing irked me. I tried explaining that we were sending him the wrong message, but it always ended up in an argument. Deb's a crier when she gets upset, so I finally went along with her to keep the peace.

As time went on, Rudy turned into a lazy, mouthy bum. I'm not one to tolerate nonsense like that, so I was all for taking a tough approach with him. But Debra disagreed. She thought we needed to show him more compassion. She seemed to think that throwing love at him would somehow magically transform him into a decent person, but in reality, she created an entitled monster who knew how to manipulate her to get his own way.

The downhill slide worsened over the course of Rudy's junior and senior years. He'd shown an interest in the advanced STEM classes his school offered, so I'd been volunteering for all the overtime I could get, and was socking the extra income away in a college fund for him. He had the potential to get into a good college, but he lacked motivation. His grades went steadily down the tubes, to the point where his guidance counselor advised him that his best option was to enroll at Onondaga Community College for a semester or two, and see how he did.

I never went to college myself, so I was proud of him anyway. He registered for a full load of math and science classes, and bought his own car with the few thousand dollars his grandfather on his mom's side left him when he passed away. It seemed like Rudy was on track for a fresh start, but after the first few weeks of college, he began sleeping through his alarm in the morning, and Debra had to go down cellar to wake him so he wouldn't miss his early classes. His grades for the fall semester were straight C's. He tried to hide it from me, but since I was paying his way, I made him show me his grade reports. In the spring semester, they sank even lower. I sat him down for a serious talk, and told him I wouldn't continue supporting him if he kept slacking off. He said he was sorry for not making more of an effort, and promised to do better.

But in the middle of his second year, he withdrew from school without giving us any warning at all. I was furious. "I invest my time and effort supporting you," I yelled when he broke the news, "and you go and repay me by *quitting?*" I demanded he get a full-time job immediately, and start paying us rent. Trying to peddle someone else's junk on the internet didn't count as employment in my book, and it definitely wasn't enough to cover his living expenses.

In spite of my warnings, he kept at it, and gave me one excuse after the next for why he couldn't pay his rent—seller fees, overhead costs, business taxes, you name it. We pleaded with him to find a real job, and when he didn't, I threatened to kick him out, which threw Deb into a tizzy. She sobbed about how "unfair" I was being, and got so bent out of shape that I agreed to a compromise, and gave Rudy the remainder of the money in his college fund, to help him get set up in his own place. But instead of leasing an apartment, he used the money to buy more inventory for his useless business. When I found out what he'd done, I threw him out on the spot. But a few weeks later, he came slinking back, claiming he'd had an epiphany, and was ready to get his life on track.

Debra begged me to give him another chance. She'd become emotionally fragile from all the turmoil in our home, so I caved in to her, to avoid any further hysterics. What a sucker I was. Before too long, Rudy slid right back into his shiftless ways, and refused to contribute a single cent toward the household expenses. Looking back, I realize I allowed things to drag on far longer than I should have, because I was afraid of upsetting my wife. A couple more tense years passed, during which we managed to maintain a shaky coexistence with Rudy. I finally got fed up with walking on eggshells all the time, so I went to see a lawyer, to find out what my options were. We could take Rudy to court and have him evicted, the lawyer told me, as long as we gave him proper written notice, and allowed him adequate time to move out. By that point, eviction seemed like the only choice.

* * * * *

Debra places the empty laundry basket on top of the washing machine and starts up the stairs to the kitchen. I'm about to follow her, then pause a second to look over my shoulder at the closet in the back corner of the laundry room. The door is closed tight, the padlock in place. *Good*, I think. *No worries there.* Rudy doesn't have any idea what's in that closet anyway, since I've always been so careful about it. When he was little, I told him it contained bottles of powerful insecticide and rat poison that needed to stay locked up, and he believed me. I always keep a loaded handgun in the drawer of my nightstand anyway, just in case, so the rest of my guns can stay right where they are for now, safe and secure under lock and key. I flip the cellar lights off and follow my wife up the stairs.

4

Debra

After Mitch has gone up to bed, I go into my office, close the door and try calling Rudy. As usual, he doesn't pick up, so I have to leave yet another voicemail. "Hi honey, it's me again. Just calling to check in. Hope you're all settled in your new place and, um…" There isn't much else for me to say, since he hasn't responded to the half dozen text and voice messages I left for him over the weekend. "Please call me back when you can," I go on, trying to keep my voice bright. "I'd really like to talk to you, and make sure everything's going okay. Love you. Bye."

My heart is heavy as I disconnect the call. I'm not expecting Rudy to mend fences with Mitch right away, but it hurts that he won't talk to me. I'm not the bad guy here, after all—it was Mitch who consulted an attorney, and made the final decision to take legal action against Rudy. I was unsure about the eviction, but Mitch pressured me to go along with him, like he always does. My husband is a formidable opponent when he gets his mind set on something, and pushing back against him is almost always futile.

I wander back out to the kitchen and microwave a cup of leftover coffee, then sit down to drink it at the table, in the chair facing the backyard. The sky above the trees has clouded over, and the glass of the slider is streaked where I wiped those creepy handprints away earlier. Before he went upstairs, Mitch told me he'd picked up an open shift for this evening, and I shiver at the prospect of the lonely night ahead of me. I might have to call my sister before I go to bed, which will be a welcome distraction. Denise always has plenty to prattle on about, concerning her family or the latest drama at the doctor's office where she works. And when Mitch gets up later this afternoon, I'll be sure to keep my chin up in front of him, because I don't want him worrying about me when he's at work. He's extremely conscientious about his job and he needs to stay focused, so his pushy supervisor doesn't find any more infractions to write him up about.

Mitch has been a hard-working guy for as long as I've known him, which is most of my life. We grew up on the same street in Fairmount, a middle-class suburb west of Syracuse. Even though he was two grades ahead of me in school, I had a huge crush on him for years. He was handsome and athletic without being conceited about it, and he was always polite and friendly to everyone he met. I used to doodle his name all over my notebooks, then scratch it out with heavy jabs of my pen, so no one would see it.

From the fifth grade on, I was best friends with a girl called Ann Marie whose family moved in three houses down from mine. She was prettier and more outgoing than I was, and the two of us would sit as close to Mitch as we could on the school bus, hoping to catch his eye. Later on in high school, Ann Marie used her daring and charm to push herself into Mitch's orbit every chance she got, often dragging me along with her. Neither of us seriously believed we stood a chance with him, but we kept on trying. It was a game we played without any expectation of success.

But guess what? Ann Marie won. I can't say I didn't expect it. I was lanky, quiet and studious, while she was curvy and sassy in a way that appealed to the boys. When Mitch asked her out when we were sophomores and he was a senior, she basically dropped me as a friend. I was demoted to the status of dreary wallflower, and a few months later, I watched in silent indignation as Ann Marie chewed up Mitch's earnest devotion and spit it out in favor of a pot-dealing, motorcycle-riding lout named Leo Moore, commonly known as Morbid within his older circle of friends. At the end of the school year, Ann Marie rode off into the sunset on the back of Morbid's Harley, while brokenhearted Mitch went down to the local Army recruiting office and enlisted. I didn't feel the least bit sorry for her later that summer, when I heard she'd gotten pregnant. After the heartless way she'd dumped Mitch, I thought she deserved whatever bad luck came her way.

I read an article once, about how we should accept the misfortunes life sends us, and try to transform them into something positive. Ann Marie took the social stigma of her teenage pregnancy in stride, and in her usual determined manner, she got what she wanted in the end. When Mitch came home from the service a few years later, he and Ann Marie reunited, their romance bursting back into bloom as if nothing had ever happened. Before I knew it, they were married, and Mitch had accepted Rudy as if he was his own.

Bad luck has a tendency to recur before it finally turns. Two weeks shy of their one-year anniversary, Ann Marie died in a tragic accident, leaving Mitch grief-stricken and bewildered. But in a welcome twist of fate, the universe finally opened his eyes to me, allowing me to step in and help him put the pieces of his life back together. For me, it was a long-overdue dream come true.

Syracuse isn't that big of a city, so Mitch and I eventually crossed paths several months after Ann Marie's death. Denise and her husband had invited me to go with them to a fundraiser for the Wounded Warriors at the American Legion post in Centerport, and to my pleasant surprise, I spotted Mitch there, tending the smoky barbecue pit.

I'd been praying every night for heaven to send a nice young man my way, because I was striking out at finding a boyfriend. I wasn't asking for movie star good looks or tons of money, which didn't matter much to me. All I wanted was a decent, honest guy who was ready to commit to marriage and a family. Someone like Mitchell Bateman. When he took a break from sweating over the grill and sat down at a nearby table with a plate of chicken and a cold Bud Light, I worked up the nerve to go over and say hi.

Mitch was as polite as I remembered him, though understandably more subdued. I asked him about Rudy—a hopefully neutral subject that wouldn't trigger sad memories—but talking about his stepson didn't seem to cheer him up any. By the look on his face, I could tell he was still reeling from Ann Marie's death, so I tried to steer the conversation in a more cheerful direction. We traded opinions on Coach Boeheim and the Syracuse Orange, and discussed the musical acts that were scheduled to play at the upcoming New York State Fair. After we'd been chatting a while, I could see him loosening up.

I got the sense that he didn't have anyone who was willing to listen to him about his current troubles, so I was more than happy to fill that need. Over the course of an hour, I coaxed him into sharing a good deal of personal information with me. He told me how Ann Marie's parents had offered to take Rudy in, but Mitch had turned them down. His affection for Rudy and his loyalty to my old friend touched my heart, and I wished there was something I could do to ease his pain. In a burst of courage, I gave him my phone number and told him I was available to talk any time. I wasn't trying to take advantage of his vulnerable state or weasel my way into a relationship, I swear. I truly felt for him in his unusual predicament, and just wanted to help.

Mitch called me the next day, and we went out on our first date the following weekend. Our romance remained casual at first, mainly because he was still rooted in his grief, and I didn't want to push him into anything he wasn't ready for. We saw each other regularly, usually going out as a threesome with little Rudy. We were rarely able to go anywhere by ourselves, because Rudy had some behavior issues—a result of the tragic loss of his mother—and finding the right babysitter for him was a challenge. Instead, Mitch and I would cook dinner together at his place a few nights a week, then watch a family-friendly movie with Rudy snuggled between us on the couch. Afterward, we'd share a few brief moments of intimacy that always had to be cut short because of Rudy asleep in the next room. It wasn't the passionate affair I'd been dreaming of, but it was okay. I'd finally landed the guy I'd been crushing on since my adolescence, and that was good enough for me.

One Sunday morning, after another at-home date the evening before, I sat brooding over coffee in my cramped apartment. I'd been involved with Mitch for six months, and I was yearning for more. Despite the professions of love that I'd managed to wheedle from him during our quiet moments together, Mitch wasn't moving any closer to making our relationship permanent. I suspected he was still weighed down by his memories, and the burden of caring for Rudy by himself. The problem for me was that most of the girls I knew from high school were already engaged or married, and I felt like I was in danger of falling behind. If this thing with Mitch sputtered out, I didn't have a fallback plan.

I was more than willing to become a mother to Rudy, who I'd discovered was an endearing child, once he'd warmed up to me. Marriage was my goal, and I saw my future union with Mitch as a way of evening things up. Ann Marie had edged me out of the way twice before, but now fate had presented a way for me to step back in. I could pick up with Mitch where she'd left off, and I had every intention of treating him way better than she ever had. I'd be a faithful and dedicated wife—the exact opposite of Ann Marie, who'd taken her husband for granted, and abused his trust in her.

The facts of the matter were plain as day to me: Mitch needed me, and I needed him. It was time for me to step up my game and push things along to an engagement. What better tonic for Mitch's doldrums than a brand-new wife by his side, to help him shoulder the responsibilities of parenthood? My campaign of steady hints and encouragement soon paid off. Mitch proposed to me on New Year's Eve, and we were married in the spring.

It turned out we were unable to have children of our own, so we threw ourselves into bringing Rudy up with love—until he reached his teens, and everything began to go off the rails. He got in trouble at school, mouthing off to his teachers and picking pointless fights with other kids, which he usually lost. You'd think he would have learned after getting a few black eyes, but he lacked impulse control. He and Mitch argued constantly, and there were many occasions when their disagreements turned physical. One time, when I scolded Rudy for not keeping his cellar bedroom clean, he turned on me in such a rage that I was terrified he was going to hit me, and Mitch had to jump between us to protect me. After that, I was too scared to speak up anymore, and allowed him to do whatever he liked down there. I couldn't imagine what I'd ever done to make Rudy behave violently toward me, when I'd always tried so hard to be kind to him. I was on his side, didn't he understand that? I just wanted him to be happy.

Mitch and I did our utmost to be supportive of Rudy as he struggled to find his path in life, but as the years went by, it became more and more difficult to maintain our patience with him. When Mitch first brought up the idea of evicting him, I couldn't stand the thought of it. How could we do such a cruel thing to him after all he'd been through— losing his mother when he was only five years old, and barely knowing his absent father? There had to be a better solution, but I couldn't fathom what it might be.

Mitch's reasons for wanting to evict Rudy were understandable, in a way. Mitch believes in the tough love approach, where the parents stop giving handouts to their wayward adult child, in order to get him to take responsibility for himself and change his behavior. Our stepson's lack of ambition frustrated Mitch to no end, and I get that. But I also felt sorry for Rudy. Growing up a virtual orphan would be hard enough on anyone, let alone a painfully shy little boy. It was no surprise to me that Rudy struggled with social anxiety throughout his teen years, and had so few close friendships. Like many people, he wasn't cut out for the rigors of college, and then when he tried to make a go of his internet business, his lack of experience got in the way.

When Rudy refused to grow up and pursue a more practical occupation, I knew he and Mitch had hit a crisis point. But *evicting* him! That was too much. I cried and begged Mitch not to take such a drastic step, but my pleas fell on deaf ears. My husband was dead set on his chosen course of action, which he believed was perfectly justified. When I realized there was no point in arguing any longer, I grudgingly agreed to go along with it.

I'm holding out hope that we'll all get past this ugliness one day, and come around to healing. I have faith that Rudy will get his life in order one day. He'll forgive Mitch for what he's done, and we'll be a happy family again. With all my heart, I want to believe that underneath his resentment and angry behavior, Rudy's still the innocent little boy who used to cuddle in bed with us on Saturday mornings, and draw colorful pictures for me with his crayons. Despite the tragedy in his past, he's still an intelligent, capable young man. If he puts his mind to it, I have no doubt he possesses the ability to overcome his emotional wounds and achieve great things. I want to help him unlock his potential, and see him go on to a life of success and happiness.

It's just that he scares me sometimes.

5

Rudy

Fudgie agrees to loan me his car for the afternoon, thinking I need it to apply for jobs. I sneak out to the shed to retrieve the gun, and stuff it into my backpack. Once I'm in the car, I put on the stiff new Pirates ball cap that I recently bought, and twist the bill around to the back. I'm a Yankees fan, but I read on the internet that street thugs are partial to the Pirates, and I want to fit in with their vibe. I adjust the cap and twist the rearview mirror toward me to check my look. I was going for tough, but with my pudgy cheeks and bad complexion, I see I've missed the mark. *Oh well*, I think with a shrug. Nothing I can do about it now.

The drive out to Centerport takes twenty minutes, due to a fender bender on Genesee Street. I go past the entrance for Spruce Tree Knolls and turn onto the wooded road that runs behind my stepparents' subdivision. A half mile down the hill, I come to a sprawling housing project called Woodland Homes, a place I've never dared venture into before.

When I was growing up, I spent my free time playing by myself in my backyard, because I didn't have any friends. One summer morning, as I was trying to build a fort out of a few pieces of scrap lumber I'd scrounged from an empty lot down the street, these two grubby boys came walking out of the woods and stopped at the edge of my yard. I'd never seen them before. They lived in Woodland Homes, which is in another school district, so we went to different middle schools and rode different buses.

Kids my age pretty much hated me back then. I had this skin condition called pediatric rosacea, which made my eyes get all swollen and crusty, and turned my nose and cheeks bright red. The boys mocked me and the girls steered clear of my grossness, so you can imagine how excited I was when these two boys showed up out of nowhere, and asked if they could help with my fort.

The older one, Dion, was tall and slender, and had a weird, pale scar where his left eyebrow should have been. The younger, shorter one was Trey, Dion's cousin. Dion was the alpha male of the pair. He had the brains and did most of the talking, while Trey stayed quiet, and deferred to his cousin in everything they did. I wasn't used to kids like them. They threw f-bombs like confetti, and used all sorts of crude lingo that I didn't know the meaning of, but pretended I did, in hopes of looking cool. They were eager to get to work at first, but after slapping a couple of two-by-fours together and pounding a few nails, Dion said he was bored with my lame fort, and asked if we could go inside my house.

Debra was at work and Mitchell was asleep upstairs in their bedroom. Dion and Trey followed me into the kitchen, where I gave them orange popsicles and cans of Pepsi. We watched television in the family room until Dion got bored again. "C'mon," he said, reaching across the couch and prodding my shoulder. "Let's see the rest of your house."

After warning the boys to be quiet because my stepfather was sleeping, we tiptoed upstairs to my room. They poked around on my shelves, examining my collection of LEGO Creator sets. I was worried they'd get too noisy playing with my Hot Wheels track, but Dion only scoffed when I mentioned Mitchell again. "You gotta stepfather?" he said as he followed me back downstairs. "Big deal. That ain't nothin'."

"He *is* a big deal," I insisted. "He was in Special Forces in the Army." This was a flagrant falsehood, but I wanted to take cocky Dion down a notch.

"Oh yeah?" Dion looked genuinely interested for the first time all morning.

"Yeah. I can show you." I led the two boys down to the basement, and made them turn their backs while I slipped beneath the staircase and took the key off the nail. Their eyes grew wide as I unlocked the padlock and swung the closet door open, revealing Mitchell's collection of guns and knives.

Dion swore in appreciation, and reached a covetous hand out. "Don't," I snapped, pushing him away. "If we touch anything, he'll know we've been in here."

Dion curled his lip at me in disdain. "You're a pussy."

"I am not!" I retorted. "We need to be careful, that's all. I'll be in big trouble if my stepfather finds out I messed with his stuff." I slammed the closet door shut and clicked the padlock back into place. Dion waved his hand and said "big deal" again, then punched his cousin's arm. "We leavin' now." Trey jumped to follow him up the stairs, and they went home a few minutes later.

I hung out with them on and off over the next few summers, but only ever at my house. One time they invited me over to their apartment, where they'd told me they lived with their doped-up mother and her string of druggie boyfriends, but I was too chicken to go. My family circumstances were no picnic, but Dion and Trey's home life was way more screwed up than mine.

I lost touch with them after high school, but every now and then I see Dion at the Sunoco station on Genesee, filling the tank of a shiny black Monte Carlo with a serious set of rims. He looks like a gangbanger with his shaved head and tats covering his arms, but whenever he sees me, he always nods in a friendly way. I'm hoping I can find him today, and talk him into doing business with me. But even if he's not, he might be able to hook me up with someone else who's in the market for a stolen gun.

I cruise the streets of Woodland Homes, rolling past neglected brick apartment buildings with litter strewn about their bare front yards. A couple of old men are hunched on a concrete stoop, staring at the cigarettes between their fingers. As I slow down for a stop sign that looks like it's been used for target practice, I spot a group of people in hoodies and sagging jeans, hanging out under a tree on the opposite street corner. They turn as one to stare me down, and I feel like a big-time jackass for invading their territory. I'm about to move it along, but then I notice an older dude nudge the shoulder of a hefty kid standing next to him. The kid detaches himself from the group and sidles up to my car window. I roll it down a few inches and pray he isn't going to try and sell me crystal meth.

"Whatchu want?" the kid asks. His two front teeth are sticking out so far that his mouth won't close all the way. Behind him, the knot of people is watching me in a curious but not necessarily hostile manner.

I try for a friendly smile, then shut it down and go businesslike. "I'm looking for Dion. You know him?"

The kid looks surprised, then bobs his head and jerks a thumb toward a car parked down the block. It's the flashy Monte Carlo I've seen Dion tooling around in, so I cautiously pull up beside it and lower my window. I'm blocking the street now, and I cross my fingers that another car doesn't come along and get ticked off.

The driver's window of the Monte inches down and there's my old buddy Dion, with that same pale scar on his eyebrow, and a dark soul patch etched on his chin. He gives me the nod, then grins and stretches his tattooed arm out to clasp my hand. "Hey, man. Long time."

"Yeah, long time." My stomach spasms. I'm about to attempt to sell a stolen gun to a probable drug dealer, with a half dozen eyewitnesses standing by. I take a deep breath. "Mind if I talk to you?" Dion shrugs one shoulder, so I pull my car in front of his and get out, bringing along the backpack that contains the Glock. There's a guy sitting in the front seat with Dion, and I do a double take when I realize it's Trey. He's considerably more muscular than he used to be, and his eyelids are heavy, as though I've woken him from his afternoon nap. He doesn't acknowledge me beyond a curt nod of recognition.

I get in the back seat, take the gun out, and hand it over for them to inspect. Dion lets out a low whistle. "Where'd a 'burbs boy like you get holda this?"

Something tells me to keep it vague. "It belongs to a friend of mine. He's hard up for cash and asked me to sell it for him." Dion raises his missing eyebrow and gives me a hard look, like I'm yanking his chain. "There's more where this came from," I add. "Lots of ammo and some knives, too."

"Yeah," Dion says with a slow, sly smile. "I remember."

Shit. He sees right through my flimsy cover story, but it's too late to change it now. After a brief confab with his partner in the front seat, Dion stows the gun in the glove compartment, then pulls a thick wad of bills from his pocket, thumbs a few off the top and hands them to me. "You come back and see us again," he says in a pleasant manner. "I'll tell the boys to keep an eye out for you."

With shaking hands, I open my door and climb out of the car. The buck-toothed kid is hovering a few feet away, his head swiveling back and forth between me and the older dude on the corner, as if he's waiting for instructions. When the dude gives the okay sign, the kid bobs his head at me and backs off.

I get back in my own car and drive out of Woodland Homes in a daze. *That was too freaking easy!* I'd been super nervous going in, but now I've happily discovered that dealing with street hoods isn't such a big deal after all. Not like on TV where they rob you first, then beat the crap out of you, and leave you for dead. You just have to keep your cool when approaching them, and know how to establish the proper rapport.

I stop for the traffic light at Genesee Street, jerk the Pirates cap off and toss it into the back seat, then pull out the folded bills Dion gave me and count them—something I was reluctant to do in front of him, in case he got offended. The few hundred bucks in my hand isn't as much as I'd hoped for, but it's enough to cover groceries and my share of the rent. Since I'm going to be sleeping in the living room, Fudgie's only charging me fifty dollars a week. Plus, I've still got a hundred left over from when Mitchell tried to bribe me to move out, so I can coast for another week or two, until I get a job.

Amazed at myself for what I've just pulled off, I decide to celebrate by treating myself to Buffalo wings. I pull into Gregorio's Pizza and order a dozen extra hot, with celery and blue cheese. When my wings come up, I grab the styrofoam box and take it out to the car. I'm chowing down when all of a sudden I'm like, *Duh!* There's got to be a thousand dollars' worth of weapons sitting in the closet in my stepparents' basement. I'd be an imbecile not to go back there and clean Mitchell out, then pay another visit to Dion, to unload the goods. I could smash the doorknob or something on my way out of the house, and plant the Pirates cap on the scene, to make it look like it was someone other than me who broke in.

It seems like a good plan, and I might as well make use of Fudgie's car while I've got it. Mitchell's probably working, and I'm pretty sure Debra has her girlie book club thing tonight, since it's the third Thursday of the month. I'll have to cool my heels until it gets dark out though, so no one sees me going into the house.

I finish off the wings and mop my saucy fingers with a handful of paper napkins. Instead of going back to Fudgie's place and rousing his suspicions, I think the smartest thing is for me to sit in the parking lot of a nearby shopping center until it's time to roll. I briefly consider filling out a few job applications while I'm there, but I'm not in the mood for the hassle. I've got the prequel to *The Hunger Games* in my backpack, and I'd rather kill the time by reading. I toss the dirty handful of napkins on the floor and start the car. *Let's do this.*

I find a parking spot behind the KeyBank, and get settled with my book. Several cars come and go from the lot, but no one looks twice at me. As the afternoon stretches into evening, the sky begins to cloud over, and it looks like there might be a storm coming. When it's time for me to go, I put my book away and head for Spruce Tree Knolls.

The homes there are spaced far apart on wooded lots, and there aren't any streetlights, so it's already fairly dark. I take the back way along Crestview Drive, and park around the bend from the house. I'm pleased to see Mitchell's truck isn't in the driveway, confirming he's gone to work. The house is dark as well, which means Debra isn't home either, and I feel a thrill of excitement. It's all systems go. I get out of the car and walk down the street. There's a tall lilac hedge that runs up the lawn alongside the driveway, and I scuttle through the shadows of it to the side door of the garage.

I insert my house key in the lock, but it won't turn. *What the—?* I jiggle the knob several times, but no luck. Blowing out a frustrated breath, I try to figure out what to do next. I didn't want to chance using the front door, in case someone drove by and saw me, but now I have to. After checking that the street's still deserted, I dart across the driveway and sprint up the walkway to the front steps. My key doesn't work on that door, either. *Frigging Mitchell changed the locks.*

Rage smolders in my gut. I can't keep standing here exposed like this on the front steps, so I return to the concealment of the lilac bushes, and try to think what to do. The only other way into the house is through the sliding door in back, which might be easy enough to jimmy. I run around the house to the patio. The vertical blinds on the inside of the slider are drawn and the kitchen is dark. The door is firmly latched, and it doesn't even budge when I yank hard on the handle.

I stare up at the house with clenched fists, swearing under my breath. I didn't come all this way, only to be shut out. The wind has picked up and thunder is rumbling in the distance. Peering around the dark yard, I notice the black outline of the storage shed beneath the swaying pine trees at the back of the property. I activate the flashlight on my phone, charge across the lawn and throw the door open. The shed is filled with Debra's gardening supplies—dirt-crusted flower pots, bags of potting soil, spades and rakes of various sizes. I grab a large shovel and run back to the patio, and try to use the heavy metal blade to pry the slider off its track. It doesn't work. Taking a step back, I flash my light at the door so I can reposition myself for another try, and that's when I see the security bar.

Those assholes. Not only have they kicked me out, they've gone and barred me—literally—from my home. The fiery ball of anger swells and fills my chest, and there's a roaring sound in my ears. Fat raindrops pelt my head and shoulders, but I barely notice. I'm so livid, I can't stop myself. Gripping the shovel in both hands, I raise my arms over my head and smash the blade against the glass. The door shatters with a resounding crash, spraying shards of glass across the kitchen floor. My breath catches in my throat, and I get an odd sense of wonder and pride as I observe the damage I've done.

I hear whimpering coming from inside the house, and realize I've scared poor Cocoa. I'm about to step through the broken door to comfort her, but then a light comes on in the back hallway, and I hear Debra's frightened voice, calling for the dog. I freeze with the shovel clutched in my hands, then whip my head left and right, wondering which way I should run. I turn back to the shattered door and see a petrified Debra in the kitchen, shouting into her phone that there's an intruder in her house. She backs out of the room, then turns and bolts for the front door, her voice becoming fainter as she runs outside, babbling her address to the 911 operator.

Emboldened by her swift retreat, I push the blinds aside and peer into the house. There's a light on in the back hall by the mudroom, which illuminates the kitchen just enough for me to get a view through to the front door, which is wide open. I can't see Debra anymore but I can hear her voice, high-pitched and panicky in the front yard. "*Hurry!*" she shouts. "*Please.*"

I step all the way inside, glass crunching beneath my feet, and stand in the center of the kitchen. A surge of power fills me, like I've never experienced before. I have a sudden, crazy urge to run down to the basement and grab as many guns as I can carry out of here, but that would be suicidal. The police will be here any minute, I've got to get out of here. I go back out through the broken door and run across the yard to the woods. It's pouring rain now, which makes it extra difficult to find my way in the dark. Moving as fast as I can, I stumble through the trees and tangled brush to the Scanlons' property next door, cut through their side yard, and run down the street to where the car is parked. There's no sign of the police yet, so I get in and take several deep breaths to calm myself, then try to execute a rapid U-turn with my headlights off, to position myself for a stealthy getaway. The car's manual transmission grinds as I fight with the temperamental clutch and gearshift, and I'm terrified I'm going to stall out in the middle of the street. In my rearview, I spy the flash of blue lights approaching through the rain, and my mouth goes dry. The Nissan finally shifts into gear, and I put the pedal down and speed away in the opposite direction.

I'm sweating through my t-shirt, and my trembling hands are slippery on the steering wheel. When I turn out onto Genesee Street, an oncoming vehicle flashes its high beams at me through the rain, and I realize with a jolt that I've turned on my wipers, but forgotten my headlights. I check my mirrors every few seconds, to see if there's a police car behind me. The high I was on when I bashed in the door of my childhood home has evaporated, leaving my mind racing with anxiety.

It's probably a good thing I wasn't able to steal any more of Mitchell's guns. Things could get dicey, teaming up with a shady guy like Dion. I should never have done it to begin with, it was too foolish and risky. What if he uses the Glock to commit a crime, and gets arrested? The cops will have no trouble tracing the gun back to Mitchell, who will then point the finger at me. I slam my fist on the steering wheel. It was so fricking *stupid* of me to think I could get away with this! Dion lives in a completely different world than me, with shadowy rules and ways of doing things that I don't understand. I'll have to pray he doesn't get himself into trouble with the law, and bring me down with him.

I check my phone as I drive. Fudgie has texted me five times, demanding in all caps to know what the hell's happened to me. It's going on ten, so I've been out with the car way longer than I told him I would, which might be a problem. I can't afford to make him mad when I'm so dependent on his goodwill. I really ought to call and tell him I'm on my way, but I'm so shook up right now, I'll probably come off sounding like a whack job, and my hands are too shaky to text him back.

My world's caving in. I've got hardly any money, no way of getting more, and a roommate who may be on the verge of telling me to get lost. And on top of everything, in less than a week's time, I've committed three serious crimes that probably have me headed for a long stretch in the joint.

I reach the west side, driving way too fast. There's a busy four-way stop coming up ahead, but it doesn't register in my brain until the last second. Stomping on the brakes, I screech to a halt, my tires skidding on the wet pavement. When I accelerate through the intersection a moment later, the gears grind loudly again, and the Nissan shudders violently. I've fucked it up, for sure. Just like everything else in my life.

6

Debra
Earlier the same night

I was supposed to go to my book club meeting at the town library tonight, but the group leader has gone on vacation and postponed it till next month. I'm disappointed, because it's one of the few social groups I belong to that I enjoy participating in.

With Mitch at work and nothing else to do for the evening, I decide to call my sister and ask if she'd like to go see a movie, or grab a bite to eat somewhere. Denise lives only five minutes away, but we began to drift apart a few years ago, due to her obsessive concerns about Covid, and our long-simmering sisterly rivalry. She's only a year older than me, but we couldn't be more different. Denise loves shopping and going on expensive trips, while I'm a homebody who's more interested in gardening and quilting, and volunteering at church. If we weren't sisters, we probably wouldn't be friends at all. But I've always believed it's important to stay close to one's family, so when the pandemic ended, I started making an effort to reach out to her regularly, even when I didn't really feel like it. She seems to appreciate the gesture but rarely reciprocates. Our girls' nights usually play out the same way every time—Denise talks at length about her personal issues, while I listen in silence and try to empathize with her. That's what a sister's supposed to do.

Denise agrees to meet me for a 6:15 movie. We've both been busy lately and haven't had the chance to get together in weeks, so I expect we'll have a good bit of catching up to do. I arrive at the theater first, so I go inside and buy the tickets, then wait by the entrance where my sister will be sure to see me when she arrives. She shows up ten minutes later, her stylish blonde bob bouncing with every step, a white jean jacket draped over her shoulders. It's much too muggy out tonight for her to need it, but she always complains that the air conditioning in the theater makes her cold.

The movie is a formulaic rom-com that drags on for nearly two hours. Afterward, we go to Tully's, a local sports bar and restaurant. I steer us toward a high top in the bar area, where I can distract myself with the TV in case the conversation lags, which it often does. Denise fussily arranges her spotless jacket on the back of her stool. "How about a glass of wine?" she says, then flags down a passing waitress and orders two house chardonnays.

The wine comes, and Denise says "cheers," and clinks her glass against mine. I take a small sip and feel it go straight to my head. Neither Mitch nor I are big drinkers, but my sister's a champ. She says she needs her wine to maintain her sanity when her husband's out of town and her girls are acting up. The waitress left us a bowl of mini pretzels, and Denise scoops up a handful and pops one into her mouth. "So," she begins. "How does Rudy like his new place?"

It's a loaded question. As my older sibling, Denise still thinks she can comment freely on everything I do. "Rudy's doing fine," I say lightly, even though I haven't heard a peep from him since he moved out. "He's busy getting settled."

Denise crunches another pretzel. "Has he found a job yet?"

Her superior tone is already rubbing me the wrong way. I struggle to stay composed, and tell her Rudy's been applying at businesses all over town. I don't know if that's true, but I sincerely hope it is. Without a full-time job, I don't know how he'll get by. Mitch won't allow me to lend him any more money, after what happened the last time.

Denise plays with one of her dangly earrings. "It's too bad he never finished college, or he might have been established in a profession by now."

This is a brag in disguise. My sister's husband is a bigwig insurance executive who earns six figures, and they began grooming their three daughters for college as soon as the girls started kindergarten. "Have you talked to him about getting into a job training program?" Denise asks. "I heard something on the news, about the state providing assistance for unskilled people like Rudy. It might be worth looking into."

I feel myself tensing up. "Mitch and I have given him every suggestion we can think of. You know we did, Denise. We've helped him as much as we possibly can, but it's time for him to make his own choices, and live with the consequences. It's up to him if he wants to pursue job training or not. We're staying out of it."

The waitress returns to take our food orders. I can tell by the way Denise is wagging her head that she's not done with her jabs at Rudy yet. "It was so sad, the way you had to take him to court," she says with a dramatic frown. "I can't imagine having to do that to one of my children."

I hate conflict, so I rarely push back when my sister touches a nerve, but I'm not in the mood for her criticism tonight. I lean across the table and look her straight in the eye. "Yes, it was very sad for us, but I'd rather not talk about it tonight. Could we please change the subject?"

Denise sniffs and barely hides an eyeroll. I sit back and cross my arms, keeping my gaze on the TV screen above the bar. The Yankees are playing the Red Sox, and the score is tied.

My sister drinks more wine, then places her hand on the stem of her glass when she sets it down, as though someone might come along and try to snatch it from her. "I've been meaning to tell you about Peyton. She's not coming home for a visit after all."

Peyton is Denise's oldest daughter, a rising junior at a college in North Carolina. She's a biology major, currently taking summer classes and working part time in one of the school's research labs. "She's got this new boyfriend," Denise explains. "He invited her to his parents' house the weekend before the fall semester starts. Sounds like they've got money. Peyton says they live on the coast in a gated golf community."

I raise my eyebrows but don't respond. Denise has a hangup about our working class upbringing, and tries to hide it from people. Personally, I could care less what anyone thinks about my economic status. I try for a positive spin. "That's nice, she'll get to meet his family. Maybe they'll go to the beach."

Denise purses her lips. "They're probably rich snobs. I hope they don't look down their noses at Peyton, coming from nowheresville Centerport and all. She's doing well in her classes, though. I'm so proud of the way she's making the most of her education." Denise reaches for another pretzel. "I'm just disappointed that she's not showing more loyalty to us. That weekend was supposed to be our special family time at home, since we hardly see her anymore. I've been trying to guilt her into changing her mind."

I can't quite relate to my sister's family travails, considering how Rudy has no interest in college, and the past year has been so turbulent. Denise drains her wine and orders another, but I decline. When her fresh drink arrives, she takes a big gulp, then looks at me and sighs. "I treasure my time with Peyton, and I hate having to give up even a few days with her. It's a mother/daughter thing, I guess. At least I have a few more years left before the other two go off on their own. I just hope they stay close by, like your stepson did. That must be a comfort to you."

I can't stand the way Denise always emphasizes that Rudy is my stepson, and throws her motherhood in my face. It makes me feel like a failure, since I never had a baby of my own. Mitch and I tried, but after a string of miscarriages, the emotional toll was too much on us, and we gave up.

"Yes, I'm lucky to have Rudy," I murmur as my eyes drift back up to the TV. The broadcast has cut to highlights from another ballgame that I have no interest in. Our salads come, so we pick at them and make aimless small talk for a while. I'm out of sorts with my sister, and I start thinking about excusing myself and going home early.

Before I can say anything, Denise reaches for her phone to check her weather app, a favorite habit of hers. "The hourly forecast's calling for a severe thunderstorm to start soon. We'd better skip dessert and get going, so we don't have to drive home in it."

That's fine by me because I don't have the energy to spar with her anymore. We split the bill, and promise to get together again soon. Outside, the sky has turned an ominous gray and it's grown quite dark. We hug each other goodbye and hurry to our cars.

The wind rises and lightning flashes, so I drive faster, hoping to get home before the sky opens up. My house is completely dark because I forgot to leave the lights on before I left, and I chide myself for the oversight. Ever since we found those mysterious footprints in the backyard, Mitch has been after me about keeping the doors locked and the exterior lights turned on at night. I promised him I'd be more careful, but I sometimes forget if I leave the house when it's still daylight out.

I turn into the driveway and press the remote to open the overhead garage door. The door goes up, but the light inside the garage doesn't come on like it's supposed to. *Oh, great,* I think. I'm going to have to grope my way into an empty house in the dark. I pull my car inside, leaving the headlights on so I can see my way around all the junk we've accumulated over the years—riding lawnmower, snowblower, a set of old tires, a pair of bicycles we haven't used since Rudy was a boy. Feeling my way in the dim light, I open the door that leads from the garage into the mudroom, reach my hand around the doorjamb and flip on the ceiling light, then return to the car and turn off my headlights. All this fumbling around in the dark has my nerves fluttering. Stepping quickly into the mudroom, I close the door behind me and twist the knob on the new deadbolt.

The door to the kitchen is closed, and Cocoa is scrabbling her paws against the other side of it, anxious to greet me. After slipping my shoes off, I'm about to open the door when I hear a terrific crash from the kitchen. I stop dead with my hand on the knob. *Oh my God, what was that?* My heart bangs against my ribs and I hold my breath, listening.

Cocoa's whimpering jerks me back into action. *She's hurt, I've got to help her.* I cautiously open the door a few inches, and see the glimmer of broken glass covering the kitchen floor. My eyes fly to the damaged slider, and my heart nearly jumps out of my chest—there's a man outside on the patio. Our eyes meet for a split second, and I catch a glimpse of a pale face before he turns and disappears.

I can't see very well in the dark room, so I shout Cocoa's name, only to find her cowering at my feet. Scooping her under my arm, I pull my phone from my purse and hurriedly dial 911, then make a run for the front door. It's pitch black and raining outside, but that doesn't slow me as I hurtle down the front steps. Cocoa squirms free and gallops beside me, down to the foot of the driveway. I stand in the middle of the street, gasping for breath with my hands braced on my knees, and wait for the police to arrive.

7

Mitchell

The lights are blazing in my house and two police cars are parked on the street when I arrive home in a rush, after getting Debra's panic-stricken phone call saying someone broke into the house. I burst through the front door to find two Centerport police officers standing in my living room, and Debra perched on the edge of the couch, her face pale and tear-stained. She stretches her arms out to me as I stride across the room. I embrace her, and ask if she's okay. Instead of answering, she nods her head weakly, then sinks back onto the couch and wraps her arms around her middle.

I recognize one of the officers—Gary Scanlon, a guy I've known since grade school. He was promoted to detective several years ago, so he thinks he's hot stuff. Scanlon can't let go of the glory days of the 80s, when he played left tackle on our high school football team. He's one of those people who no one really likes, but everyone has to try to get along with because he's such a fixture in the community. Besides being a cop, he's the head of Centerport's parks and rec committee, and volunteers with Kiwanis. He goes around boasting about the good works he does on behalf of the citizens of this town, without getting paid for it. I generally try to ignore him, but his arrogance really sticks in my craw.

Scanlon nods a greeting, then gives me the rundown in cop speak. "Mrs. Bateman states that she returned home from an outing at approximately 9:00 p.m. As she accessed the domicile by way of the garage, she heard the sound of breaking glass. Upon entering the kitchen, she observed that the sliding door had been shattered."

Holding a hand up, I step into the kitchen and see broken glass all over the floor. The back of my neck tingles, the same as it did when I found those handprints on the door the other morning. *Rudy did this.* My hands curl into fists as the heat rises in my chest. I give myself a moment to cool it, then return to the living room. "Do you know who did this? Did anyone see them?"

Scanlon raises a finger and goes on reading from the notepad in his hand. "Mrs. Bateman then exited the domicile via the front door, and utilized her cellular phone to contact 911 for assistance." He pauses to gesture at his female partner. "Officer Tobin and I responded to the call, and conducted a thorough inspection of the interior of the home, which determined that no intruders were present. We then inspected the exterior of the property, and discovered a garden-type shovel on the patio, but no additional signs of forced entry. Mrs. Bateman states that to her present knowledge, no items are missing from within the home."

Officer Tobin turns to me, hands gripping her belt. "Have you experienced any previous disturbances here, Mr. Bateman? Suspicious characters in the neighborhood, or anyone trespassing on your property?"

"No," I say. "Not really."

"What do you mean by 'not really'?"

My eyes flick to Debra, then back to the lady cop. "We saw footprints in the backyard earlier this week, when neither one of us had been out there."

"Anything else?"

"No." I look at my wife again, hoping she hasn't figured out that I never reported the incident, like I'd said I would; but she just sits there hugging herself. "Did you see anything else outside?" I ask Scanlon. "With that storm that came through, there might've been muddy footprints or something?"

Scanlon shakes his head. "If there were, the heavy precipitation obliterated any traces of them."

Tobin addresses Debra. "Mrs. Bateman, you said you caught a glimpse of the intruder, who you believe was a young male. Are there any other details of his appearance that you can recall?"

Debra looks away with a quick shake of her head. "No. Only what I already told you."

She's hiding something. I look from Tobin to Scanlon, but neither of them seems to have noticed Debra's slip.

I'm certain it was Rudy who smashed through that door, in a brazen attempt to scare us. He's angry and unstable, and his behavior is escalating. I think Debra suspects him too, but for some reason, she doesn't want to say it. Looking directly at Scanlon, I ask him again: "Who do you think it was that did this?"

Scanlon studies his notepad before answering me. "There have been recent incidences of misdemeanor activity over at the Woodland Homes apartment complex. Underage drinking, disorderly conduct, vandalism—the usual teenage shenanigans. I would advise you to keep your doors locked at all times, in case the behavior spills over into your neighborhood. Keep a sharp lookout, and report any suspicious activity promptly."

Debra speaks up in a shaky voice. "Mitchell works the night shift. What if those troublemakers come back when I'm here alone?"

She's covering for Rudy. I can't imagine why, but I'm not about to reveal anything to a blowhard like Scanlon without talking to my wife first. Sitting down beside her, I take her hand. "You don't need to worry, Deb. I'm going to put surveillance cameras up outside, so I can monitor things while I'm at work. I may even look into getting a home security system."

"Good idea." Scanlon stuffs his notepad into a back pocket. "You're a security guard, aren't you, Mitch? You must be an expert with that sort of thing."

I brush off the veiled insult. I'm used to morons like him calling me Officer Friendly, Guardzilla, Robocop, you name it. I let go of Debra's hand and stand up. I've had enough of the useless Q & A. It's time for these officers to leave, so I can have a private conversation with Debra, and get my house back in order. I thank them both for their assistance, and show them to the door.

Once they've gone, I grab a throw blanket and wrap it around Debra, then sit beside her and give her shoulders a squeeze. "Is there something you're not telling me?"

She pulls the blanket snugly around her neck, and stares at floor. "No, of course not."

"Are you sure you told the police everything? You didn't leave anything out?"

Debra frowns, keeping her eyes on the floor. "Why would you even ask me that?"

I tilt her chin toward me. "Tell me the truth, Deb. You saw who it was, didn't you?"

She jerks her head away, and the blanket falls to the floor as she jumps to her feet. "What are you implying, Mitchell? That I lied to the police?"

"No, I don't mean you lied, exactly—"

"Yes, you do! I told Gary I never saw anyone because I didn't. Not really, anyway—it was only a quick glimpse of something in the dark. And now you're calling me a liar." Tears fill her eyes, and she covers her face with her hands. "I cannot believe you'd accuse me of a thing like that, after what I went through tonight."

Now I've done it. I stand there helplessly, wishing I'd said it differently, and hadn't gotten her so upset. It's true—she has been through a lot tonight, and I shouldn't have jumped to conclusions. Maybe she *didn't* see anyone, and my hunch that she's withholding information is way off the mark.

Fine. I'll deal with Rudy myself. If he did this, he's crossed the line, and he's going to regret it. I rise from the couch and pick the blanket up from the floor. "I didn't mean for you to take what I said the wrong way. I just want to be sure the police have the whole story." Debra frowns at me through her tears, so I quickly add, "And it sounds like they do."

I drop the blanket on the couch and clap my hands together. On to the next thing. "How about you clean up the kitchen, while I get started on the door? There's an old tarp out in the shed that I can duct tape to the frame. Just for tonight, to keep the rain out. Tomorrow, I'll go to Lowe's to buy a new door, and I'll install it myself." Debra nods in weary agreement. She goes into the kitchen and gets out a broom and dustpan, while I grab a flashlight and go out back to the shed.

My anger bubbles up again as I'm taping the heavy tarp in place. How dare Rudy scare Debra like this? I've got half a mind to call the police station right now and report my suspicions, but I can't do it with Debra hanging over my shoulder, listening in. Better to wait till tomorrow, when I can go there and talk to Scanlon in person.

Debra goes out to the garage to dump the last dustpan of broken glass in the bin, then returns to the kitchen and leans her elbows on the counter. She looks exhausted. I hug her and tell her she should go to bed, and promise I'll keep watch all night. It's my normal shift hours anyway, so I won't have any difficulty staying awake. If Rudy is foolhardy enough to come back tonight, I'll be here waiting for him.

I go upstairs with Debra, and while she's in the bathroom brushing her teeth, I open the drawer of my nightstand and check the handgun I keep in there, a full-size Sig Sauer P320 with night sights. I confirm there's a round in the chamber, and set it down on the nightstand within easy reach. Deb dislikes guns, but she agreed to let me keep this one in the bedroom as long as it stayed out of sight. She'll have to allow an exception tonight. I'm the one who's responsible for protecting her, so she's gonna have to deal with it.

Debra comes out of the bathroom in her flannel nightgown, and gets under the covers on her side of the bed. I spoon up behind her and we talk quietly, until I feel her begin to relax. As we're lying there, I think of the many times in the past when I urged her to take a self-defense course and learn how to shoot, but she just wouldn't do it. She claimed she had no interest in guns, but I think the real reason was that she was too scared to try. "I have you to protect me," she always used to say. And she did—until I changed shifts, and left her on her own at night. The guilt is weighing heavy on me tonight, so I lie there until I'm certain she's asleep. Cocoa pads in and jumps up on the bed, and I wait till she's curled up next to Deb before I take the Sig from the nightstand, tiptoe out of the room and go downstairs.

After checking to make sure the tarp is securely in place with the kitchen table and chairs pushed up against it, I head down to the basement, take the key from its hiding place beneath the stairs, and unlock the closet. It's full of mementos I've saved since my days in the service—a desert camouflage jacket, a pair of lace-up boots that I never wear, a shoebox of photos that I'll probably never look at again. My handguns are lined up in a padded metal rack, revolvers on the left, semi-automatics on the right, arranged by caliber and size. I take them out one by one, first verifying that they're unloaded, then performing function checks. I need to find one that's suitable for Debra, but they're all too big and heavy for her delicate hands—except for the Walther P22, which I set aside. It'll be perfect for her, I think. A few lessons at the range and she'll be good to go, and my mind will be at ease.

I tuck the Walther into my hip pocket and go to close the closet door, but wait a minute—there's an empty slot at the far end of the rack. My Glock 17 is missing. I search the other shelves in case I misplaced it, but I don't find it. I'm sure I haven't taken that gun out in a long time, and I can't even remember when I used it last.

It could be in my truck. I go outside and check the truck's storage compartments, then look under the seats, but it isn't there. I stand in the driveway, my fingers pressed to my forehead, sorting through the possibilities. I might have left it in the safe at work, or dropped it off with old Frank, the gunsmith at the Centerport Rod & Gun Club, to adjust the sights or something—but it isn't like me to lose track of such a valuable item.

My thoughts jump to Rudy. First there was the stolen drill, followed by the unexplained footprints and handprints, and then the shattered door. And now I've got a missing firearm. Something weird and potentially dangerous is going on here.

But as I think about it, I realize Rudy couldn't have taken the gun. He didn't enter the house after he broke through the sliding door, so there was no opportunity for him to get into the basement tonight. He also doesn't know where the key is hidden, and there's no sign that the closet's been tampered with.

I massage my temples, deep in thought. Or *does* he know about the key? He might have had a copy made, and gotten back into the house before I installed the deadbolts. It's possible that Rudy's been craftier than I ever would've given him credit for. Then again, I doubt it. He's simply not that smart.

I close the closet door, but instead of putting the padlock back on, I go out to the garage and get a different one from a drawer in my workbench. When the new padlock is securely in place, I slide the key for it onto my keyring for safekeeping.

I go back upstairs and settle myself in a kitchen chair for the remainder of the night, with the loaded Sig at my side. I'm worried about Debra. I can't have her living in fear like this. She's got to learn how to defend herself, in case something else happens when I'm not here. I think it will probably be best if I wait a week or two before giving her the gun I picked out for her, to allow tonight's uproar to subside. Once she's calmed down, I'll tell her I'm going to teach her how to use it. Or better yet, I'll sign her up for a class at the Rod & Gun Club. She'll learn useful skills and gain some confidence. It's exactly what she needs.

•   •   •   •   •

The security cameras I buy at Lowe's the next day are equipped with motion detectors, night vision, panning functions, and live-streaming capability. I'm very pleased with my purchase. The unit I installed over the new sliding door has a 130° field of view that takes in the patio and most of the backyard, and the second camera that I'm about to mount over the garage will cover the driveway and the walkway leading to the front door. I set the ladder in place and climb up. From the corner of my eye, I notice the curtains twitch in the bay window of the living room, and see Debra looking out. She smiles and waves at me. I give her a quick wave in return, then get on with my task.

The battery in my new drill isn't holding a charge. It doesn't have enough power to drill the holes I need for mounting the camera, so I climb down the ladder, go into the garage and retrieve the spare battery from the charger that's plugged into the wall outlet over my workbench. When I come back out to the driveway, I groan inwardly when I see my next-door neighbor Merv Scanlon—Detective Gary Scanlon's father—standing at the edge of my yard.

Merv and I have had numerous run-ins over the years, mostly to do with the giant silver maple that grows between our two properties. He came after me one time, screaming like a madman about how the tree roots were damaging the foundation of his house, and clogging the water lines on his in-ground swimming pool. I told him to get lost, it wasn't my tree, and he'd better get the heck out of my yard. You can guess how that one ended. Relations went south from there, with frequent disputes over the property line, and complaints that Rudy was straying into the Scanlons' part of the woods. Merv eventually realized he wasn't going to win any arguments with me, and we've managed to steer clear of one another ever since.

I haven't laid eyes on my neighbor in quite some time. Merv's gotta be pushing eighty by now, and he's more stooped and grizzled than when I last saw him. He's being careful to stay on his side of the property line, which he's got marked with wooden stakes. "Hey, Bateman," he calls to me.

"Hello, Merv," I call back. I suspect he's out here because his son has informed him of the break-in. Much as I dislike Merv, I guess he has the right to know what's going on next door, so I might as well go over and talk to him. I cross my front lawn and stop about ten feet away from him. Up close, he looks like he hasn't been to the dentist in years. Keeping my distance, I tell him what happened last night.

"Yeah, I heard." Merv's jowly cheeks flush with displeasure. "Gary called me this morning and told me all about it, said it was probably those scummy people in that housing project, who're always up to no good. Too many Section 8 tenants over there. That's why I got my concealed carry." He pats the side of his bulky denim jacket, where I assume he's got a firearm hidden. "Can't be too careful."

I tell him I'm putting up security cameras. He seems curious, so I invite him to come take a look. He follows me over to my driveway and I show him the new camera, explaining the various functions and capabilities. After thirty seconds, I can see I've lost him. I hold the instruction booklet out to him so he can read the information himself, but he dismissively flicks it away. "Figures a rent-a-cop like you would go overboard with this newfangled techie crap," he snorts.

That brings me up short. Here I am, making a good faith effort to be neighborly, and this geezer has to go and insult me. I scowl at him. "What's your problem, Merv? Forgot your laxative this morning?"

The look on Merv's face makes me think my guess was correct. He jabs a crooked finger at me. "Don't you get smart with me, Bateman. You've got no call to speak to me like that."

I take a step closer and get in his face. "I'll speak to you any way I like, old man."

"You got a lotta nerve, you sonofabitch!" Merv shouts, shaking his bony fist at me. "With a wife like yours, you should be more careful about who you cross."

What the hell is that supposed to mean? Out of the corner of my eye, I see the living rooms curtains moving again. Glancing up, I see Debra looking down at us, and she isn't smiling anymore. She dislikes Merv almost as much as I do, and she can't stand Edith, his miserable witch of a wife.

With Debra watching, I feel ashamed of myself for getting in the old man's face, so I back off and tell Merv to take a hike. He snorts loudly again, thrusts his hands into his coat pockets, and stalks off toward his own house. I finish installing the camera, climb down from the ladder and survey my work, satisfied with the steps I've taken to secure my home. Only one thing left to do now—give that gun to my wife, and make sure she knows how to use it.

8

Rudy

I've got a job interview this afternoon, but Fudgie won't let me borrow his car because he's taking his new girlfriend Sabrina out after work. She's the same chick I saw him talking to in the courthouse parking lot after my eviction hearing, which makes me jealous. He's not that good-looking, but he's got this mysterious kind of rizz when it comes to the ladies. I don't have it, and I never will.

Girls aren't my thing. Hold on, let me clarify that—I'm not into guys or anything, it's just that I don't seem to be able to attract females for some reason. I tried a dating app once, but all the girls I sent likes to never liked me back, which made me feel like a loser. I guess my pics turned them off. Rosacea and acne scars are difficult to hide. The app was free at least, so I didn't lose any money when I deleted my profile.

Fudgie's been acting annoyed with me lately, and he's been less cooperative about loaning me his car. After the craziness at my stepparents' house, I decided to lay low for a while because I was worried Debra might've seen me, and Mitchell would be coming after me. But a week later, when I was lounging on the couch, clicking through the TV channels, Fudgie dropped a half-joke about me being a freeloader, which got me concerned. He's my only friend and I can't burn any bridges with him, especially after the way I disappeared with his car that night. To smooth things over, I offered to cover next month's entire electric bill, and promised him I'd get busy looking for employment. I was going to put it off for another week, but then

DoorDash declined my debit card when I tried to order delivery, and I realized I'd be in a world of hurt if I didn't find a job soon.

So here I am, waiting for a city bus to take me downtown, to interview for a position as a data entry clerk at an accounting firm. It sounds like a real snoozer of a job, but beggars can't be choosers, as my stepfather loves to remind me, and I do have a flair for numbers. My interview's at three and the bus is running late, which is making me mighty nervous. If I don't get there on time, I'm up shit's crick.

Even though it's summer, we're enjoying typical Syracuse weather today—gray skies and rain. The bus stop has a plexiglass shelter that's supposed to shield passengers from the elements, but the wind has shifted, driving the rain right on in. I'm hunched in a corner when a big girl comes marching up the sidewalk, bundled in a full-length black raincoat and combat boots. The ends of her hair are whipping around outside her hood, and she's got a big canvas messenger bag strapped to her chest. She glances my way as she ducks into the shelter, then sits down at the far end of the bench.

The bus finally arrives, and since I'm already standing, I go to board it ahead of the girl. She trails me down the aisle and plunks herself into the vacant seat opposite mine. I can feel her looking at me. "Hi," she says, and I get the tingles in my stomach.

I'm not used to girls talking to me because they hardly ever do. I have a few seconds of tunnel vision before I'm able to summon a response. "Hello," I mumble back. I sneak a sideways peek at her as she pulls her hood off and shakes out her longish hair, which is jet black but dyed hot pink at the ends. I glimpse fogged-up eyeglasses and a nose ring before I turn away in terror because she's still looking at me.

"Where are you headed?" she asks.

"Um," I reply. "Downtown."

"Yeah, me too. Are you transferring at Salina Street, or is that your stop?"

"No. Yeah. That's my stop."

"Do you work downtown?"

I shake my head. My mouth has gone dry. "Job interview," I manage to spit out.

"Oh, cool." She unbuttons her voluminous raincoat. Another cautious glance confirms she's about the same size as me, which makes her less scary, because I'm not exactly the slimmest guy on the block myself. She's also pretty, so I ask where she's going.

"I'm on my way to the registrar's office at City Tech." I can tell by the way she settles into her seat that I'm in for a one-sided convo, which is fine by me, since my tongue has tied itself in a humongous knot. "I'm going to switch into their Medical Laboratory Assistant program," she says. "I started out in cosmetology last semester, and I really liked it at first. They taught us about hairstyling, makeup and skin care, which was very fun and interesting, but my feet were killing me. I've got plantar fasciitis, see? It really bothers me when I have to stand for too long. I realized I wasn't cut out to work in a salon, so I researched alternative careers. That's how I found out I could earn more money as a lab tech, and not have to be on my feet so much. Plus, I thought working in a laboratory would be really cool." She pauses to check my reaction, and I nod mutely in agreement. I'm guessing she's several years younger than me, probably fresh out of high school. She seems genuinely pumped about her vocational choice.

"If I like it," she continues, "I might take some forensics courses, and get my four-year degree. I can make a ton more money that way, as a crime scene investigator." She chatters on, telling me how much she enjoys watching those TV shows about sicko criminals and unsolved murders. I mumble "uh huh" at intervals, reveling in this miracle of female attention.

The girl sticks out her hand, which is still damp from the rain. "I'm Laci, by the way."

I return the handshake. "I'm Rudy."

"What a rad name!" Laci lowers her voice to a baritone and drawls "*Ruuudy*," then bobs her head and giggles, exposing a prominent pair of front teeth. I find myself giggling, too. I'm blown away by what's happening. I'm bumping along on a city bus, laughing with a girl who seems to enjoy talking with me. Well, talking *to* me.

Laci quits her giggling and segues the conversation. "So, what kind of job are you interviewing for?" She peers intently at me. The fog has evaporated from the lenses of her glasses, and I notice her eyes are heavily rimmed with dark blue eyeliner.

I'm hesitant to admit to the lowly data entry job, so I tell her the interview is for a tech support role with a major data management company. "I'm not at liberty to discuss the details of the position until I've signed the employment contract." A total lie, but it sounds good.

Laci looks impressed. "That sounds serious. It was must pay pretty well."

"Yes," I say. "It does." I'm sweating bullets about being late for my interview. A glance at my watch tells me I've got eight minutes to get there. The bus finally wheezes up to the transfer point on Salina Street, and Laci and I rise from our seats. Even though I'm in a hellacious hurry to get off, I remember my manners this time, and gesture for her to go ahead of me. As I follow her down the aisle and descend the steps of the bus, I gird myself for the Big Ask. I can't let this girl get away without getting her phone number.

She beats me to it. Blocking my way on the wet sidewalk, Laci smiles and says, "Call me!" and rattles off a string of numbers. I don't have enough time to take my phone out and create a new contact, so I repeat the number in my head as she turns and marches off. In a daze, I check my watch again: four minutes. Ducking my head into the rain, I take off running down the street.

Luckily for me, the guy I'm interviewing with is running late himself, so he doesn't notice I'm not on time. He asks me about my education (nothing much to tell there), my work experience (limited), and how I get along with other people (not very well, but I tell him just great). I try to act intelligent and bluff my way through it, and at the end of the interview, to my astonishment, he offers me the job. "It's only a temporary position at this point," the guy cautions me, "but we may extend an offer of permanent employment at the end of your assignment, depending on your performance and our current needs."

It sounds like a cake job, where all I'll have to do is organize files and enter data into a computer base. I could care less that it's only a temporary gig—as long as they're paying me, I'm good to go. I tell the guy I'll take it, and he hands me a pile of papers to sign.

On the bus ride home, I'm feeling happier than I have in a very long time. In one afternoon, I've got a new job with decent pay, and a girl that's interested in me, which is incredible. I wish there was someone besides Fudgie that I could share my news with, but my social circle is pretty constricted. If only Mitchell and Debra could hear how well things are going for me now. They'd see I'm not the complete loser they seem to think I am.

As I think about my stepparents, my good mood drops a few notches. I've got this nagging fear that I'm gonna get busted for stealing the gun and breaking their stupid door. I'm reasonably sure Debra didn't see me, but I'm not a hundred percent certain. To be safe, I told Fudgie if anyone asks, he should swear I've been at home with him every night for the past two weeks. He doesn't know the real reason why—I only said it had to do with Mitchell getting on my case about random stuff, and he went right along with it.

I force my thoughts back to happier topics. There's no way anyone will find out what I did, so why worry? My job starts on Monday, and I'm going to be getting a nice, fat paycheck soon. Well, maybe not exactly fat, but it'll be nice to have an income again.

•   •   •   •   •

I have to wait for my first paycheck to hit my bank account before calling Laci and asking her out. I go into the bathroom to make the call because I'm nervous as hell and don't want Fudgie staring me down the whole time. Closing the toilet lid, I take a seat, psych myself up, and dial Laci's number, which I hope I memorized correctly. Her voice is gruff when she answers, as if she was expecting it to be a telemarketer, but she brightens up when I tell her it's me. "Oh, hi!" she says. "I've been wondering about you. Did you get the job?"

She's been wondering about me! "Yeah," I say. "I did."

"How do you like it?"

"It's all right." I want to tell her more, but my throat's constricting. There's an awkward pause that I don't know how to fill. I tap my feet on the floor and clear my throat. This is the part where I'm supposed to ask her on a date. I've got the words planned in my head, but when it comes to saying them out loud, I choke. It's embarrassing to admit, but I've never really gone out with a girl before. The extent of my experience is a prom date that derailed when the girl ditched me for a guy from another school. There was one other girl when I was going to OCC, but she ghosted me after a week. Then the Covid lockdown interfered with everything, and I never went anywhere anymore, except to the grocery store and the post office.

After stammering a string of "ums" and clearing my throat several more times, I finally succeed in asking Laci if she'd like to go out with me on Friday night.

"Sure," she says. "I'd love to."

I almost fall off the toilet. "Oh! Okay. Wow."

The standard dinner-and-a-movie date is more than I can afford just yet, so I suggest a visit to Destiny USA, the local mega-mall where there are plenty of less expensive things to do.

"Great!" Laci says. "I love the mall. We could play Glow Golf, maybe."

Glow Golf is an economical choice. We agree to meet by the carousel at seven on Friday evening. When I get off the phone, my head's so high in the clouds, I can hardly see straight.

9

Debra

I'm heating up leftover spaghetti sauce on the stove when Mitch comes into the kitchen with one hand hidden behind his back, and says he has something to show me. Wiping my hands on a towel, I turn to him with a smile. "What is it?"

He brings his hand around and sets a small handgun on the table. "This is for you, so you won't be uneasy when I'm not here."

I instantly recoil, and feel the smile melt from my face. I've long been resigned to the fact that my husband is a firearms fan—a holdover from his Army and hunting days. But I wish he'd respect my fears, and not try to push this on me. "No, Mitch," I say. "I don't want it. You shouldn't have—"

He holds up his hand. "Wait a sec, Deb. Hear me out first. After what happened the other night, I don't feel good about you being in the house alone, with no way to defend yourself. Most of my guns are way too big for your hands, but this one's just the right size." He picks up the gun and tells me it's a .22 caliber semi-automatic, as if that means anything to me. "It's lightweight with low recoil, and the trigger pull is very smooth, which is perfect for a beginner like you. It's also got a manual safety, which should make you feel more comfortable about using it."

I keep shaking my head, but he pays no heed. "I'm going to sign you up for a handgun safety class," he says. "You'll need to complete that first, in order to get your concealed carry permit."

"But I don't want to carry a gun, Mitch! You know I don't like them."

My husband is unmoved by my protests. "You need to learn how to protect yourself, Deb. There's no telling what else might happen, when the police haven't caught whoever broke in yet. I called that doofus Gary Scanlon for an update today, and all he gave me was a lot of BS about 'assessing the evidence' and 'surveilling potential suspects.' I think he's full of it, and he's just covering for the fact that our police force doesn't know what it's doing. We've got to look out for ourselves, Deb, that's all there is to it."

I regard the gun doubtfully, but I can't dispute anything Mitch has said. He's right—we do have to look out for ourselves. It took the police nearly twenty minutes to respond to my 911 call, when Centerport's not that big of a town. I'll never forget how scared I was, standing in the street in the rain, thinking an assailant was going to rush out of the dark and attack me.

"Here," Mitch says. "I'll show you how to hold it." Grasping my right hand, he tries to push the gun into it, but I reflexively clench my fingers. "It's not loaded," he says, reaching for my other hand. "You don't have to be afraid to touch it." I relax somewhat, allowing him to mold my hands around the grip. "Always keep your gun pointed in a safe direction," he says, aiming the gun toward the floor, "and always keep your finger off the trigger until you're ready to shoot." He steps back and smiles at me. "See? It's not that scary."

I feel ridiculous, standing stiff as a statue with the gun in my hands. It would take an act of God for me to get over my aversion, and there's no way in the world that I'd ever be able to shoot someone. I gingerly set the gun back down on the table and return to the stove, to stir my bubbling pot of sauce. "Do you really think it's the smartest thing, me having a gun?" I say over my shoulder.

"Yes, I do. You're only nervous because you've never learned how to use one. Once you get used to handling it, it won't scare you anymore." Mitch comes over and slides his arm around my waist. "I know the guy who teaches the handgun safety courses over at the Rod

& Gun Club. He's a certified instructor, and he holds classes one weekend a month. I asked him to hold a spot for you in the next one. He's really knowledgeable, and I think you'll enjoy it."

It's a done deal, I can see that. As usual, my husband's mind is made up, and I won't get any peace until I go along with what he wants. Mitch senses I'm wavering. "There's one other lady taking the class," he says, "so you won't feel out of place."

I suppose it can't be that bad, if another woman has signed up. I'll take the class and learn how to shoot the darn gun, then I'll put it away somewhere, and only take it out if there's an emergency. I tap my wooden spoon on the rim of the saucepot and set it down with a long sigh. "All right Mitch, I'll do it, but don't expect me to turn this into a hobby. I'm only doing it because you want me to."

"I won't, hon. Thank you." He gives my shoulder a squeeze, then goes over to the table, removes a handful of cartridges from his pocket and loads the gun. When he's done, he glances around the kitchen, then opens the drawer beside the stove and places the gun inside, underneath my flowered potholders.

"Wait a minute," I say. "Isn't it safer to keep it locked up?"

Mitch looks at me in surprise. "It's no use to us if we don't have access to it. This way, you can get hold of it easily when you need it. Just don't touch it till you've finished your training."

Of course, I won't touch that damn thing until I know how to use it! Returning to my dinner preparations, I slam cupboard doors and bang another pot onto the stove, then notice Cocoa sitting beside the slider, patiently waiting to be let out. I take a careful look outside first, scanning the edge of the yard where the lawn meets the trees. Satisfied no one's lurking out there, I lift the latch and slide the door open, then wait while Cocoa trots over to the grass and does her business. When she comes back inside, I close the slider and reset the latch, then tug on the door handle to ensure it's locked.

Before turning back to the stove, I do one last scan of the yard. It's late afternoon and the shadows are deepening in the woods. A breeze shifts the tree branches, and for a second, I think I see something moving out there, and the sound of breaking glass echoes in my head. A shiver runs down my spine and my eyes dart to the drawer beside the stove. Maybe having my own gun isn't such a bad idea after all.

I'm glad we've got the new security cameras, but Mitch still hasn't shown me how to use the app so I can control them from my phone. He had promised to give me a tutorial after he installed them, but he got too tired and put it off. Thinking about that day, I'm reminded of the argument I witnessed between him and Merv Scanlon. I couldn't hear what they were saying, but it looked like it got heated. I'm always nervous when they quarrel, because I'm afraid Merv's wife Edith will get mixed up in it somehow, and then I'll be in trouble.

I worked with Edith Scanlon a long time ago, before Mitch and I were married. After high school, I got my Associate's degree in human resources, and took a job with a local real estate developer. It didn't pay very well, so I supplemented my income by waiting tables on the weekends, at an Italian restaurant a few blocks from my studio apartment on the edge of downtown. Edith was the restaurant manager.

My first night on the job, I was surprised to find Ann Marie working there too, as a full-time employee. She was a few pounds heavier than she used to be, but she was cute and sassy as ever, and seemed genuinely glad to see me again. Due to our history, I was standoffish at first, but we often worked the same weekend shifts, which gave us the chance to start talking again. Ann Marie wasn't one to shy away from the mistakes she'd made, and she joked openly about her poor life choices. Pretty soon, her friendly chatter and lively energy pulled me right back into the familiar grooves of our former friendship.

Edith didn't like me for some reason, probably because I didn't kiss up to her the way Ann Marie did. In return for Ann Marie's opportunistic brown-nosing, Edith gave her first dibs on the busiest shifts, and assigned her the best tables to wait on. It bugged me, but I went along with it without arguing. It was only a part-time job for me anyway, so it didn't really matter.

Ann Marie put on a good show of being a self-assured, upbeat person, but underneath the sunny facade, her life wasn't all that great.

She complained that the guys she was interested in didn't want to go out with her because she had a kid, and she was tired to death of living at home, and having to follow her parents' rigid rules. She was desperate to get out of their house, but couldn't afford to live on her own, which gave me an unaccustomed edge over her.

Compared with Ann Marie's dead-end state of affairs, my life was in much better shape, and I came away feeling rather proud of myself. Although my salary was minimal, it was enough for me to live independently in my own place. For a time, Ann Marie got an idea in her head about us renting an apartment together and splitting the bills, but I told her I'd signed a long-term lease agreement, and had to stay put where I was for the time being. The actual truth was that I was worried her luck would turn, and she'd find an eligible man to move in with, and leave me in the dust again. I was twenty-one years old, but I was already convinced my plain looks and dull-as-dishwater career choice had destined me for dried-out old maidhood. My life was a boring routine of work and more work, with no time for a social life. I'd gone on only two dates in the past two years, and nothing had come of either one.

Ann Marie's outlook brightened unexpectedly a few months later, when Mitch was discharged from the Army. It really bothered me, seeing her throw herself so blatantly at him, after the way she'd treated him in high school. She obviously saw steady, reliable Mitch as her ticket to a more prosperous and respectable life, and she wasn't about to let him slip through her fingers. Mitch was such a nice guy too—so clean cut and mature from his time in the service. Too nice for his own good, I guess. He fell back under Ann Marie's spell in an instant, and despite my feelings for him, which were more ardent than ever, he once again chose her over me.

God, how I envied her! When she dragged me into the storeroom about two seconds after I'd clocked in one evening, and squealed the news in my ear that Mitch had proposed to her the night before, I was so envious, my stomach hurt. They got married right before Christmas, but I pretended to be down with the flu, so I didn't have to go. I stayed hidden in my tiny studio the entire weekend, burying my loneliness beneath a mind-numbing barrage of cable TV and Byrne Dairy ice cream. After the wedding, I persuaded Edith to change the nights I worked, because listening to Ann Marie gush about married life had become too painful to bear. Our friendship gradually faded, just as it had before.

Mitch has no knowledge of the part I played in what happened after that, and I will never, ever tell him. It's my burden to carry with me for the rest of my life. Edith knows, of course; but she's never said a single word about it to me or, as far as I know, to anyone else besides her nasty husband. She's got her own reasons for concealing the truth, but she's getting old and senile now, and I'm scared that one of these days, she's going to let something slip. I can only pray she continues to keep her mouth shut.

10

Rudy

Friday afternoon, I fly into a full-blown panic over my impending date with Laci. As I dig through my limited wardrobe, I look at my clothing through her eyes, and realize how grubby everything is. In the end, I choose my least worn pair of jeans, and the collared shirt from Target that I wore to my eviction. Fudgie's got the day off from Jiffy Lube, so I'm thankful he's here to talk me down. "Relax, man," he says. "You got this. Be yourself, and let her do most of the talking."

Now that I'm gainfully employed—for the time being, anyway—Fudgie has chilled out about loaning me his car. I drive to the mall and wait for Laci near the carousel, growing more jittery every second. Ten minutes pass before I spot her coming my way through the throng of shoppers. She's in the same long raincoat she was wearing when we met on the bus, but with a fuzzy purple scarf to dress it up this time, and jeans that are cuffed a few inches above her combat boots.

We exchange a shy greeting, then I ask her if she wants to get something to eat, since that's what you do on a date. "Sure," she says with a big smile, and we head toward Taco Bell in the food court. We order off the Value Menu, and I pay for both of us with my debit card. When our food comes up, we carry our trays to a vacant table.

Laci shrugs off her coat and hangs it over the back of the empty chair next to her. Her black-and-pink hair is piled on top of her head, and she's got these really big gold hoops dangling from her ears. She looks so pretty, it makes me dizzy. I can hardly believe she's *my date*.

Too scared to start a conversation, I focus on scarfing down my meal, and my Classic Combo disappears in about two seconds flat. "Wow," Laci says. "You must've been really hungry."

I haven't eaten a thing all day because I was too nerved up. I'm still unable to make eye contact, so I study Laci's hands as she eats her burrito. Her nails are short and polished black, and there are dimples where each of her chubby fingers joins her hand. I notice she's got lipstick on tonight, in a shade of purple that matches her fuzzy scarf. "That's a nice color," I say, pointing at the scarf. It's an idiotic comment, but Laci smiles again and says thanks.

Remembering to mind my manners, I gather our discarded wrappers and toss them in a nearby trash can, then sit down again. Without food to occupy me, the jitters return and my leg starts jumping like crazy beneath the table, causing it to vibrate. Laci pretends not to notice, and gives me another broad smile. "Thanks for buying me dinner. I haven't had Taco Bell in ages. It's my absolute favorite fast food." I grin back at her, and the ice is finally broken.

Glow Golf is on the lower level of the mall, so we take the escalator down. Laci offers to pay her own way, but I won't hear of it. I'm in the groove now. Rudy Hodgens, Date Master. We each select a putter, then choose our golf balls—neon orange for me, hot pink for Laci. "Ladies first," I say, gesturing with a goofy flourish that makes her laugh.

The first hole is a simple L-shape, and it takes only a couple of strokes for us to finish it. Laci cheers when I sink my ball. We move on to the second hole, which has a Day-Glo mural of a rising sun on the wall behind it. Laci wants me to go first this time, so I step up to the line. My ball ricochets gently off a bright yellow divider and stops in prime position for my next shot.

"How's your job going?" Laci asks as she readies herself for her turn.

"It's not too exciting, but not too stressful, either. My supervisor's kind of a butt, but it doesn't really matter, since it turns out it's only a temporary position. Six weeks from now, I'll have to start applying again."

"Oh, that's a bummer." Laci swings her putter and hisses a *yessss* as her ball rolls cleanly through a pair of fake Roman columns.

I recall our bus conversation, when I pretended the job paid quite well. I don't want her to get the wrong idea about my cash flow, since I'm only making minimum wage. "The salary isn't what I was expecting, either. I'm definitely going to be on the lookout for something else."

"Good," Laci says. "I'm sure you can do much better."

We move on to the third hole. There's a big green windmill in the middle of it that completely jacks me up, but I don't care—we're vibing and having fun. Laci asks more questions about my job, and I can feel myself loosening up. It's nice to talk to someone who's interested in getting to know me, instead of nagging and telling me what to do.

Laci leads the way to the next hole, which has an underwater theme of seahorses and funky-colored fish. "I forgot to ask you before—whereabouts do you live?"

I take a practice swing with my putter, like the pros do. "Over on the west side, near the old chemical plant." When I describe Fudgie's place, she wants to know how long we've been roommates, and I tell her only a few weeks.

"Where'd you live before that, then?"

"Out in Centerport. Long story."

Tilting her head to one side, Laci waits for me to go on. I consider for a moment, wondering how much I want to share with this girl who I've only just met. Telling her why I moved in with Fudgie means I'll have to explain how I got evicted. She'll think I'm a loser, and this date will be over. I decide it's best to reveal only the basics. "I wasn't getting along with my stepfather, so I moved out."

"Oooh, I see." Laci nods her head knowingly. "I can relate."

We continue playing, but neither of us is concentrating on the game anymore because we're having too good of a time talking. Laci tells me about her laboratory classes, and gets me laughing when she describes one her instructors, who looks like a zombie straight out of *The Walking Dead*. She talks about the stray cat she adopted and named

Lady Gaga because of its long white hair, and I tell her about Cocoa, and how much I've missed the little bugger since I moved out. "Maybe you could go over to your stepparents' house and borrow her," Laci suggests. "Take her for a walk or something."

It's a nice thought, but—no. We finish our game and turn in our equipment, then take the escalator back up to the food court, to grab milkshakes at Johnny Rockets. "I love this retro fifties decor," Laci says as she climbs onto a shiny red stool at the counter.

"Me too," I say, even though the black-and-white checkered floor is making my eyes freak out. To steady myself, I keep my gaze on Laci, who's swiveling her stool back and forth like a kid. I'm no longer afraid of making eye contact with her, but now I'm concerned about the brightness of the lights in here. The stress of moving out and starting a new job has caused my rosacea to make an inconvenient reappearance. Laci might have overlooked the clusters of ugly red bumps on my nose and cheeks in the awkwardness of our initial meeting, followed by the dim lighting in Glow Golf, but there's no way she won't notice now.

A dude in a paper hat and bowtie sets two tall glasses topped with whipped cream in front of us. Laci stops her twisting and takes a big slurp through her straw, then swivels back to me. I decide to face it head on. "I suppose you've noticed—" I say, gesturing toward my face. "I've got this skin condition?"

She looks at me. "Yeah, I noticed. So?"

I can't believe it—she literally doesn't care what I look like! My worries drain right out of me, like water swirling down a sink. "I just wanted to mention it, in case you were wondering. I've had a hard time dealing with it, especially when I was younger. Kids at school used to call me Rudolph the Red-Nosed Reindeer. Original, huh?"

Laci nods in sympathy. "Kids can be so cruel." She touches my knee, and I get tingles up my leg. "You know, Rudy, I really appreciate that you opened up to me about not getting along with your stepfather."

I wasn't aware that I'd particularly "opened up" about anything, but when Laci smiles at me, I feel my chest expanding, like there's a loaf of homemade bread rising inside my ribs. She wipes a stray blob of whipped cream from her nose ring. "My family's screwed up, too. My parents split up when I was little, and then my mom died last year, so I had to go live with my dad and this woman Tiff that he's been calling his fiancée for like the past ten years." She pulls a face. "Good luck with that. They treated me okay and all, but my dad's an alcoholic who's incapable of taking responsibility for anything. I think the booze has rotted his brain cells."

She pauses to take another sip of milkshake. "He and the quote unquote fiancée live in this dinky duplex in Woodland Homes. It's a sucky place, you've probably never even heard of it."

Oh, but I have. "Woodland Homes? I'm familiar with it. The neighborhood I grew up in is right near there, on the other side of the woods."

"Really?" Laci pokes her straw deeper into her shake, then licks a dollop of ice cream off the end of it. "Anyway, Tiff already has two children of her own by two different fathers, plus there's my half-brother Jayden, who she had with my dad, so there really wasn't enough room for me to stay with them."

"So, what did you do?"

"My aunt let me move in with her. She lives on the west side too, in those rowhouses on Charles Street, where it dead-ends by the old railroad tunnel."

I know the area, which is within walking distance of Fudgie's place. It's borderline ghetto, but who am I to judge? If not for Fudgie's generosity, I don't know what I would've done. Probably ended up in a homeless shelter downtown, panhandling on Salina Street.

"I used to babysit Jayden all the time when he was younger," Laci goes on, "so we're really close."

"How old is he?"

"He just turned fourteen. Here, let me show you a pic." She takes her phone out and scrolls through her photos, then hands it to me. "This is us last Christmas." The picture is a selfie of Laci with her arm hooked around the neck of a husky boy with buck teeth. He looks like the kid who came up to my car the day I went to Woodland Homes, but they can't be the same person, because the boy in the photo is too young. I admire it for a polite second, then hand the phone back.

"He's a smart kid," Laci says, "but I worry about him. He's been hanging with an older crowd, and I'm worried they're going to drag him into some bad stuff. I don't know what I'd do if he got hooked on drugs, or got into trouble with the law."

I make supportive *mmm hmm* sounds, to show that I care. Being an only child, I honestly don't know what it's like to worry about a sibling's welfare. It's been more than enough, worrying about myself.

Looking around, Laci notices the diner has emptied out. "They must be getting ready to close soon. I guess we'd better go." She slides off her stool, and I follow her out. When we reach the main entrance of the mall, we both hesitate. I'm guessing Laci took the bus here, and I'm not about to let her ride it home again by herself, especially when we're heading back to the same part of town. I offer her a ride, and she accepts. I'm thrilled that I've earned her trust.

We drive back to the west side. I turn onto rundown Charles Street and pull up in front of a row of rundown houses at the far end of the narrow lane. There's only one streetlight, which casts a weird multi-colored glow across the graffitied stone arch of the abandoned railroad tunnel beyond it. Panic is rising again. I'm not sure what I'm supposed to do next—shake hands with her? Kiss her? On the cheek, or on the lips?

To my relief, Laci knows what to do. Leaning over, she kisses my cheek. "Thanks for a fun night, and for the ride home."

By some blessed miracle, I know what to say next. "I had fun, too. Would you like to go out again sometime?"

Laci's toothy grin reappears. "Yes, definitely!" She goes to open her door, then pauses and turns back to me. "By the way, there's an open house coming up at City Tech. I'm volunteering as a student ambassador, to help answer people's questions, and show them around."

Not sure what she's getting at, I look at her blankly. She reaches her hand out and touches my forearm, which sends a ripple of excitement through me. "You said your job was only temporary, and it doesn't pay that well. I was thinking you could check out the courses they offer at CT, maybe sign up for something that interests you. There's tons of programs—electronics, automotive, computer technology, all kinds of stuff. And they've got a placement center that helps you find a job when you finish. There are still openings available for the fall semester. It could be a great opportunity for you."

A warm glow fills me. It feels so good to have someone care about what I do. Though I'm loathe to admit it, Mitchell was right—I do need to get serious about my life, and Laci seems willing to help me. "That sounds awesome," I say. "I think I'd like to go."

"Great!" Laci grins at me again, then plants another quick kiss on my cheek. "Text me," she calls as she pushes the car door open and climbs out. I watch her go up the walkway and let herself into her aunt's unit, then I drive away in a daze, marveling at the completely unexpected and wonderful turn that my life has taken.

11

Rudy

Laci and I meet up again at the bus stop, to go to the open house at City Tech. Since our first date, we've gone out twice more—once to see a movie, and another time when we hung out at a coffee shop and talked. We've also been texting constantly. Laci's always joking and sending me goofy emojis, and I feel a little zing of excitement every time I see her name pop up on my phone. The awkwardness between us has completely disappeared, and we embrace like old friends inside the bus shelter.

The City Tech building in downtown Syracuse is a repurposed former high school that was built in 1900. The open house is on the first floor, in a high-ceilinged room that was the old gymnasium. Tables are set up around the perimeter, each with a display board behind it, showing photographs of smiling young people engaging in work as plumbers, machinists and healthcare techs. Because Laci has volunteered to help out today, we've arrived early and there aren't that many people here yet. While she goes to check in with the event coordinator, I find a folding chair in a corner, sit down and look over a brochure about careers in computer programming.

I'm starting to have my doubts about all this. My previous experience with college was dismal. I liked math and science when I was in middle school, and I joined the robotics team with all the other nerds, which was kind of fun. But after I graduated and it came time for me to register at the community college, Mitchell pressured me into the pre-engineering curriculum, which I ended up hating. The classes were boring, and way harder than the ones I took in high school. I tried to study, but failed all my tests anyway, so I eventually gave up. When the school put me on academic probation, I thought I'd save them the trouble of expelling me, and dropped out. Mitchell was irate, but he has no idea how difficult college is, since he never went himself.

The gym fills with people, and the open house gets underway right on time at 1:00. I'm unwilling to get up and walk around by myself, so I stay put where I am, wondering where Laci's gotten to. A short while later, she comes and finds me. "They've got more volunteers than they need," she says, "so I'm free to show you around. Where would you like to go first?"

I have no frigging clue. "Um," I say. "Whatever you think."

"Perfect!" Laci leads the way to a nearby table with a sign over it that says Culinary Arts. "Does this interest you?"

You've got to be joking. I like to eat all right, but I hate cooking anything more elaborate than toast or an omelet. "No," I answer. "Not at all."

We move on, to Dental Assisting. The literature on the table shows jolly dental assistants hovering over reclining patients, getting ready to do scary shit to their teeth with sharp instruments. I shake my head. "Nope. No way."

The next stop is Early Childhood Care—definitely not for me. We breeze past it to Phlebotomy. "I considered switching into this after I changed my mind about cosmetology," Laci says, "but I decided the Lab Assistant program was a better fit for my long-term career plans."

We continue on to the table for Teaching Assistant, which doesn't excite me in the least. Laci's beginning to look discouraged, which concerns me. She's going to think I'm a slacker with no future if I don't show an interest in something pretty soon. Our next stop is Automotive Repair. I enjoy figuring out how things work, but all those complicated tools… I take the brochure anyway, and Laci smiles at me. Machining is next, so I take that brochure too, to make her think I'm really getting into it.

The last stop on this side of the gym is the HVAC program—
Heating, Ventilation and Air Conditioning. The fortyish guy behind
the table reminds me a little of my real father, with his working man's
sturdy build, flannel shirt and scruffy beard. That's about all I
remember of my dad, who stopped coming to visit after I finished the
eighth grade. For all I know, he could be dead or have disappeared into
the wilds of Alaska.

The HVAC guy shakes my hand, and asks how I'm doing today. He
waves a brochure at me. "Did you know the number of jobs in the
HVAC field are projected to increase at a faster than average rate over
the next few years?" I tell him I was not aware of that fact. He nods and
informs me that the industry also offers excellent entry-level salaries,
which catches my interest, and he shows me some literature to back up
his claims. "You can't go wrong with the HVAC program here at CT.
There's high demand for technicians right now, so you'll begin your
career in a good job with plenty of room for advancement."

Laci's standing close behind me, listening over my shoulder. She's
wearing her hair long and loose today, and I can smell her perfume, or
shampoo, or whatever it is that's filling my head with a delicious
fragrance. I feel her pressing against my back as she reads the brochure
along with me. I need to say something intelligent, so I turn back to the
guy. "What does an HVAC technician do, exactly?"

He's psyched to tell me all about it. "We'll teach you the mechanics
of motors and pumps, and how electronic systems operate. You'll get
hands-on training that will prepare you for a job as a refrigeration
installer, maintenance mechanic, or home appliance repair tech."

"This might be a good one for you," Laci says, "since you're so
dexterous. I could tell by the way you played golf so well at the mall."

Dexterous. It's not a word that anyone's ever used to describe me
before. I like the picture of myself that it brings to mind—a capable,
skillful person, instead of the useless being that Mitchell can't stand to
be around.

"It's a certificate program," Laci points out, "so you'll be done in only two semesters. Think about it—you could have a full-time job by summer!"

Despite my reservations about going back to school, I'm tempted. I could work with my hands, but still use my brain. I know I can do it, if I stay focused and apply myself. Laci prods me in the back. "What do you think, Rudy?"

I might as well go for it, since nothing else has appealed to me so far. I reply after reflecting another moment or two. "I think I might like this."

The HVAC guy gives me a card with a QR code on it, that he says will take me straight to the City Tech application form. "Classes begin a week after Labor Day, and financial aid is easy to apply for online. If you have any questions, you can call the admissions office and they'll help you out."

Laci is practically jumping out of her skin next to me. "Oh my gosh, Rudy!" she says, squeezing my arm with both hands. "Are you really going to do it?"

Yes, I tell her, I am. At long last, here's a chance for me to find a direction in life, which makes me feel like a real human being. I'll have to figure out how to pay the tuition, and have a talk with Fudgie about crashing with him long term. But once I graduate and get a good-paying job, like the HVAC guy said I would, I'll be able to get my own place. I grab Laci's hand. She responds with that cute buck-toothed grin of hers, and my insides do an excited flip.

We stop for sodas at McDonald's on our way back from the open house. Sitting across from each other in a booth, we discuss my new academic plans. "You're going to *love* City Tech," Laci gushes. "Let me know when you're ready to set up your class schedule, so I can make sure we have the same free periods." Smiling sweetly, she nudges my knee. "Maybe we could eat lunch together in the caf." She checks the time on her phone. "Darn, I've got to get back. I promised my aunt I'd make dinner, and she likes to eat early."

Fudgie's there when I get home. His girlfriend Sabrina is working tonight, so we settle in for an evening of hardcore gaming. In between rounds of *Halo*, I tell him about my school plans. "A year from now," I say proudly, "I'll be a certified professional technician with a salary and benefits."

My roommate is impressed. "Maybe I oughta do that. Jiffy Lube's gettin' old. I applied for Crew Chief but they turned me down cuz I haven't been there long enough. I might hafta bail and find something else." He tosses his controller aside, lifts his skinny legs onto the battered coffee table, and massages his shins. "How 'bout that girl you been seeing? Anything going on?"

I can't help smiling. "Yeah, I really like her. It was her idea to go to the open house. She's gonna show me how to apply for a Pell Grant, so I don't have to pay for anything at school."

Fudgie nods. "That's the way."

"I'll need to crash here a while longer though, bro. That okay with you?"

"Sure," he replies. "That's cool with me, long as you can keep chipping in."

I lean back on the couch and cross my arms behind my head. "Laci's great. She's smart and ambitious, and she's got this whole career plan laid out for herself once she finishes at City Tech."

My phone dings—a text from Laci, saying goodnight. "Hang on a sec," I tell Fudgie, and type a quick reply: *Sweet dreams. CYT.* I put my phone down. "We get along really well, and she's so easy to talk to. It's only been a couple weeks, but it already feels like we've known each other forever."

"I'm happy for you, man." Fudgie punches my shoulder. "Look at us, we both got a girl now. Who'd a thought?" I punch him back, grinning like a fool.

•   •   •   •   •

Fudgie's staying at his girlfriend's place, so I invite Laci over to hang out on the following Saturday night. I haven't kissed her properly yet, but tonight's the night I'm gonna make it happen. After she arrives, we order a pizza and get settled on the couch with a movie, but we wind up talking instead.

We're both excited for school to start in a week. Laci helped me set up my schedule and apply for financial aid, so I'm ready to roll. She's been researching salaries for her future career as a crime scene investigator. "If I go on to get my bachelor's degree," she says, "I could be earning six figures one day."

"Holy," I say. "That's a lot."

"Yeah, it's amazing. Do you know what the entry-level salary is in the HVAC field?"

I don't. The guy at City Tech said I'd be earning an "excellent" salary, which was enough info for me. I grab my laptop to look it up. My screensaver is a picture of Cocoa when she was a puppy. "Oh, she's adorbs!" Laci coos. "So darn cute. How can you stand to not see her anymore?"

"Why would I miss her when I've got this?" I point toward the kitchen counter, where there's a Mason jar of water containing Blueberry, Fudgie's betta fish.

Laci swats my arm. "Silly! A fish isn't a real pet. Don't you miss your dog?"

"Of course, I do. I love Cocoa." I tell her how my stepparents surprised me with a puppy on my thirteenth birthday, to cheer me up after my father's disappearing trick. "She was the cutest, fluffiest little thing. I played with her all the time since I didn't have any friends. I used to walk her around the neighborhood after school every day until Mrs. Scanlon, the weird lady next door, started creeping me out. She'd jump out of the bushes between our yards like she was stalking me, and say stuff about my stepmother that didn't make any sense."

Laci pats my arm. "Hold on a sec. You keep calling them your 'stepparents.' I don't get it—how can they both be your stepparents? Shouldn't it just be one or the other?"

I explain the whole thing about my mother's teenage pregnancy and my fly-by-night father, and how Mitchell saved the day by marrying my mom and becoming my stepfather. "But then when I was five years old, my mother was killed in a car accident."

Laci looks stricken. "Oh my gosh, you poor thing!"

"Yeah, it was tough. Then Mitchell married Debra, so she became my stepmother, see? They never bothered to legally adopt me, though. They obviously didn't care enough, or thought it would be too much trouble. It's not something I like to talk about it. Besides Fudgie, you're the only person I've ever told."

"But wait," Laci says. "Your real father was still alive, right? You said he used to visit you."

"Yeah, he did for a while, but then he stopped coming. I guess he didn't want to be inconvenienced by any of my adolescent crap."

"Are you sure? Maybe he died or something."

I shrug. "All I know is that he never came to see me anymore. That's why Deb and Mitch gave me a puppy, to make me feel better. I've tried looking him up on the internet, but I can't find anything."

Laci won't let go of this bone. "If your biological father was still living, your stepparents couldn't have adopted you, unless your father gave up his parental rights, or neglected his financial obligations." She leans into me, and her wonderful Laci scent fills my senses. "I know a lot about this, because of my own screwy family. Was he still paying child support?"

"Yeah, I guess so. A check would come in the mail from him every once in a while, and Debra would put it in the bank for me."

"Okay, then. That means your stepparents had no legal recourse. I'll bet they wanted to adopt you, but they couldn't."

Damn, this girl is a wonder. I'm barely registering the movie droning in the background. I reach out and tuck a strand of hair behind Laci's ear. This is it, the moment when I make my move. Before I can chicken out, I lean in and plant one on her. Her lips feel soft, and taste faintly like grape soda. We pull apart and she gazes back at me, then we kiss again, closing our eyes this time. "You're awesome," I murmur.

I'm ready for more action, but Laci wants to keep talking. Locking hands, we scooch closer together, and she tells me more about her own family. "It's so screwed up, Rudy. I was too embarrassed to tell you all this before. My mother was an addict, and she went to jail for possession. After she got out, she fell right back into her drug habit, and died of an overdose. I was the one who found her."

This is a level of dysfunction way beyond my experience. "That must have been awful," I say, squeezing her hand.

"It was, but I'm over it." Tears glint in her eyes, but she brushes them away. "She wasn't a very good mother anyway."

All of the sudden, I'm thankful for my comparatively normal upbringing. My life is way less chaotic than Laci's, and I'm slowly beginning to recognize the fact that I've brought a lot of my problems on myself.

I feel so comfortable sharing things with Laci like this, in a way I've never felt with anyone else before. Since we've opened up to each other, I figure I might as well go for full disclosure, and tell her the real reason I moved out. She already knows that Mitchell and I don't get along, so it's not like I've been withholding a big secret.

"Um…" I begin. "There's something else I should tell you."

Laci strokes my hand and gives me an encouraging smile. "What is it?"

I talk fast, taking care to spin the story so I'll come across as the victim. "They pressured me to leave. Mitchell, especially. He was a savage, always bawling me out and making threats, and throwing shade on everything I did. He shut off the heat in my room too, in the middle of winter." That last thing is completely made up, but it fits my narrative.

I'm on the verge of telling Laci how my stepparents lawyered up and had me evicted, but at the last second, I lose my nerve. Dropping a bomb like that might turn her off, and spoil the current comfy mood. It'll be safer to save that topic for another day, so I gloss over the details instead. "Mitchell didn't give me any choice, he just told me I had to get out. So, I took my stuff and moved in here with Fudgie."

Laci stares at me. "Are you serious? Your stepfather kicked you out?"

"Yeah, he did." Blood roars in my ears and my palms are sweating. I brace myself—any second now, it's going to dawn on her that I'm a loser, a total waste of her time.

Instead, Laci bristles in my defense. "I can't believe he did that to you!" She brandishes her can of White Claw. "What a complete jerk!"

Her righteous anger exhilarates me. I've never had anyone stick up for me like this besides my Grandma Nan, before she lost her marbles and had to be carted off to memory care.

Laci nuzzles my cheek. "That is so awful, Rudy. You poor thing."

I'm relieved that my sob story hasn't put her off, but I'm suddenly wiped out from talking so long about myself, which I'm not used to doing. Laci quickly picks up on the shift in my mood, and switches the conversation to a new crime drama she's watching. We turn off the movie we've been ignoring this whole time, and search for the first episode of her show on Netflix. It's Fudgie's account, but he's cool with me using it.

We snuggle together under a blanket, but before I press Play on the remote, I ask Laci if she'll be my girlfriend. She giggles and says yes, and my heart soars as we begin kissing again. It feels fantastic to be cozied up with my very first girlfriend like this, but in the back of my mind, a persistent worry keeps nagging at me—if the police catch up with me, I'm screwed.

12

Debra

The firearms safety course that Mitchell signed me up for is scheduled for the last weekend of September. Mitch drops me off early, so he'll have a few minutes to catch up with his buddy before the class begins. The Rod & Gun Club is out in the country, on 100 acres of open land that borders a disused branch of the Erie Canal. I've never been here before. The gravel entrance drive leads to a gray cinderblock building that Mitch says is the clubhouse. Beside it is a long, low shed that houses the indoor pistol range, and the outdoor shooting range lies beyond it at the end of the road.

We're the first ones to arrive. A muscular man with a buzz cut greets us at the door of the clubhouse, and introduces himself to me as Patrick. He and Mitchell exchange handshakes and backslaps, then we go inside. The main room is divided in two, with a small kitchen and dining area on one side, and a classroom section on the other. Three rows of rectangular tables and folding chairs are set up on the classroom side, with instruction books, pens and paper arranged neatly at each place.

After a few minutes of listening to my husband and his friend reminisce about the days when they used to go hunting and fishing together, I excuse myself and take a seat in the back row. Class doesn't begin for another twenty minutes, so I've got time to kill. I thumb through my instruction book, browsing the lesson content: state and federal laws, situational awareness, the use of deadly physical force. It all sounds very intimidating.

Setting the book aside, I take my phone out of my purse. I've given up on calling Rudy, but I texted him again last night, to ask how his first weeks of school went. I'm hoping he's texted me back, but he hasn't yet. To make myself feel better, I send him another text full of encouraging words, and remind him that I love him.

My classmates have begun to arrive, and to my dismay, they're all outdoorsy-looking men in plaid shirts, jeans and boots. I get a pit in my stomach, worried I'm going to make a fool of myself in front of them. As the chairs fill, Mitch wraps up his conversation with Patrick and walks back to where I'm sitting. He brought his fishing gear with him today, and I can tell he's eager to get to the creek. "I'm heading out now," he says, giving me a quick kiss on the cheek. "Have a good time. I'll be back to pick you up at four."

The two young men seated in front of me are talking to one another as if I'm not even here, so I'm sitting silently in my corner when another woman finally walks in. She's about ten years younger than me, with stylish eye glasses and dark hair arranged in a messy bun. She hesitates when she sees that all the seats up front are taken, but Patrick points her to the empty spot next to me in the back row. I smile as she approaches, relieved to have female company. "Hi, I'm Joanne," the woman says as she pulls out her chair and sits down.

"I'm Debra. Nice to meet you."

Joanne flips through the instruction book for a minute, then turns to me. "I'm really nervous. I've never handled a gun before, except for my brother's Red Ryder when we were kids. How about you?"

The pit in my stomach shrinks a little. "Same here. My husband signed me up for this class. He bought me a gun, and said I had to learn how to use it."

Joanne laughs. "My brother made me sign up. I'm recently divorced, so he thinks I need to learn how to protect myself at home."

"Oh my gosh, my husband said the exact same thing! He works nights, so he doesn't want me being alone and defenseless." I make air quotes with my fingers as I say that last part, and Joanne rolls her eyes.

"Okay folks, let's get started." Patrick moves to the front of the room and stands with his feet apart, the tips of his first two fingers resting on his hips. He looks like the kind of guy who'd gladly throw himself between the president and a would-be assassin. "To remind you, this is an 18-hour class. The coursework will be spread over two days, and we'll end with two hours of instruction in the basic principles of marksmanship, using live ammunition on the shooting range tomorrow afternoon." Joanne and I glance at each other with identical *Oh my God* expressions.

Class begins with a lengthy discussion of the general safety rules involved in the handling of firearms. After that, we learn about safe storage, conflict management, and New York state law regarding the duty to retreat. At noon, we take a thirty-minute break. The men gather in the kitchen area to eat the lunches their wives packed for them, but Joanne and I stay in our seats and chat.

"Do you live around here?" I ask her as I unwrap the cheese sandwich I brought.

Joanne stirs her container of salad. "I'm down the road, in Elbridge. I used to live in Centerport though, when I was married."

"How long have you been divorced?"

"Almost a year now."

"Oh," I say. "I'm sorry."

Joanne wrinkles her nose. "No need to be sorry. It was a long time coming. He found someone younger, and I didn't feel like competing. Good riddance, I say."

I'm impressed by her self-assurance. I can't imagine getting divorced at my age, and having to take care of myself after all these years of Mitchell being in charge. "Well," I say, "I'm glad you're here. I thought I was going to be the only woman in the class."

Joanne gestures toward our classmates with her fork. "How much do you want to bet that we turn out to be better shots than any of those fellas?"

Her cheeky attitude makes me laugh. "Who knows?" I reply. "Maybe we will."

•   •   •   •   •

When Mitchell comes to pick me up at four, the first thing he wants to know is how did I enjoy the class. I give him a noncommittal answer. I'm tired from sitting on a plastic folding chair all day, and for a good deal of the time, I was bored. The only bright spot was my lunchtime conversation with Joanne.

"You'll have a better time tomorrow," Mitchell says as he turns into our neighborhood. "The range work will be fun, you'll see."

I seriously doubt it, but keep my opinion to myself.

Mitch has to work Sunday night, so the next day he stays home to catch up on his sleep, and I drive myself to the club. The classroom instruction moves along more quickly than yesterday, and ends with a written test, which I ace. I guess I was listening better than I realized.

"We'll head to the outdoor range now," Patrick says, collecting the papers. "Grab your coats, it's getting cold out." The class follows him down the gravel road to a wide clearing bordered on two sides by dense rows of trees that are beginning to drop their leaves. On the far end, there's an enormous earthen berm that serves as a backdrop. In the center of the clearing is a row of paper targets with bright red bullseyes, mounted on stands made out of PVC pipe.

Patrick pairs us up, putting Joanne and me together, and distributes the firearms we'll be using for the drills. The men look excited, but I feel the pit growing in my stomach again, much bigger this time. We've already practiced loading and unloading with dummy rounds in the classroom, but now it's about to get real. Glancing at Joanne, I can tell she's as nervous as I am.

"The first person in each pair will now load and make ready," Patrick says. "Five rounds. Follow the safety rules you learned." Joanne and I widen our eyes at each other. She agreed to go first, since I'm too scared to. She loads her gun, then steps up to the firing line with the others in her group. Following Patrick's commands, she successfully completes the drill.

Now it's my turn. I load my gun as I was taught, then step up to the line with my hands in the low ready position, and wait for the next instruction. My heart's banging like mad, so I breathe deep, to try and slow it down.

"Fire all five rounds, slow and steady," Patrick says, "then drop your mag and show clear to your partner. All ready on the line?" Those of us who are preparing to shoot call out "Yes" in unison. "Okay," Patrick says. "Fire at will."

I take another deep breath, which doesn't slow my pulse any. Raising my arms, I adjust my stance, align my sights, tighten my grip and pull the trigger, counting the shots in my head. *Bang. Bang. Bang. Bang. Bang.* The slide on my gun locks open. I release the empty magazine, and Joanne verifies that the chamber is empty. My heart's still pounding wildly, but it's with elation this time, instead of fear. *I did it!* Squinting at the target, I see my shots have landed all over the place, but one round hit fairly close to the bullseye. I'm immensely pleased.

As the afternoon goes on, we progress through a series of drills. My confidence grows as my aim improves, and I begin to enjoy myself. At the end of the day, I'm exhausted but exhilarated, and relieved that it's over.

For a couple of beginners, I think Joanne and I did pretty darn well, and we even outperformed a few of the men. When Patrick hands out our certificates, we've each earned a Level 3 out of four, which is better than I'd expected. I'm surprised at how happy it makes me. I faced my fears and learned a new skill, and I'm feeling extremely proud of myself.

"Let's stay in touch," Joanne says as we walk to our cars. "Maybe we could meet up for a cup of coffee some time. Once we get our pistol permits, we could practice shooting together."

I think it sounds like a wonderful idea. To be honest, I've been getting bored with my circle of church lady friends. They're all lovely women, but none of them are interested in doing anything besides attending our weekly Bible Study group, and organizing the annual parish bazaar. I'm craving something more exciting than my tame hobbies of gardening and quilting, and seeing movies with my sourpuss sister.

An afternoon shooting guns at the range almost seems like too daring of a pastime for a stodgy gal like me, but I'm on a roll now, and I want to keep Joanne as a friend. "Sure," I say. "I'd love to get together again." We exchange phone numbers and hug goodbye as if we've been best girlfriends for years.

•   •   •   •   •

My husband is waiting for me when I get home. "How'd it go today?" he asks, the moment I walk in the door. "Did you have fun?"

I try to hide a smile. Unrolling one of my paper targets that I kept as a souvenir, I invite him to admire the grouping of my shots. "Believe it or not, I really enjoyed it. You were right, Mitch. It was fun, once I got over being so scared about it. Patrick was a really good teacher."

Mitch looks gratified. He tries to kiss me, but I shoo him away and carefully roll the target back up. "I made a friend, too—that woman Joanne, who you met yesterday. We might meet for coffee next week." I suddenly notice that Mitch is dressed for work. "Oh gosh, I forgot you're going in tonight. Have you eaten yet?"

"I'm all set, but I've gotta run. I'm really proud of you, Deb." He leans over me again, and I allow him to kiss me goodbye. "Stay safe," he calls over his shoulder he heads out the door.

After he's gone, I notice a neat stack of papers sitting at my place on the kitchen table. Upon closer inspection, I see that Mitch has printed out an application for a pistol permit for me. Smiling at his tenacity, I fix myself a sandwich and a cup of tea, then take the application into my office, sit down at my desk, and begin to fill it out.

13

Rudy

I wake up to the comforting weight of Laci's arm flung across my chest. Her breathing is soft and rhythmic, wafting a sweet and sour fragrance from beneath her tousled hair. It's the first time she's spent the night, and we're squashed together on the futon. Fudgie went somewhere with his girlfriend for the weekend, so we have the apartment to ourselves. With Laci living with her aunt and me sleeping in the living room, we haven't had the chance for this kind of alone time till now.

We've officially been boyfriend and girlfriend for two and a half months now, and it's going great. I wake up in the morning thinking about Laci, and I fall asleep texting her at night. Sometimes she'll say something that sparks this heady feeling, like I've never experienced with any other person before. It makes me feel incredible. I think maybe I'm in love.

Laci's lying on my right arm, giving me pins and needles in it, but the moment is too peaceful—and novel—for me to do anything but lie still and savor it for as long as I can. I'm utterly amazed by the change that has come over my life. This girl actually likes spending time with me. We ride the city bus to school together every morning, and study side by side in the evenings. She makes me feel like I can do anything I put my mind to, as long as she's there to do it with me.

I continue gazing at her till the numbness becomes too uncomfortable. As gently as I can, I try to ease my arm out from under her without waking her, but her eyes flutter open. "Hello," she murmurs. She caresses my cheek, and I crane my neck to kiss her on the forehead. What a lucky, lucky guy I am.

It feels funny to wake up in bed with her, and I'm not sure how I'm supposed to act. Laci's a lot younger than me and equally inexperienced, so she's not sure what to do, either. We're both in our underwear, which is awkward. She sits up on one side of the futon, pulling the sheet with her, and asks me to look the other way while she pulls on a T-shirt. It happens to be my T-shirt, but I don't care, because it's so cool that my girlfriend wants to wear my clothes. It's Sunday morning, so we don't have to get ready to go to class. I roll off the futon on the other side, dress quickly in a fresh T-shirt and jeans, then offer Laci a pair of my sweatpants to put on. We're about the same size, so she doesn't mind borrowing.

We walk five feet into the adjacent tiny kitchen, to scrounge up some breakfast. In the fridge, there's a package of Oscar Mayer bacon that Fudgie bought last week, but I'm sure he won't care if we use a few slices. Laci gets to work cracking eggs into a bowl, then scrambles them up with lots of butter, while I fry the bacon. The breakfast we create is a masterpiece—white toast and eggs, orange juice and coffee. We sit beside each other at the counter, munching away on our food, and talk about school.

I really like my classes, and I'm doing pretty well so far. I'm taking advanced algebra and physics, both of which are a breeze for me, along with basic refrigeration and air conditioning theory, which are more interesting than I expected. My teachers are cool and the tests aren't that hard. Laci's studying laboratory procedures and human anatomy, but the class she's most looking forward to next semester is phlebotomy, where she'll learn how to take blood samples. She says it'll be a stepping stone to her future career as a crime scene investigator.

It's chilly in the apartment because Fudgie likes to keep the heat turned down, to save money. I slide off my stool, cross the small living area, and bump the thermostat up a notch. My phone's sitting on the coffee table and I pick it up as I walk by, to see if I missed any texts last night. There's another lengthy one from Debra. I skim through the caring words she routinely sends and I never respond to; but at the end of this message, she invites me to come over for Thanksgiving dinner next week. I make a face, set the phone on the kitchen counter and push it away. *As if, Deb. Sorry not sorry.*

"Who was that text from?" Laci asks.

"My stepmother."

Laci spoons more sugar into her coffee. "I didn't know you two were talking again."

"We're not, but she keeps texting me all the time, and I haven't felt like responding. That last one was her inviting me for Thanksgiving."

Laci looks surprised. "Are you going to go?"

I laugh. "Why would I want to do that?"

Laci shrugs and stirs her coffee. "I don't know, I was just wondering if anything had changed. I mean, she's been reaching out to you, right? Maybe she wants to make amends."

My laugh turns into a derisive snort. "I seriously doubt it. There's no way they actually want me to come for dinner. Debra's only making a show of inviting me because she feels guilty."

Laci regards me for a long moment, her coffee mug poised in her hand. "Did you like her when she and your stepfather first got married?"

I think about it for a second. "Yeah, I guess I did, at first. She used to drive me to school every day because the kids in my neighborhood were mean, and I didn't like taking the bus. She was really nice that way. I can't say the same for Mitchell, though. He hated me for being a burden to him, after my mom died."

"Oh, come on," Laci says, flapping her hand. "I'm sure he didn't think that. He was probably in over his head, and didn't know how to handle it."

The giddiness I felt when I woke up next to Laci is quickly evaporating. "Whose side are you on here? We're talking about the guy who kicked me out of my house! Mitchell's glad I'm gone, and he doesn't have to deal with me anymore."

"I'm on your side, of course!" Laci pats her hand on my thigh. "Wait a minute, Rudy, let me explain where I'm coming from. I've been thinking about this a lot. Sure, your stepparents treated you like crap, but maybe they had a point? I mean, they only wanted what was best for you. Maybe you should've done something to improve your life a long time ago, like they were always telling you."

I can't believe she just said that. I draw myself up straight on my stool. "I *was* trying to improve my life, but they didn't give me enough time to do it." Deep down, I know this is bullshit. My perspective has changed since I enrolled at City Tech. I'm more focused than I was before, and I'm seeing things more clearly now. But that focus comes from inside me, not from anything Mitchell or Debra has ever said. There's no way in hell I'll give them credit for what I've done for myself.

"I'm just saying," Laci goes on, "from what you've told me, it sounds like they were trying to steer you in the right direction for a long time. They wouldn't have done that if they didn't care about you, so maybe you shouldn't be so mad at them anymore."

I fold my arms across my chest. "I have every right to be pissed as hell at them! What they did to me was wrong. You thought so too, when I told you about it."

Laci waves her hands. "Okay, okay, I did, at first. And I agree with you that it was an awful thing for them to do to you. It's just that—" Her face becomes red and blotchy, and I realize she's about to cry. "You have a mother—a *step*mother, I mean—who actually cares what you do, while I don't have anyone. So, if Debra's inviting you to come for Thanksgiving dinner—" She pauses for a second because she's choking up. "—I think you should go."

She looks so sincere, and I can't stand to see her in tears. "Aw, Laci." I fold her into my arms and hold her for a few moments, stroking her hair. "Please don't cry." When she's calmed down, I pull back a little. "What do you mean, you don't have anyone? You live with your aunt, and you've still got your dad."

Laci's face squinches up again, but she holds back her tears. "My aunt could care less about me, Rudy! The only reason she allows me to live with her is to have someone to help with the cooking and cleaning, and to pick up her insulin prescriptions. She doesn't do holidays, anyway. And as for my dad, he's too effed up to know what day it is. If I go over there for Thanksgiving, all he and Tiff will do is drink, and it'll end up in a fight. Either that, or they'll both pass out before the turkey's even in the oven." She sniffles and wipes her nose. "The only person in my family that I'm close to anymore is Jayden, and he's been blowing me off."

I hug her close again. "I'm so sorry. That really sucks. I didn't know it was that bad."

Laci pulls free and settles back onto her stool. Her eyes are sad, and she uses a torn piece of paper towel to dry her tears. It occurs to me that she's angling for a Thanksgiving invitation. I'd love to help her out, but I can't stomach the idea of going back to my stepparents' house and sitting down to a meal with Mitchell. Even if I could stand to be in the same room with him, I'd be totally paranoid the whole time, remembering what I did the last time I was there.

But then I think what a trip it would be, to go over there and flex about how far I've come in the short time since they kicked me out. I'm enrolled in school now, with a high-paying job to look forward to when I finish in the spring, and I've got this awesome new girlfriend, besides. With Laci backing me up, I could prove to Mitchell that I'm not the degenerate loser he thinks I am, and I could rub it in that I've achieved all of this on my own. It's a double opportunity—if I accept Debra's invitation, I can give Laci the happy holiday she's craving, and throw my success in Mitchell's face.

Laci is looking at me expectantly, and I feel a rush of—love, maybe? My body is humming like a live electrical wire, and I want to grab her and kiss her. With the tips of her fingers, she nudges my phone toward me, and I heave a big sigh. "All right, I'll do it," I say. "For you." Laci beams, which makes me feel terrific.

I dial Debra, and she picks up on the first ring. Our conversation lasts only a minute, but it's long enough for her to tell me how glad she is that I've finally called, and for me to tell her I'm coming for

Thanksgiving dinner. I don't want the call to drag out, so I'm about to cut her off, but then I feel Laci's eyes on me. "Um, Debra?" I say. "Would it be all right if I brought someone with me?" My girlfriend's mouth forms an *O* of delight. My stepmother says I'm welcome to bring whomever I'd like, probably assuming I was referring to Fudgie. *Ha ha,* I think. She's in for a big surprise.

I end the call and Laci flings her arms around my neck. "Thank you, Rudy! This means so much to me!"

We kiss for a minute. Happiness bubbles up until it spills over, and I blurt the words without thinking: "I love you."

Laci pulls back, her big brown eyes staring at me in astonishment. "Oh, Rudy," she whispers. "Do you really mean it?"

"Yes," I whisper back. "I do."

14

Mitchell

When Debra told me she wanted to invite Rudy to come for Thanksgiving, I was opposed to the idea. In my opinion, he didn't deserve an invitation from us, and he needed to apologize for his past behavior before we could even think about mending our relationship. But my wife disagreed with me, as usual. She said it's up to us to make the first move, because we're the grown-ups. Boys take a long time to mature, and Rudy's still an awkward young man with a lot of personal baggage to overcome. As his parents, we should be offering our guidance and encouragement as he finds his way into the adult world, and inviting him to join us for a family dinner is the perfect start. After listening to her argue with me for an entire evening, I grudgingly agreed with her. I figure it'll at least be a chance for us to find out what Rudy's been up to since he left.

•   •   •   •   •

My jerk supervisor has been making work a misery for me lately, so I'm in a crabby mood on Thanksgiving afternoon as Debra bustles around the kitchen, peeling potatoes and making dressing. She's gone all out this year, with extra side dishes and two kinds of pie for dessert. She says Rudy's bringing someone with him—probably that multi-cultural roommate of his with the dumb nickname, since he doesn't have any other friends—so she wants to make sure there's plenty of food.

"I know you don't care for Fudgie," Debra says as she sprinkles brown sugar over a dish of sweet potatoes, "but please be courteous to him." She wipes her hands on a towel and smooths the skirt she put on for this special day. "He offered Rudy a place to live, so I think he deserves our thanks for that."

I wonder if the louse also deserves my thanks for swiping my drill and my gun. With every day that goes by, I'm growing more worried about the missing Glock. I checked the safe at work but it wasn't there, and when I asked the gunsmith at the club, he said he didn't have any record of servicing it, which could've been extremely embarrassing for me. I'm a trained security officer, so I shouldn't be losing track of my firearms like this. I had to make up a story on the spot, about the gun being registered to my wife's permit as well as my own, and that Debra probably put it away somewhere, and forgot tell me.

Now I'm reluctant to tell the police because legally, a missing firearm is supposed to be reported within twenty-four hours, even if you believe you simply misplaced it. If I report it now, I'll have to admit how long I've been aware the gun was missing. I looked up the laws on the internet, and learned that my negligence could result in a thousand-dollar fine, and up to a year in jail. Knowing how much that bastard Gary Scanlon dislikes me, I'm sure he'd do whatever he could to make sure I got the maximum penalty.

I wander restlessly around the house, looking for something to occupy myself with, then go back to the kitchen and gripe about Rudy some more. Debra's bent over the open oven door, basting the turkey. "Please be nice, Mitchell," she pleads.

I dig through the food in the fridge, reaching for the six-pack of Genesee beer in the back. "I'll be polite, as long as he's civil to me in return. You know how he can fly off the handle sometimes."

Debra closes the oven door, and the delicious smell of roasting turkey fades. She blows a wisp of hair out her eyes and straightens her apron. "I want us all to have a pleasant time together, without any arguments. Can you do that for me, Mitch? For one afternoon, that's all I'm asking."

"I'll do my best, but if Rudy starts playing his blame game with me again, I'm telling you right now, I'm not gonna put up with it." Debra huffs and turns back to the stove.

•   •   •   •   •

The doorbell rings at five minutes past three. Debra jumps from her post in the kitchen, and practically runs to the door. I finish off my beer and mentally brace myself. It's been over three months since I've seen Rudy, and despite my earlier blustering, I'm feeling apprehensive about it.

I wait in the kitchen, peeking into the covered dishes on the stovetop, and thinking about cracking another beer. Rudy walks into the room a minute later. He crosses the kitchen and extends his arm for a handshake, which gets us off on the right foot. Then I notice the person standing behind him. I was expecting crippled Fudgie, but Rudy's brought a big-boned teenaged girl with him instead. I immediately don't like the look of her. She's wearing an olive-colored overcoat similar to what the Nazis wore in World War II, and she's got pink hair and a damned nose ring, of all ridiculous things. *For godsakes, Rudy*, I think. *What the hell is this?*

"This is Laci," Rudy says, taking the girl's hand. Debra is hovering behind her, nodding vigorously at me with wide eyes, in a silent reminder for me to mind my manners.

"Hello, Mr. Bateman," Laci says. "It's very nice to meet you."

I mumble something in return. It's gonna take more than one beer to get me through this dinner. While Debra takes their coats and hangs them up in the front hall closet, I grab another Genny from the fridge. We assemble in the living room, and sit looking awkwardly at one another for a minute. The arrival of Laci has caught Debra by surprise as well. I can tell by the way she's looking at Rudy that she's trying to figure out if Laci is just a friend, or a bona fide girlfriend.

"Well then," Debra says, crossing her legs and clasping a knee. "Isn't this nice? Rudy, how have you been since we've last seen you?"

I lean forward, curious to hear what he has to say. He's sitting beside Laci on the loveseat, gripping her hand. He sits up a bit straighter as he answers. "I'm enrolled at City Tech now."

"Oh my!" Debra says. "And how is that going?"

"Good. I like the program."

"What program is it?" I ask.

"HVAC. You know, heating, ventilation and—"

"I know what it stands for," I cut in. "What classes are you taking?"

Rudy describes his first semester curriculum, then Laci interrupts. "He's doing very well. He gets 90s on all his tests, and his teachers really like him." She turns and gives him a smile. "Don't they, Rudy?"

My stepson looks embarrassed, and I wonder if the girl is exaggerating.

"That's good to hear!" Debra says. "I'm so proud of you, Rudy."

Laci speaks up again. "He recently started a new job, too."

All eyes turn to Rudy. "Yeah," he says. "I got a part-time position in a warehouse that sells heating and air conditioning equipment. I help keep track of inventory, which is great experience for me, because I'm learning about the business end of things, along with the practical stuff they're teaching me at school."

I'm surprised he's taken such a sensible view of things, and it makes me mad. Why the heck couldn't he have done this a long time ago? And what was the point of me and Debra wasting our time and effort supporting him for so long, if he had it in him to do it on his own the whole time?

"How about you, Laci?" Debra asks. "Do you go to City Tech as well?"

"Yes," Laci says with an enthusiastic nod. "I brought Rudy to the open house, and persuaded him to sign up for the fall semester. I'm in the Medical Lab Assistant program. I'm planning to eventually get my bachelor's degree in forensic science."

I certainly wasn't expecting her to be that ambitious, and judging by her slovenly looks, I doubt she'll ever get there. "You must be good at math and science," I say. "Have you taken calculus yet, or any chemistry classes?" I'm fishing for clues about her age, since she looks awfully young to me.

Laci's face turns pink. "Not yet, but I'm going to."

Debra comes to the girl's rescue before I can say anything else. "That's wonderful! You must be very excited." Turning to Rudy, she says, "Why don't you tell us how you and Laci met?"

Laci jumps in, and tells a cutesy story about them riding a city bus together. Her overly familiar manner is getting on my nerves, and it annoys me that she's trying to take credit for Rudy's progress, when it was me who pushed him to go back to school in the first place. "How long have you been at City Tech?" I ask her, fishing again.

"Since I graduated. I started in the cosmetology program this summer, but I switched to med lab this fall."

"Since you graduated? Do you mean from high school?"

Laci's expression turns wary. "Ye–es."

Debra senses where I'm going with this, and tries to head me off with an alarmed shake of her head, but I press on. "High school! So that makes you how old—?"

"Eighteen."

"I see." There's an uncomfortable silence. "You do realize," I say, "that Rudy's twenty-five?"

Rudy bristles. "What's your point, Mitchell?"

"Never mind that!" Debra says. "It doesn't matter. Don't forget, Mitchell, I'm two years younger than you." Returning to Laci, she asks, "Do your parents live around here?"

It's a simple question, but Laci seems embarrassed by it. "I live with my aunt, actually. On the west side, not too far from Rudy's place."

"That must be convenient for you," I say, "since Rudy doesn't have a car."

Debra shoots me a warning look. "Do you have any brothers or sisters, Laci?" she asks.

"Yes, I have a half-brother who's a few years younger than me."

"A half-brother," I say. "Does he live with you and your aunt?"

Laci looks uncomfortable again. "No, he lives with my dad."

"With your dad. That's interesting." Debra is glaring at me now, but I don't care if she disapproves. This Laci girl looks to be about one rung above white trash, and I mean to find out what her story is. "What about your mother? Where is she?"

"For your information, Mitchell," Rudy cuts in angrily, "her mother's dead, just like mine, so you can quit with the third degree, okay?"

Debra draws in a sharp breath at Rudy's outburst, but quickly recovers her composure. "I'm so sorry to hear that, Laci. It must be very hard for you."

Laci nods and stares at the floor. An awkward silence follows, but it's soon broken by Debra, who jumps to her feet. "Who's ready to eat? I know I am. Come on, everyone, let's sit down at the table."

I finish my beer and help myself to another. Debra gives me a dark look when she sees the fresh bottle in my hand, but I ignore her. If she expects me to keep my cool through this ordeal, she's gonna have to give me a break. We take our places at the dining room table. Debra says grace, then hands the dishes around. The meal passes relatively peacefully, filled with meaningless small talk and a discussion about college basketball.

When we're done eating, Laci gets up to help Debra clear the table, and I drain the last of my beer. "How are you paying for school, anyway?" I ask Rudy when the girls have gone into the kitchen. "Since you frittered away all that money I gave you."

"Mitchell," Debra calls to me in a warning voice.

"He got a Pell Grant." Laci stands before me, twisting a dish towel in her hands. "I helped him apply for it. His tuition and books are covered for both semesters, so he doesn't have to pay for anything."

Pointing a thumb at my chest, I say, "That's because I'm paying for it, indirectly. A Pell Grant is taxpayer money, you know."

Debra comes back into the dining room. "There will be more funds available one day, for Rudy to put toward his educational expenses," she reminds me. She's referring to the modest inheritance Rudy will receive when his Grandma Nan dies. I wish she hadn't brought it up in front of Laci. Rudy's financial affairs are none of this girl's damn business.

"Time for dessert." Debra sets an apple and a pumpkin pie on the table, along with plates, silverware, and a carton of vanilla ice cream. "Laci, would you mind scooping the ice cream while I slice the pies?"

Our holiday meal proceeds, with only Laci daring to break the silence. "I love pumpkin pie," she says, helping herself to a large piece. "Your crust is perfect, Mrs. Bateman. So tender and flaky."

Debra thanks her for the compliment, then launches into a detailed explanation of the proper way to roll out pastry. "I learned a few tricks from my grandmother," she says. "She was an excellent baker."

"Speaking of which," I say, "when was the last time you saw your grandmother, Rudy?"

Rudy stops with his fork in mid-bite. "What's it to you?"

Nan is my former mother-in-law, so I think I should be allowed to inquire about her without getting an attitude from anybody. "I was only wondering, because you two used to be so close. It'd be a shame if you've been neglecting her."

Debra slaps her palm on the table. "That's enough, Mitchell. Rudy doesn't—"

Laci chimes in: "Rudy was just talking about his Nan the other day. He said he's planning to go visit her soon, and I said I'd go with him."

"How thoughtful of you!" Debra forces a smile. "Mitchell, wasn't that nice of Laci to offer?"

"Oh yes," I say. "Very nice." The stony expression on my wife's face tells me it's time for me to shut up. I'm feeling a little woozy from the alcohol, so I excuse myself and go upstairs to the master bathroom. When I come back down a few minutes later, Rudy and his friend are standing at the front door with their coats on, ready to leave. Debra hugs them each tightly, and whispers something in Laci's ear. The girl listens with her head bowed, then looks up and smiles shyly. Watching them, I realize I've made a hash of things. All Debra asked was for me to be civil for a few hours, and I had to go and blow it.

Later that night, when we're getting ready for bed and my hangover is already setting in, I try to deflect the blame my earlier boorish behavior. "It was the beer," I tell Debra as I pull the blanket up to my chin. "It always loosens my tongue and makes me say stupid things. I shouldn't have had so many."

My wife isn't ready to let it go. "You shouldn't have had *anything* to drink, Mitchell. You know you don't handle alcohol well. You nearly spoiled Rudy's visit. There was no need for you to keep needling him like that, when he's finally showing some maturity."

"I couldn't help it. That girl's a pushy know-it-all. She hardly gave Rudy a chance to speak for himself."

Debra yanks the covers back and climbs into her side of the bed, deliberately making sure our arms and legs don't touch. It's a tried-and-true avoidance tactic that she uses when she's annoyed with me. "I thought she was perfectly pleasant and polite," she says into her pillow. "She helped me wash up the dishes and put the food away, which I thought was very considerate of her."

"Well, you sent her home with enough leftovers for an entire week. I think she's a gold digger. Did you see how her ears perked up when you mentioned Rudy's inheritance?"

Debra sits up in the bed. "She's not a gold digger! How can you say something like that, when she's working so hard to put herself through school? I never said anything specifically about the inheritance anyway, so she wouldn't have known what I was talking about. She was just trying to stick up for Rudy. You made her feel like she needed to defend him, which I think is a good sign. He needs someone who's on his side, unlike *you*."

I raise myself on my elbow. "You think I'm not on his side, after all I did for him?"

Debra glowers at me. "Oh please, Mitchell, stop your self-righteous complaining! I've heard it a million times already, and I don't want to hear any more of it. I'm going to sleep now." With an exasperated huff, she rolls over away from me and turns off her lamp.

15

Rudy

Despite the Thanksgiving family drama, which played out pretty much the way I'd expected it to, Laci sticks with me. Things are moving fast with us, but that's okay, because we're so into each other. We spend every minute of our free time together, usually hanging out at my place because it's cheaper than going out. Laci likes to dream out loud about our future together, when we'll both have good jobs and can afford to move into our own apartment. I can hardly wait for it to happen.

·   ·   ·   ·   ·

Two weeks before Christmas, we go to visit my grandmother. Aside from Laci, Nan's the most important person in my life. My memories of my mother have grown fuzzy over the years, and my grandmother's the only connection I have left to her. When I was a kid, I used to love spending the night at Nan and Grampa's house. My grandfather wasn't well, so he didn't stir from his recliner in the den much, but Nan was lively, and always had fun things for me to play with, like a board game or a new LEGO set. She showed me how to make milkshakes in the blender, and every spring, she'd take me outside with her, to tromp around the backyard in search of the first crocuses poking their heads out of the snow. Nan was my best ally when my father stopped coming to visit, and she helped me get past the crushing rejection I felt. She loved telling funny stories about my mom, and I loved hearing them—until she got Alzheimer's, and the memories disappeared.

Since then, I've come to realize that Nan and I have one main thing in common: we don't fit into the real world very well. I think that's why I can relate to her so easily, and I'm unfazed by her dementia. It's weird, in a way—I'm bonding with a person whose mind is only half there. But I don't care about that. I still enjoy spending time with my grandmother because it makes me feel safe and loved, despite the fact that she doesn't always recognize me at first, and sometimes thinks I'm my grampa, when he was my age.

I thought it was really generous of Laci to offer to come with me for the visit, and I'm excited to introduce her to Nan. The bus ride takes forever. It's cold out, and we have to walk four slushy blocks up to Avery Avenue to catch a Centro, then change buses at the downtown transfer hub. The second bus is running behind schedule due to the messy road conditions, but that doesn't bother us. It's fun to be going someplace together, holding hands and talking about school. We both ended the semester with decent grades, and we're looking forward to finishing our programs in the spring.

It's over an hour before we arrive at our stop and climb the steep hill up to Autumn Meadows. Since it's a memory care facility, the receptionist has to buzz us in at the front entrance. "I'm kind of nervous," Laci whispers as the doors close behind us. "I'm not used to being around old people."

"Don't worry," I tell her. "You'll be fine. Just follow my lead."

Autumn Meadows has got its Christmas cheer on in a big way. The entrance is decorated with wreaths and garland, and there's a big fake Christmas tree in the lobby, covered with plastic ornaments and strings of blinking lights. We stop at the reception desk to sign in. I put my name and Laci's down in the visitor logbook, then notice the name *Edith Scanlon* in spidery handwriting on the line above. I've known for a long time that Nan and my former next-door neighbor used to be friends back in the day, but I'd like to avoid the old bat if I possibly can.

It's been so long since my last visit that the receptionist doesn't recognize me. She looks up from her computer. "Who are you visiting today?"

"My grandmother, Nancy Garber. Is her friend Edith still with her? I don't want to disturb them if she is."

"Mrs. Scanlon came for lunch, but she left right after. You picked the perfect time to come. They're having live music in Magnolia today, with Denny Lutz. He's doing a holiday sing-a-long." *Oh, goody.*

Laci follows me toward the double doors that enclose Magnolia, the "neighborhood" my grandmother lives in. The decor at Autumn Meadows is designed to dupe the residents into thinking they're living in a real place, rather than inmates at a high security cracker factory. The vibe is cheery 1950s, the era in which most of the residents came of age. The main lobby is disguised as a Town Square, with lampposts, street signs, a soda fountain and a barbershop. Each of the three neighborhoods has its own formal dining room, plus a living room with a television and comfortable wingback chairs arranged around an artificial fireplace.

We step into Magnolia's spacious living room, where a bald-headed man is cranking out "Jingle Bell Rock" on an electronic keyboard, surrounded by residents seated on folding chairs. Joyce, the energetic activities director, is cavorting about the room, trying to get people to sing along. "Come on, y'all!" she calls out to a pair of gentlemen seated in the front row, who are staring at her in astonishment. "Get up and dance!" She grabs one of the men by the hand and pulls him to his feet. The gentleman is surprisingly nimble. He swoops Joyce into an enthusiastic twirl, which prompts a few of the ladies to get up and join in.

"Oh, my goodness!" Laci says with an appreciative laugh. "They're so cute!"

I scan the room, looking for Nan. She usually likes to sit in the armchair beside the fake ficus tree, but the chair has been pushed into a corner to make room for the musical equipment. I have to speak loudly so Laci can hear me over the music. "I don't see her anywhere. Let's go check her room."

As we walk down the short hallway that leads to my grandmother's wing, I explain to Laci that the walls throughout the building are painted different colors, to help the residents find their way. Nan's room is "Two Blue," which the staff have to constantly remind her of. I raise my hand to knock on her door, then notice another resident has followed us. She's holding a cardigan in her hands and frowning. "This belongs to Ralph Lauren," she says, showing me the label. "I need to return it to him. Do you know where he is?"

"I'm sorry, I don't."

The woman looks distressed. "Oh dear. What should I do?"

"Try checking the living room. He might be in there watching TV."

"Yes!" she says, relieved. "That's where I saw him last!" She doesn't seem to know which way to go though, and keeps standing there looking at me.

"The living room is that way," I tell her, pointing back down the hall. "Follow the music."

The woman walks away and Laci gazes at me admiringly. "Wow, you handled that well, Rudy."

When Nan first moved in here, I did some reading about Alzheimer's, so I'd know what to expect. I learned that the trick is to enter into the other person's reality, instead of trying to correct them when they forget things. You avoid confrontation that way, which helps keep them calm. No one likes to be challenged, especially someone who's struggling to remember what day it is, or who their children are.

Smiling at Laci's compliment, I knock on Nan's door. There's no answer, so I open it and we go in. Nan is fast asleep on her bed, curled up on top of the covers with her shoes on. "Nan," I call softly, so I won't startle her. "Wake up, Nan." She stirs, then opens her eyes and looks up at me without recognition. "It's Rudy," I tell her, pointing at myself and giving her a big grin. "Your grandson?"

Sitting up, she studies my face. She's small and round, with shapeless gray hair and pale blue eyes that used to always have a mischievous twinkle in them, but are now dull with age. "Yes, of course," she says after a moment, her face lighting up. "Rudy!" She reaches her wrinkly hands out and grasps mine. "How wonderful to see you!"

I sit down beside her on the bed and give her a kiss on the cheek, then gesture toward Laci, who's standing nearby. "Nan, I'd like you to meet my girlfriend. Her name is Laci."

Nan is all smiles. "Hello there, young lady. I'm pleased to meet you." Laci smiles back, but seems to be tongue-tied. She's fiddling with her hat in her hands, nervously shifting her weight from foot to foot. To make her feel more comfortable, I invite her to sit down in Nan's flowered armchair.

"Christmas is almost here," I tell my grandmother. "Two more weeks."

"Yes, it is," she says, even though I know for a fact that she doesn't have a clue what day it is, despite the digital clock on the dresser that says TODAY IS TUESDAY, DECEMBER 11 in three-inch letters.

"Have you got all your shopping done?" I ask.

"I have, indeed," Nan answers pleasantly. "I drove to the mall yesterday and bought a million things."

This is obviously not true, but I play along. "Was the mall very busy?"

"It certainly was! So many shoppers everywhere. I always enjoy it."

As far as I can recall, my grandmother always disliked the mall, and avoided it whenever she could. I decide it's best to change the subject. Smiling brightly, I say, "Laci and I go to school together. She's training to work in a medical lab, and I'm learning about heating and cooling systems."

"My goodness!" Nan says. "What smart young people you are. Before you know it, you'll be the ones in charge here!"

We all chuckle at that. Laci glances questioningly at me, as though she wants to join in the conversation, so I give her an encouraging nod. She leans forward in the chair and says to Nan, "I like your red nail polish."

"My what?"

"Your nail polish. You have red fingernails."

Nan looks down at her hands. "Oh yes, I do. How about that." She seems mystified by this discovery.

"It's very Christmassy," Laci says. "The red."

Nan is confused. "The red what?"

"Your nails. They're—"

Waving at Laci, I redirect the conversation. "They've got Christmas music in the living room today, Nan. Would you like to go listen to it?"

My grandmother is delighted with the idea. We all get up to leave the room, and find the Ralph Lauren woman lurking outside the door. "Were you smoking in there?" she asks suspiciously.

I assure her we weren't. "It's okay if you were," she whispers. "I won't tell anybody."

We walk down to the living room, where Denny Lutz is winding up a bouncy rendition of "Frosty the Snowman." When the song ends, it's break time, and Joyce's helper wheels in the snack cart. I find chairs for us next to an empty book case, the books having been carried off by the residents, never to be seen again. The three of us sit in a row, with Nan on one side of me and Laci on the other. When the snack cart comes around, I make sure Nan gets a cup of apple juice and a handful of Fig Newtons, which she loves. As she's eating, a stocky fellow named Bill sneaks into the room and turns out the overhead lights, then scurries away with a shit-eating grin on his face.

Denny returns to his keyboard, and launches into a rollicking version of "Deck the Halls." Joyce circulates throughout the room, encouraging the residents to clap their hands and sing along. The next number is "Rudolph the Red-Nosed Reindeer." I've hated that stupid song forever, so I've learned to block it out. Laci knits her eyebrows at me, then grins and squeezes my hand when she sees it isn't bothering me, and we join in the singing. I glance over at Nan, and she looks jolly, too. She's tapping her feet and waving a Fig Newton in time to the music.

After another lively sing-a-long, Denny takes things down a notch and segues into "White Christmas." The slower tempo short circuits Nan's joyful mood and she begins to fret, thinking she needs to pay for her juice and cookies. "It's all right," I tell her. "I already took care of it."

"No," she says. "I need my pocketbook." She gazes down at her lap, then looks past me to Laci. "Where is my pocketbook?"

"I don't know," Laci says. "I don't think you brought it with you."

"Yes, I did. Give it back to me."

"I don't have it." Laci turns her palms up and shows them to Nan. "See?"

Nan narrows her eyes. "I know you took it."

Laci's face goes red. "No, I didn't!"

"Look, Nan," I say, tapping her arm to distract her. "I've got more Fig Newtons! These ones are free." I press a cookie into her hand. She gives me a mistrustful look, but accepts it. I glance sideways at Laci, who looks mortified at having been accused of theft. "Never mind," I whisper. "She's confused, that's all."

The music transitions to "Silent Night." Nan adores classic Christmas carols, so I'm hoping this one will calm her down and restore her good cheer, but it doesn't. When we get to the part about the holy infant, Nan's face crumples and she bursts into tears. "My daughter," she says, her mouth contorted in sorrow. "My poor Ann Marie." Her sobs grow louder, which sets off another little old lady who's sitting nearby. Heads start to turn in our direction.

I speak to her with soothing words, but it doesn't help. Laci tries patting her hand, but Nan pulls away. She stares at Laci, her eyes distant, like she's reaching way back into the past, then, "Debra," she says slowly, her eyes narrowing to slits. She points a shaking finger at Laci. "It was your fault. You think no one knows, but I do!"

Without warning, Nan lunges across me and grabs Laci's hair. Laci shrieks and tries to pull herself free. I'm caught in the middle, trying to pry Nan's fingers open without hurting her. The commotion catches the eye of an aide, who runs over to help.

Nan releases her grip and falls back into her chair. The aide squats beside her, rubbing Nan's shoulder. "What's the matter, Mrs. Garber? How about another glass of juice?"

Nan gives her a tearful nod. The aide slips her arm through Nan's, helps her out of her chair and leads her away.

Laci is rubbing a bright red spot on her scalp, and looks like she's about to die of embarrassment. "I didn't do anything, Rudy! I don't know why she got so upset with me."

"I know you didn't. It's the dementia, not you. She gets agitated sometimes, out of the blue."

"But she called me Debra. I don't look anything like your stepmother! Why would she do that?"

I can't give her an answer because I don't have one. It makes no sense to me, either.

"And she mentioned her daughter. Was she talking about your mother?"

I shrug my shoulders. It's been twenty years since my mother's death, but when the memory pops up at random in my grandmother's head, it's as fresh as if the accident happened yesterday. I obviously know the story of how my mother died, and vaguely remember Mitchell sitting me down one day and explaining that Mommy had gone to heaven and couldn't come back. When I got older and started asking questions, he told me about the accident. Beyond that, he never talked about it, and I tried not to think about it. But the last few times I've come to visit Nan, she's been saying some weird stuff, making it sound like there was something else that happened.

Hearing my mother's name and seeing Nan sobbing has left me with a sick feeling in the bottom of my stomach. I recall her saying something odd about Debra once, but I brushed it off as a figment of her dementia. When I was young, I remember Nan letting a comment drop about my stepmother once, which left me with the impression that she viewed Debra as an interloper who roped Mitchell into marriage way too soon after my mother's death. I tried to get her to tell me more, but Nan got flustered and changed the subject.

I don't want to discuss any of this right now, but Laci persists. "I don't get it. What did she mean about it being Debra's fault? What was—"

"I don't know!" I snap. "Sometimes there's no sense in anything she says. There's no point in analyzing it, so can we just drop it?"

I've never snapped at Laci like that before. She looks hurt and I'm afraid she might cry, so I put my arm around her and we start walking down the hall. "Nan didn't mean anything by it, she was just confused. Don't give it another thought."

We exit Magnolia through the double doors and cross the pretend Town Square. "Wait a minute," Laci says, stopping short and tugging on my sleeve. "We didn't say goodbye."

"That's okay, it's better if we don't. If we go back, it might upset her all over again." I sign us out at the front desk, then we go outside and head down the hill to the bus stop. It's very cold and the afternoon light is fading. The sidewalks in front of Autumn Meadows have been heavily salted so there's not a speck of snow or ice on them, but as we get closer to the plexiglass bus shelter on the main road, we have to watch our footing as we crunch over the frozen mounds of slush.

The bus arrives and it feels good to climb into the warmth of it. It's packed with people heading home from work, so we have to stand near the front, gripping the metal pole and leaning on each other for balance. "I'm sorry for being short with you," I say quietly in Laci's ear. "Nan sort of freaked me out with that outburst."

"I'm sorry the visit didn't go so well," she says in return. "I know you were looking forward to it."

"It was all right. There've been a few times when I came, and she didn't even recognize me."

Laci looks happy again. "You were amazing, Rudy. I wouldn't have known what to say to any of those people, or how to act around them."

I grin back at her. "It's not rocket science."

The bus rumbles up Valley Drive, stopping frequently to let passengers off. I'm thinking about Nan's worsening dementia, and how disastrous it is to challenge her when she's confused. That pretty much sums up the bad blood between me and Mitchell. I hate the way he questions everything I do, and he doesn't like it when I push back. Round and round, year after year. Our contentious Thanksgiving dinner was only the latest in a long list of examples of his inability to give me a frigging break.

The bus turns a sharp corner and Laci's body sways in my direction. I brace one foot to counter her weight, and marvel once again at how fortunate I am to have found her. I have the urge to kiss her, but I don't feel comfortable doing things like that in public, especially on a crowded city bus. The romantic turn of my feelings reminds me that I need to get her something for Christmas. My new boss gave all the employees Target gift cards last week, as an early holiday bonus. I think I'll use mine to buy Laci a special present, to show her how much I care about her. The trouble is, I have no clue what a girl wants. I nudge her with my elbow. "What do you want for Christmas?"

She gives me a coy smile. "I don't know. What do you want?"

I want a lot of things, but money can't buy them—a successful next semester of school, a full-time job, the endless love of the beautiful young woman standing next to me. Putting my mouth close to her ear, I whisper, "I only want you."

Laci blushes and giggles. "Oh, Rudy," she whispers back, "you're so sweet."

Our bus ride continues with the two of us holding tight to the pole and giving each other meaningful looks. We transfer downtown and continue our journey home. The second bus is less crowded and we don't have to stand anymore, but when an elderly woman boards at the next stop, I get up so she can have my seat. She's carrying a tattered paper shopping bag, and has a vacant expression that reminds me of the folks at Autumn Meadows. "We could get something for Nan," I say to Laci. "Maybe a pair of slippers."

Laci nods her approval. "I think she'd like that. Besides you, Jayden's the only other person I'm going to get anything for." She chews her lower lip. "I'm really worried about him, Rudy. I heard he may have gotten involved with some older boys who might be in a gang. I tried calling my dad, but he's always so wasted, he's clueless about what's going on. I don't know what to do about it."

I don't know, either. I tell her I'm sorry to hear it, and we ride the rest of the way in silence.

16

Debra

When the intruder returns, I'm ready.

It's four thirty in the afternoon, one week before Christmas. I finish up the report I've been working on and log out for the day. I've been at my desk since early morning, so I feel justified not working all the way till five, like I'm supposed to. Mitch has been called into work again, so he's upstairs getting changed. After going outside to get the mail, I start heating up dinner for him.

I'm gazing idly out the kitchen window when I notice movement in the trees. Dusk is falling, so I go over to the slider and peer into the gathering darkness. There's someone standing in the yard. A shudder of alarm runs through me, but instead of panicking, I keep my wits about me. I confirm that the sliding door is securely latched, then hit the switch for the floodlight. The snow-covered patio lights up, bright as day, and I can't see the person anymore. I run to the foot of the stairs and shout up to Mitch that there's a trespasser outside, and then I call the police.

Mitch comes racing down the stairs with his gun in his hand, runs outside and searches the yard. Ten minutes later, when I see a Centerport Police vehicle pulling up in the street out front, I yell to him to come back inside, then go answer the front door.

It's Officer Tobin, the one who responded to the August break-in along with Detective Scanlon. I didn't get a very good look at her before, because of being so shaken up by what had happened. She's younger than I remember, but without Gary Scanlon lording it over her this time, she has a more confident manner and seems to know what she's doing. She takes out her notepad and follows me into the kitchen. Mitch is back inside now, the gun put away.

I tell the officer what happened. "I was standing here in front of the sink, and I noticed someone in the yard." I point out the window to a spot near the edge of the woods. The floodlight doesn't reach that far, so the trees beyond it are cloaked in darkness. "They stood there for about a minute, then disappeared into the woods."

"Male or female?"

"It looked like a male, from the way he was moving."

"How old, would say? Can you make a guess?"

"Not an adult, but definitely not a child. I'd say it was a teenager."

"Can you describe what he was wearing?"

I squeeze my eyes shut. "He had on a black hooded top and black jogging pants."

"Could you see his face?"

"No, it was too dark out, and it was hidden by the hood."

"Did you take note of his build?"

I think about it for a second. "He wasn't very tall, and he was sort of husky." I'm surprised at how much detail I'm able to recall, now that I'm really thinking about it. I hope it helps.

Officer Tobin taps her pen on her notepad and turns to Mitch. "When I was here after the August incident, you mentioned you were going to get security cameras. Did you follow through on that?"

"Yes," Mitch replies. "I put one up over the garage, and another one out back, over the patio."

"Do they have night vision?"

"They sure do. Here, I'll show you the feed." He takes out his phone and we all sit down at the table. He pokes around in the app a second, then hands the phone over to Tobin.

Mitch and I watch over her shoulder as the recorded video plays. I see a grainy image of a person standing at the edge of the woods. The figure is difficult to distinguish against the dark backdrop of the trees, but I can see him staring toward the house. After a minute, he crosses the yard and moves out of range of the camera. Thirty seconds later, he reappears and stands facing the house for a moment, then melts back into the woods.

I shiver. "That's scary. He was out there watching me through the window."

"Hmmm." Tobin taps her fingers on her chin. "Can you email this to me?" She takes out a business card and hands it to Mitch, then says she's going to take a look around the yard. Removing her flashlight from her belt, she goes out through the sliding door. Five minutes later, she returns with nothing else to report. She tells us she'll investigate further, and reminds us to call her if anything else comes up.

After she's gone, Mitch goes around the house double-checking that the doors are deadbolted and the outside lights are on. He offers to stay home from work, but I know that will get him in hot water. "I'll be fine," I tell him. "I can take care of myself now." He reluctantly gets ready to go, and promises to monitor the camera feed throughout the night, since I still don't know how to use the app. "Your pistol is in the kitchen drawer," he reminds me. "You know you're not supposed to touch it until your permit comes, but don't hesitate to use it if you think you're in danger."

I don't have any appetite for supper, so I bring my knitting basket into the family room and spend the evening watching a lighthearted holiday movie on TV. By 10:00, I'm getting sleepy. Setting my needles and yarn aside, I stand up and stretch. The past couple hours of mindless handiwork have helped settle my nerves, but with bedtime approaching, I'm starting to feel anxious again.

I go out to the kitchen and let Cocoa outside one last time, watching her closely and listening for any unusual sounds in the yard. When she returns to the house, I put the security bar in place across the slider and draw the blinds. As I'm leaving the kitchen, I flick the lights off out of habit, then switch them back on, knowing I'll sleep better if I leave them on all night.

Time to get ready for bed. I start up the stairs, then stop halfway, thinking of the gun Mitch gave me. It would be foolish of me to not keep it handy tonight, to defend myself with in case something really bad happens. Turning around, I go back down to the kitchen. The Walther is right where Mitch left it, in the drawer with the potholders. Before I took my class, I was scared to touch it, but I'm not afraid anymore. It feels much more comfortable in my hand than it did before, when I didn't know how to handle it yet. I check that the magazine is fully loaded and there's a round in the chamber, and set the manual safety. It's only a .22, but Patrick told me if I'm ever in a life-threatening situation, I should fire multiple rounds, until the aggressor stops.

Upstairs, I change into my nightgown and brush my teeth, then get into bed with the gun under my pillow. The idea of shooting someone makes me queasy, but I'll do it if I have to, to defend my own life.

17

Mitchell

My phone wakes me the following day around noon, as I'm sleeping off the extra night shift I picked up. It's Gary Scanlon. "You missing a gun by any chance, Bateman?"

I bolt upright in bed, wide awake. "What are you talking about?"

"I'll get to that. First off, I have good news to share. Upon closer examination of the video you provided Officer Tobin with, the suspect's garment was determined to be a black hooded pullover with red sleeves, with a small logo on the front. With the assistance of this more detailed description, we tracked down a teenaged boy residing in the Woodland Homes complex. The suspect denied trespassing on your property, but was nevertheless placed under arrest due to an exacerbating circumstance."

Huh? I wish the guy would speak in plain English, instead of this highfaluting cop language. "What was the, uh, circumstance?"

"The youth was found to be in possession of a firearm."

"Oh. That's not good."

"No, it isn't." There's a pause. "The firearm in question was a 9-millimeter Glock 17. Does that happen to ring a bell with you?"

Holy cow. It's my missing gun. I don't know how to respond. I've got to cover my back somehow. After a second, I say, "Why would that ring a bell with me? The kid obviously stole it from someone who lives in the housing project."

Scanlon clears his throat before he lowers the boom. I can picture his chest swelling as he enlightens me. "We traced the serial number. The gun belongs to you."

"But how can that be?" I try to sound incredulous. "My gun wasn't stolen! There must be some mistake." Scanlon doesn't respond. I know this is a common police tactic, intended to get me to say something incriminating, but in my panic, I fall for it anyway. "At least, I don't think my gun was stolen. I mean, I haven't used it in a while, so I can't say for sure. Maybe that kid stole it when he broke into my house back in August." I know that's not possible, but if the police pursue this theory, it might get me off the hook.

"That's a probable scenario," Scanlon says, "but it's a long time for you to be unaware that a gun was missing from your home. Failure to report a stolen firearm is a crime in New York state. You could be fined or jailed."

I already know this, of course. I also know that if the owner is honestly not aware his gun's been stolen, he can use this in court as a valid defense. "But I had no idea he stole it," I insist. "I swear, I didn't know the gun was missing from my house until you told me just now."

"I see." Scanlon sounds unconvinced, but he must have bigger fish to fry down at the station because he shifts the topic. "The suspect has been classified as a juvenile because he's fourteen years of age. However, burglary and unlawful possession of a weapon by persons under sixteen are serious offenses, so the charges against him may be severe."

"Good. I hope they throw the book at him." Scanlon has no comment. "So, where's the kid now? What's going to happen to him?"

"After taking him into custody this morning, we made a good faith effort to contact his parents, but thus far, we've received no response. Due to the severity of the crimes, the judge ordered him to be held in a juvenile detention facility. He'll be assigned a lawyer when he goes to court."

I'm glad the punk is off the streets. He was undoubtedly up to no good if he was running around the housing project with a gun, but I know he couldn't have stolen it from my house. Even though Scanlon seems to think it's an open-and-shut case, I'm afraid this matter isn't settled yet, and I'm going to have to watch my step.

18

Laci

It's been weeks since I've seen my brother Jayden, and it's stressing me out. He doesn't have a phone of his own, so he usually uses his mom's, to check in with me every now and then. I haven't heard from him since Thanksgiving, which he spent with his mother at a friend's house. Sounds like Tiff, the terminal fiancée, might be getting ready to kick my father to the curb—which might not be a bad thing. I called him two days ago, but he had nothing useful to tell me, besides calling Tiff a skank, and complaining that Jayden hasn't been coming home at night. Where does a fourteen-year-old boy disappear to, one week before Christmas? I'm making myself sick, worrying he's run away or joined a gang.

Jayden and I have always been super close. Before my mom went to jail, the two of us lived in an apartment on the opposite side of Woodland Homes from my dad and Tiff's duplex. Since I'm four years older than Jayden, I was often called on to babysit him during the occasional stretches when both his parents had jobs. Tiff's teenaged daughters were too busy with their own lives to be bothered looking after Jayden, but I liked doing it because it was fun.

Jayden didn't have a bike to ride or many toys to play with like other kids, because his parents were imbeciles that never had any money to spare, but he loved music more than anything. My dad had an old turntable and a plastic milk crate full of classic rock albums—Aerosmith, Van Halen, Bob Seger, ZZ Top. I would play deejay, picking out the rockingest tracks that Jayden could dance to. He was the cutest thing to watch, shaking his chubby tush to songs like "Sharp Dressed Man" and "Walk This Way." We spent hours listening to our favorite records over and over, trying to pick out tunes on my dad's acoustic guitar.

When Jayden was eleven and I was fifteen, I took him on the bus to go Christmas shopping at the Fairmount Fair shopping center. We had a blast digging through the discount bins at Five Below, filling our baskets with items that cost only a few dollars. Afterward, we browsed through Target, then went to the café, where I treated him to a giant cookie and a hot chocolate. Jayden told me about school, and the few friends he had. He was unathletic and overweight like me, so he was an easy target for teasing. "I wish I was more like you, Laci," he said to me one time. "You don't let stuff like that bother you."

Our shopping trips have become an annual tradition for us, so I'm disappointed we're not doing it this year. Either Jayden has outgrown his big sister, or something's wrong, and I need to find out what it is.

•   •   •   •   •

The Saturday before Christmas, I take the bus out to Woodland Homes, hoping I'll find Jayden at my dad's place. As I'm walking down the hill from the bus stop, I hear a car coming behind me. There's no sidewalk, so I move over as far as I can without falling into the snowbank. The car slows and draws abreast of me. The windows are tinted, so I can't see who's inside. I pick up my pace, trying to act like I belong here, and turn into the block of duplexes where my father and Tiff live. The car trails me around the corner, then passes and stops a few yards ahead of me, and I feel a twinge of fear as the rear window goes down.

A girl I used to know hooks her spiky fingernails over the top edge of the window, sticks her head out and calls to me. "You lookin' for your little brother?"

I cautiously approach the car. "Yeah. Have you seen him?"

She blinks her fake eyelashes. "He been hangin' with Dion's crew. I think they up to somethin'. You best get him away from that mess, before he gets hisself into trouble." The window goes up before I can say anything, and the car speeds away.

I've never met Dion in person, but I know him by his bad reputation, and I've always been careful to avoid him. He has a pack of thuggish pals that I have no doubt are engaged in drug dealing and petty crime. If they've lured my naive little brother into their vile web, I don't know what I'll do.

At my dad's duplex, I find him lying on the couch in a stained T-shirt and sweatpants, with the TV blaring. The last time I saw him was back in the summer, and he looks like he's lost a good deal of weight since then. He reaches for his cigarettes on an overturned cardboard box that he's using as an end table. "What're you doin' here?" he says as he lights one up.

I take the remote control from the box and turn down the volume on the TV. "I'm looking for Jayden. Is he here?"

"Little shit ain't been around in weeks. Police came banging on the door this morning, said they wanted to talk to him."

I'm immediately on edge. "About what?"

My father exhales a stream of smoke through his nose. "I dunno. I told 'em go find his mother and ask her where he went."

I look around the room and notice some of the furniture is gone, and the television is smaller than the one that used to be here. After grilling him with more questions, I learn that Tiff finally got fed up with his drinking and left him, so he's drowning his sorrows in Southern Comfort and orange juice, which is remarkably ironic and ignorant, even for him. "Did she take Jayden with her?" I ask.

My dad splashes more whiskey into his plastic cup and maneuvers it towards his mouth. "No clue."

"You're useless, you know that?" I don't normally waste my breath sassing my father because he doesn't care what anyone says anyway, but I'm extremely upset about my little brother's disappearance. He's only fourteen, someone should be looking after him. "I tried calling Tiff," I say, "but she's apparently changed her number again." Tiff is famous for doing this periodically; it's her brilliant way of staying one step ahead of the bill collectors. I hold my hand out. "Give me your phone."

My father digs into the couch cushions and tosses a battered phone in my general direction. It lands on the floor and I stoop to pick it up. Scrolling through his contacts, I find Tiff's latest number and dial it, and get a recording that says her voice mailbox is full. I enter the number into my contacts, then throw the phone back at my father. It smacks him on the shoulder and he looks up at me in surprise.

"Where did she go?" I ask.

"Who?"

"Who do you *think?* Tiff. Where's she living now?"

He swirls the putrid mixture in his cup. "Don't know, don't care."

"You're a disgusting waste of a human being."

"Yeah," my father replies, narrowing his eyes at me through a haze of cigarette smoke. "Uh huh."

I stomp down the short hallway to Jayden's bedroom. Some of his clothes are missing from the beat-up chest of drawers, but his Percy Jackson books are neatly arranged on top of it, and the NASCAR poster I gave him last Christmas is still hanging on the wall. He would've taken those things with him if he moved someplace with his mother. I go back out to the living room, where my father is trying to light a fresh cigarette with the stub of his last one, but keeps missing. "Your son has run away." No response. "Do you even care?"

"Not much."

I spit a few choice words at him, then leave without saying goodbye.

•   •   •   •   •

When the bus reaches the stop near my aunt's house on Charles Street, I get off and head in the direction of Rudy's place instead of going home. It's a relief to see him. He wraps his arms around me and pulls me onto the couch, and asks where I've been all day. I tell him I went looking for Jayden, and describe the disgusting condition I found my father in, even though it's embarrassing to talk about. "He's such a wreck, he doesn't even know where his own son is."

Rudy is sympathetic, like I knew he'd be. He kisses my cheek and rubs my back. "I'm sorry you didn't find your brother. I know you've been worried about him. Is there anywhere we could go to look for him?"

"I wouldn't know where to start." I rub my forehead in frustration. "My dad couldn't tell me anything. I'm so sick and tired of the useless adults in my family."

"Speaking of family, guess who called me?"

I roll my eyes in wonder at how swiftly Rudy has deflected the conversation away from my problems. "Your stepmother, I suppose. She's the only person in your family who ever calls you."

"Yeah. She invited us over for brunch on Christmas. I'm not exactly dying to see them after the way Thanksgiving went, but look at it this way—it's a free meal. What do you think?"

Honestly, I'm torn. I hated the way Mitchell spoke so condescendingly to Rudy during dinner, but Debra was nice. Before we left, she hugged both of us and told Rudy she loved him, and whispered an apology to me for her husband's rudeness. Then the next day, she called Rudy to tell him that Mitchell had said he was very sorry, he'd had too much to drink, and she hoped I wasn't offended by his behavior. I was offended, but with me, an apology can go a very long way in making things better.

"Debra promised there'd be no drinking this time," Rudy says. "My stepfather doesn't hold his booze so well."

I can relate to that. But still, I'd trade my drunken dad for Rudy's stepfather in a heartbeat. At least Mitchell goes to work every day, takes care of his house and puts food on the table, while my father lives off a phony disability claim, and seems dead set on drinking himself to death.

Rudy twines his fingers with mine. "I get it if you don't want to go, Laci. We can stay home and make our own brunch right here."

I look around the room—no Christmas tree, no decorations, no gifts waiting to be unwrapped. Probably no food in the fridge either, if you don't count the moldy leftovers. It's depressing to think about us sitting around by ourselves in this cramped apartment, when we could be spending the day with other people in a warm, comfortable house, playing with the dog and enjoying a home-cooked meal.

How bad could it be? Mitchell did say he was sorry, after all. And by the way she acted so friendly and considerate towards me at Thanksgiving, I think Debra genuinely likes me. When I was a little girl, my mother used to push me away when I tried to hug her, and never once told me she loved me. It would be nice to spend more time with a nice person like Debra. Maybe we could even get to be friends.

I smile at Rudy and tip one shoulder up. "I don't mind going if you don't."

He raises his eyebrows. "Are you sure?"

"I am sure. Go ahead and call her back."

·   ·   ·   ·   ·

Debra invites us to join them for church on Christmas morning, but we decline. Bus service is limited today, so they drive over to Rudy's apartment after the service and pick us up. Debra greets us with a big smile when we climb into the back seat, and Mitchell twists around to wish us a merry Christmas. I feel almost giddy to be riding in the car with them, like they're my parents and we're a regular family. I'm wearing a sparkly black dress that I hope is appropriate for a brunch. I reach for Rudy's knee and give it a grateful squeeze. I have a feeling it's going to be a good day.

At the house, I give Debra the box of Russell Stover's chocolates that I bought for them. "How thoughtful of you!" she says, as if it's the best present in the world. "We'll save these for after we've eaten." I bend to pet Cocoa, then dig inside my messenger bag for the rawhide bone I got for her. She takes the treat from my hand and disappears down the hallway with it.

Rudy pulls me over to the Christmas tree in the living room. It's artificial, but it's pretty. The lights are white and twinkling, and there's a construction paper star on top that's lost most of its glitter. "I made that in third grade," he says. "I'm surprised they still have it."

Debra turns some Christmas music on, then comes to join us. "He made this one, too," she says with a smile, pointing out a sequined styrofoam ball. "And here's another one." She goes over to an end table and picks up a small paper plate that's got gold-painted macaroni glued around the edges. In the center is a wallet-size school picture of Rudy, red-cheeked and grinning, his two front teeth missing.

"Look at you!" I exclaim. "You were such a cute little boy."

"Ha," Rudy says. "Not anymore."

I playfully smack his shoulder. "Not true! You're still very cute."

"I agree," Debra says, beaming at me.

We eat at the round table in the kitchen this time, "to be less formal, since it's only brunch," Debra says. She serves us a delicious sausage casserole, with homemade biscuits and strawberry jam on the side. Our little circle feels cozy and comfortable. Mitchell makes an effort to talk to Rudy about a construction project that's going on at the hospital, while Debra tells me about the new quilt pattern she's piecing together. I'm not really interested, but I go with the flow because she's so enthusiastic about it. "I think it's coming along nicely," she says. "I can show it to you later, if you like."

After we've finished the meal and cleared the dishes, we all go back into the living room. Rudy passes the box of chocolates around, then sits beside me on the loveseat and slips his hand into mine. Debra takes two colorful gift bags from under the tree, and hands one to me and the other to Rudy. "It's nothing fancy," she says. "Just a little something I made for you. You can open yours first, Laci."

Removing the tissue paper from the bag, I find a beautiful knitted scarf nestled inside. The yarn is a deep, rich mauve, and the ends of the scarf are fringed. I rub it against my cheek, feel the wonderful softness of it. I feel tears welling and blink them away, and thank Debra in a voice that's barely more than a whisper.

Rudy takes his turn. He sticks his hand in his bag and pulls out a navy-blue beanie, knit with a tighter stitch than my scarf. "Look at the inside," Debra says. "It's lined with wool, to keep your head warm." Rudy pulls the hat on for us to admire. I can tell he likes it, but doesn't want to let on.

"Wait," Debra says, jumping up from her chair. "Let me get my phone so I can take a picture." She has Rudy and me pose in front of the tree with our gifts, and snaps a photo. "There," she says. "Perfect."

I don't think I've felt so happy in my entire life. Returning to my seat next to Rudy, I'm helping myself to another piece of candy when Cocoa starts barking like mad in the kitchen. Debra flinches and turns quickly to Mitchell, who jumps up and goes into the kitchen. I hear him tell the dog to be quiet, then the sound of the sliding door opening. I glance questioningly at Rudy, but he's clutching his new hat in his hands, one ear cocked toward the kitchen.

The slider thumps closed and Mitchell returns to the living room. "It was a squirrel," he says. "It knocked down the bird feeder." I notice Debra's long exhale, and see her shoulders relax.

Rudy and I must be looking confused because Debra turns to us to explain. "We had a burglary a few months ago."

I gasp in surprise, and feel Rudy stiffen beside me. "What happened?" I ask.

Debra glances at Mitchell, then turns back to me and Rudy. "I had just gotten home from having dinner with my sister one evening, when someone broke the glass on the sliding door in the kitchen. I was so terrified, I ran straight out the front door and called the police." She shudders at the memory.

"Oh my gosh! You must have been so scared. Did they catch the person?"

"They certainly did," Mitchell says with a satisfied smile. "Turned out it was one of those teenaged scumbags from Woodland Homes."

Rudy looks sideways at me, then slips his hand back into mine and squeezes it tight. I don't let on that I'm all too familiar with Woodland Homes, because I'm afraid Mitchell will think I'm a scumbag, too.

"Now, Mitchell," Debra says. "I'm sure there are plenty of good, hardworking people who live over there." Her gaze wanders up to the paper star on top of the Christmas tree, and her expression softens. "I'm a firm believer in redemption, no matter how bad off someone is. Hopefully, this young man will get the help he needs, so he doesn't fall into a life of crime."

A disturbing thought crosses my mind—what if Jayden had something to do with this? Maybe that's why he disappeared. But that can't be, because I know him too well. He's a good kid who would never do anything criminal like breaking into a house.

Debra claps her palms on her thighs. "Enough about that, anyway. Laci, would you like to go upstairs now, and see my quilting project?" I look at Rudy, hesitant to leave him alone with Mitchell; but then Mitchell asks Rudy if he wants to watch the Celtics game, and Rudy says that would be great. I get up to follow Debra upstairs, and a moment later, I hear the TV come on in the family room.

The remainder of the afternoon passes pleasantly enough. While the guys are watching the game, I look at fabric swatches with Debra. I try to look interested as she shows me how to assemble a quilt square, but my mind keeps drifting back to the teenager who got arrested. What if it *was* Jayden? He's never been a troublemaker, but that girl in Woodland Homes who stopped to warn me seemed to think he was at risk of getting sucked into Dion's gang of lowlifes. Dion might have lured Jayden into doing something bad, and now he's locked up in juvie. It would explain why the police were looking for him, and why no one seems to know where he is.

Debra sits down at her sewing machine to demonstrate some kind of fancy quilting stitch. I stand behind her, pretending to watch. I don't dare ask her for more details about the burglary, for fear of giving away my Woodland Homes connection. "Look at this," she says cheerfully, turning to show me an intricately stitched square of material. I admire it without really seeing it, because my mind is fixated on my little brother.

After a long afternoon of Debra showing off her sewing talents, she suggests we go back downstairs and have a cup of tea. I'm thankful for the reprieve from my worrisome thoughts. We sit chatting at the kitchen table until Rudy comes in to remind me that Fudgie's coming to pick us up at 4:00, on his way home from his grandparents' house. Because I've been so distracted all afternoon, I feel like I've left all the conversation up to Debra, which was impolite of me. To make up for my lack of manners, I take our empty teacups and saucers from the table, and go to rinse them at the sink.

"Don't worry about those, sweetheart," Debra says. "You've got a few minutes yet before you have to go. Why don't you and Rudy take Cocoa for a short walk around the block?"

Rudy seems agreeable, so we put on our coats and the new scarf and hat, and head outside with the dog. It's snowing and the trees are coated with powder, giving the street a magical look. We're rounding the bend in front of the house when a woman in a long brown coat appears at the foot of the neighboring driveway. The snowbanks are piled high from the snowplow, so I don't notice her right away. "Hello, Mrs. Scanlon," Rudy says politely as we approach.

We keep on walking, but the woman comes toward us and steps in our path. Her eyes are dark holes in her wrinkled face. "That woman," she hisses, gesturing toward the Batemans' house.

Startled, Rudy stops in his tracks. "What? Who're you talking about?"

"You know who I mean. Your stepmother."

Rudy takes a half-step back and tightens his grip on Cocoa's leash. "What about her?"

I recall him mentioning a creepy neighbor to me one time, who used to scare him when he was a kid. By the nutso look on this woman's face, I assume she's the one. Mrs. Scanlon steps closer, bringing a gross whiff of moth balls, and peers into Rudy's face. "God rest your mother's soul." Still staring, she makes the sign of the cross on herself and mutters something about the truth coming out, then turns and trudges back up her driveway.

Rudy tugs at Cocoa and we turn around. "That was seriously weird," he says in a low voice as we hurry back to the house. "Don't say anything when we go back inside. They'll only get upset if we tell them."

Fudgie's car pulls into the driveway as we reach the front steps. I go inside to find Debra, and thank her for the brunch and the beautiful scarf. She gives me a big hug and says she hopes I'll come over again soon, then hugs Rudy, and asks him to keep in touch. Mitchell walks me to the front door and gets my coat from the closet, and he gives me a hug as well. It's stiff and awkward, but I appreciate the gesture. Aside from that freaky woman next door and my worries about Jayden, today has been a really good day.

19

Rudy

It felt like a huge weight was lifted off my shoulders on Christmas Day, when Mitchell told us the police had made an arrest. I'll admit I felt a tiny prick of guilt about someone else taking the heat for what I did, but that only lasted a minute. The main thing is that my butt is covered. Whoever it was that got arrested is probably a pretty bad dude anyway, likely one of those shady characters I saw hanging out on Dion's street corner. As Mitchell said, they're scumbags who are probably involved in all kinds of criminal activity. One less gangsta on the street is better for everybody.

I'm pumped today because I'm getting a new car. Well, a new-to-me car, to be more accurate. It's a 1995 Chrysler LeBaron that was originally my grandmother's. Nan had to give up driving when she moved into memory care, so her brother, my Uncle Gene, said he would take her car. But Uncle Gene had a stroke a month ago and can't drive anymore, so he's passing it on to me. Not the hottest set of wheels on the road, but it'll get me where I need to go, and the price—*free!* — is right.

Laci comes with me to pick up the car. We take a short bus ride over to Uncle Gene's neighborhood, and walk two blocks to his house. He lives in a neighborhood called Tipperary Hill, where there are more Irish pubs than you can swing a cat at. His house is up the hill from St. Patrick's, the former Catholic grammar school that my grandmother went to when she was a girl.

Laci follows me up the steps and into the windowed front porch, which smells like stale cigar smoke. I knock on the door, then open it when I hear my uncle shout for us to come in. The poor guy's stuck in a wheelchair that's parked in the center of the living room, and there's a foreign nurse hovering over him, trying to wheedle him into taking his pills.

Uncle Gene is anxious to get right down to business, probably hoping it'll distract the nurse from pushing her pills. He's right-handed, but that's the side that got zapped by the stroke, so he has to use his left hand to scrawl his initials when he signs over the title. It seems like the proper thing for me to stay and chat awhile, but my uncle is tired and growing irritable. After a few minutes of me doing the talking and Uncle Gene grimacing and growling back, the nurse suggests it's time for him to take a rest. Before wheeling him into his room, she goes and gets the car keys for me, which are stashed inside one of the kitchen cupboards, to stymie any potential burglars. When the keys are in my hand at last, Laci and I make our escape.

We run outside to the detached garage behind the house. The LeBaron isn't a bad car. It's got cruise control, power locks, and a maroon velour interior that looks like it's never been sat on. There are only 60k miles on it, since Nan only ever drove it to the grocery store and church, and Uncle Gene never had reason to go anywhere farther than the Ukrainian Club and the nearest Rite Aid. There's barely any rust on the body because the both of them avoided driving in the winter.

"This is so exciting, Rudy!" Laci squeals as I back out of the garage. "Your own car!"

I feel myself grinning. I'm pretty lit at the moment—got a car, got a girl, got a job, gonna graduate soon and get an even better job. To top it all off, it looks like I've gotten away scot-free for the crimes I've committed, so I'm stoked about life in general. I'm even warming up to my stepparents. I was really touched by the hat Debra knitted me for Christmas. It showed that she still cares about me, in spite of all we've been through. Before I left that day, she told me it makes her worry when she doesn't hear from me, so I've been making more of an effort to reply to her texts. I figure it's best to stay on her and Mitchell's good side, after the damage I did to their home.

I'd love to cruise the streets for a while and get a feel for my new car, but I've got to go to work soon. The spring semester starts next week, so I'm trying to get as many hours in as I can, to earn enough money to pay for my auto insurance and registration. I apologize to Laci for being so busy, and promise to make it up to her.

I turn onto Charles Street and stop in front of her aunt's place. "See you tonight?" I ask hopefully. "I'm not sure if Fudgie'll be home, but I can check with him. Either way, we could hang out and watch a movie together."

Laci's head is bent over her phone, her hair obscuring her face. She looks up at me blankly for a second, and I notice a lengthy text message on the screen. When she sees me looking, she hurriedly clicks out of it, and sticks the phone in her coat pocket. "I don't know, I've got a lot to do this afternoon. Maybe tomorrow, instead?"

I'm surprised by her response. Since the day we first said "I love you" to each other, we've been spending every possible moment we can together, so it's unusual for her to put me off like this. I thought we were solid after she slept over on New Year's Eve and we sealed the deal, but maybe something's changed. A cold feeling settles in my stomach. "All right," I say reluctantly. "See you tomorrow." Laci nods distractedly, then grabs her bag and gets out of the car, without even kissing me goodbye.

20

Laci

After going to see my father the week before Christmas, I tried several more times to reach Tiff, but continued getting recordings saying her number was unavailable. I kept calling and texting though, but I didn't get a response from her until this morning. That was the text I was looking at right before Rudy dropped me off at home: *Couldn't respond sooner, my phone service got cut off. Your dad's an asshole (sorry). Lot of shit to deal with here. Call for update when u can.*

I go inside and head straight to my bedroom, ignoring the dirty dishes and remnants of breakfast that my aunt left all over the kitchen before she went to work this morning. I take my phone from my pocket, shrug my coat off and dial Tiff.

"Holy frick, Laci," she says in her raspy smoker's voice. "Your fucking father, pardon my English. He withdrew money from my checking account without telling me, so I wasn't able to pay my phone bill on time, and they cut me off. That's why it took so long for me to get back to you."

I have zero sympathy. My father and Tiff's relationship has always been volatile, and neither one of them has ever been capable of managing money. "I take it you moved out?" I say.

"You bet your sweet ass, I did! It got where I couldn't take the drinking anymore, and nothing I said made any difference to him. The moron thought I was bluffing, but I showed him. I took the TV and the—"

I cut her off because I need to get to the point. "What about Jayden? Is he with you?"

Tiff lets out a harsh laugh that turns into a phlegmy coughing fit. "Jesus, Laci," she says when she's recovered. "Didn't your father tell you?"

I grip the phone tighter. "Tell me what?"

"He got arrested. They're holding him in juvenile detention till he goes to court. His father refused to get involved, and they apparently didn't trust me to look after him."

I can't believe what I'm hearing. This is the exact thing I was the most worried about. I struggle to keep my voice steady. "What did he get arrested for?"

"They said he broke into someone's house this past summer, and stole a gun."

My heart skips a beat. "Whose house? Where?"

"I don't know, I think they said it was in Centerport."

I sink onto my bed. *Oh my God, Jayden. What have you done?* It's too much of a coincidence, it's got to be the Batemans' house. I try to say something, but the words won't come. Tiff keeps on talking, telling me about Jayden's upcoming appearance in Family Court. "Have you seen him?" I ask. "Where is he? Is he okay?"

"He's at Stonebrook. I went up there the day before yesterday. He's doing all right, but he's scared. They told me a lawyer has been assigned to his case, so I talked to her on the phone afterward. She promised to do everything she can to keep him out of jail. It's his first offense, so she hopes they'll go easy on him."

"I'd like to see him, too. Are siblings allowed to visit?"

"No, only parents and grandparents are allowed, but they might let you do a remote visit. I'll check with the social worker and let you know what she says."

The social worker calls me a half hour later, and tells me she's arranged a Zoom call at 3:15 this afternoon. Even though he's locked up, Jayden still has to complete his school day, which goes until three.

To keep myself occupied while I wait, I get busy cleaning up the kitchen and doing a load of laundry.

As I go through the mindless motions of housework, I think about what I'm going to say to him. I'm sure he's frightened and anxious, so I need to be calm and supportive, and assure him that his mom is ready to do whatever's necessary to get him out. I also wonder what I'm going to say to Rudy. He'll be shocked when I tell him it was my brother who broke into his stepparents' house, and I can only imagine what Debra and Mitchell will think. Mitchell especially, because he's so prejudiced against the people in Woodland Homes.

At ten minutes after three, I shut myself into my bedroom in case my aunt comes home early, dial into the Zoom link, and sit waiting with my phone in my hand. Promptly at 3:15, the call connects and my little brother's round face fills the screen. A lump forms in my throat when I see him, and I can tell he's feeling it too. "Are you all right, Jay?" I ask him first thing. I guess it wasn't the best question to ask right off, because his mouth puckers up and he starts to cry. "It's okay, buddy," I say in a soothing tone. "Don't worry, everything's going to be all right." In the background, I see a classroom-type space with inspirational words painted on the wall—*Believe, Succeed, Love, Accept.* I'm relieved to see he's dressed in his own clothes, and there aren't any bars on the windows.

Jayden grinds his knuckles into his eyes and sniffles. "Hi, Lace," he says at last in a small voice. I ask him what he did in "school" today, and he mumbles a few words about the ancient Romans. I know he likes math, so I ask what problems he worked on. He perks up a little and starts talking about algebraic equations, then describes the computer lab at Stonebrook. "It's not as good as the one at my school," he says, "and it's really small."

Now that he's calmer, it's time to cut to the chase. "Jayden," I say. "What happened? How did you get into this kind of trouble?"

He raises his chin and his eyes go wide. "I didn't do it Laci! It wasn't me!"

"Why do the police think it was you, then?"

Jayden's gaze doesn't waver. "I went over to that house a couple of times to scope it out for Dion, but that's all I did, I swear! I never broke in, or did any damage."

"*Dion?*" I shriek. "Were you out of your *mind?*"

Jayden begins to cry again, so I dial it back. "Okay, sorry, Jay. I promise I won't yell anymore. Now, go back to the beginning, and explain how you got mixed up with that creep."

Jayden stammers out his story. "I know it was stupid. It's just that things were so screwed up at home, with Dad drinking and fighting with Tiff all the time, so I started hanging out with some kids on the corner. Then Dion and this other guy came and talked to me one day. They were real nice and friendly at first—" He pauses to wipe his runny nose with the back of his hand. "But then they started pressuring me to do stuff."

"What kind of stuff?"

He shrugs. "You know, random stuff. Delivering packages and messages to people, that sorta thing."

I feel like I'm frozen in place as I listen to him. *Dion used my little brother as a drug courier.* "Then what?" I prod. "Why did Dion want you to scope out the house?"

"I heard him telling someone there were guns in the basement, and he wanted to steal them. He said something about 'eliminating the middleman' and making more money. All I did was walk around the yard and peek in the windows a few times. That's it."

"Hold on," I say. "Where exactly is this house located?"

"It's on the other side of the woods, in this neighborhood called Spruce Tree something."

Definitely the Batemans' house. *Holy crap.* I wonder how on earth I'm going to explain this to Rudy.

"You were caught with a gun on you, though," I go on. "How did that happen?"

Jayden looks like he's going to claw his way through the screen. "That was Dion's fault! It was *his* gun. We were out back of his apartment talking, and one of the other kids came running up and told him the cops were coming. He shoved the gun into the back of my jeans and ran."

"Then what?"

"I got caught. I told the cops it wasn't mine, but they didn't believe me."

Whew. This is a lot to process. "Did you tell all this to the lawyer? She needs to know exactly what happened, so she knows what to do about it."

Jayden looks away. "No," he says. "I'm too scared to. Dion told me to keep my mouth shut, or I'd be in big trouble."

"Jayden! You have to tell the lawyer, or she can't help you!" I feel like this is partly my fault, for not paying more attention to him all along. "Why didn't you call me, if things were getting that bad at home? Maybe I could've helped somehow."

"I did call you one time, don't you remember? You said you were busy with your boyfriend and you'd call me back. But you never did."

I think back to when I was first dating Rudy, and feel a stab of guilt when I realize that what Jayden's saying is absolutely correct. I *did* blow him off one night, when Rudy and I were in the middle of buying tickets at the movie theater. I told Jayden I'd call him later, then completely forgot about him because I was so caught up in the excitement of my budding romance.

"Jayden, I am so, so sorry for being such a selfish jerk." My eyes well up, but Jayden's remain dry this time.

"No, you're not," he says. "You're the nicest person I know, Laci. Sometimes I wish *you* were my mom."

That does me in, and the tears stream down my face. The social worker appears at Jayden's side, and says his time is up. "Don't worry," I tell my brother before signing off. "I'm going to get you out of this."

21

Debra

I'm so pleased that Rudy's been making an effort to stay in touch with me, like I asked him to on Christmas. He responds to my texts now, and usually picks up when I call. We had a pleasant chat on the phone the other day, and it felt almost normal. He shared his plans for the coming semester, and I told him about the Basic Pistol course I took, which impressed him. I suspect it's Laci who's behind the change in his behavior, which warms my heart. Despite her unconventional appearance, she's turning out to be a very kind and considerate person, which seems to be having a positive effect on Rudy. She even sent me a thank you note after Christmas, and mentioned how appreciative she was of the opportunity to get to know our family. She's obviously stolen Rudy's heart, and now she's close to stealing mine.

Rudy's classes begin again on Monday, and I'm excited for him. Four months from now, he'll have his certificate, and will be qualified to start work as an HVAC technician. To celebrate the beginning of the spring semester, I invited him and Laci to come for dinner last night, since it was Mitch's weekend off. We spent an enjoyable evening talking about their upcoming classes and Rudy's new car, which he's extremely proud of. The frostiness between him and Mitch is slowly but surely thawing, and Mitch appears to be getting used to Laci. She's still got the silly dyed hair and that awful nose ring, which bugs the heck out of my husband, but I keep reminding him that we need to take Laci's youth into account. I'm convinced it's a phase she's going through, and she'll soon grow out of it.

•   •   •   •   •

On Saturday morning, my pistol permit arrives in the mail. I call Joanne, and she tells me that hers arrived the day before. "As soon as I got it," she says, "my brother took me to a Bass Pro Shop and helped me buy a brand-new handgun, but I haven't had the nerve to use it yet. I'm worried I'm going to forget everything I learned in the class if I don't get some practice soon."

"I have an idea," I say. "Why don't we go to the Rod & Gun Club? My husband added me to his membership after I completed the class, so you could come as my guest. We can practice target shooting on the indoor range. They have a range safety officer on duty on the weekends, so if we have questions or run into trouble with anything, someone will be there to help." Joanne says she'd love to, so we plan to meet there in the afternoon.

At the club, the range officer goes over the rules with us, then gets us set up on a lane. Shooting indoors is quite different from what I experienced in the class, due to the noise being a lot louder and the percussion feeling more intense. But after a while, I become engrossed in the drills we're working on, and the noise fades into the background. Joanne and I are both rusty when we start out, but after an hour of practice, we're satisfied with our overall performance.

"We should do this once a month, to keep up with our training," Joanne says when we're back in the relative quiet of the clubhouse, and can remove our eye and ear protection.

"I agree. I could definitely use more practice." I set my new range bag on a bench and check the various pockets, to make sure I have all my gear.

Joanne admires my bag. "Did you get this for Christmas?"

"Yes, my husband gave it to me. Isn't it cute?" I show it off to her. "Mitch said he picked the pink camouflage pattern so I'd look hip."

"That's really sweet. My ex was never thoughtful like that."

Joanne's comment gets me thinking. Mitchell can be a thoughtful guy, in his own way. He rarely tells me he loves me, but I can see it in his actions—for example, the way he picked out my gun for me, and insisted I learn how to use it. He did that for my benefit, to keep me safe.

I zip my bag closed and loop the padded strap over my shoulder. I'm enjoying my day out with my new friend, and I'd like to stretch it longer, since there's no reason for me to rush home to my housework. "Do you have time to get coffee?" I ask Joanne. "There's a Dunkin' not too far from here."

Joanne says she has plenty of time, so she follows me there in her car. We each get a large coffee, then find comfortable seats in front of a fireplace that looks warm and cozy, but doesn't actually emit any heat. We chat about our jobs and our families. For some reason, I feel perfectly comfortable telling Joanne about my travails with Rudy. The fact that she's divorced makes her seem more real and approachable somehow, unlike my overachieving sister Denise, who I'm constantly comparing myself to, and falling short of.

I talk about Mitchell, and how he pressured me into taking the Basic Pistol class. "I resisted at first, but now I'm grateful he pushed me to do it. I have more confidence when I'm home alone, which makes me feel more independent. I mean, look at me today—I never spend a Saturday afternoon like this, going out to do something fun with a friend. A normal weekend for me is cleaning the house and running errands, or helping out with something at church." I look down at my coffee cup, and pick at the edge of the plastic lid. "To be honest, I'm a pretty boring person."

Joanne scoffs. "You are not boring, Debra! I'm sure you have your exciting moments."

I tilt my head and think about it. "I used to, I guess, back when I was in my teens and early twenties. I had a girlfriend named Ann Marie, who I grew up with. She was a riot, so bold and daring. Totally unlike me. We used to work together at this restaurant downtown. It's long gone now, but it was a very popular place back in the eighties. The manager there was an older woman who was an absolute witch. Nobody could stand her, but Ann Marie was one of her pets. We used to pull all kinds of pranks on the poor woman, to deliberately annoy her, then we'd laugh our heads off when she blew her top."

Joanne chuckles. "That sounds like fun. You must have been rather daring yourself, if you were pulling pranks on your boss."

I stare into space for a few moments, remembering. Working with Ann Marie was fun for a while, until Mitchell came home and got serious with her, and I was sidelined once again. After they got married, she continued working at the restaurant for another year, because they needed the extra income. Edith agreed to change my hours, but our shifts sometimes overlapped. On those nights, I'd have to endure Mitchell bringing Rudy to visit with Ann Marie on her breaks, and I'd hear the three of them laughing together at their table in the back corner. It was hard to take, but I tried not to let it get to me—until that fateful night.

I stare unseeing at the cardboard cup in my hand, my thoughts tangled up in the past. *I shouldn't have done it*, I murmur, shaking my head.

"You shouldn't have done what?"

I yank my thoughts back to the present. *Did I just say that out loud?* "Nothing," I reply quickly. I grab my cup and swallow the last of my coffee, then reach for my coat. "I'd better get going, or Mitch will be wondering where I am."

After saying goodbye to Joanne, I get in my car and sit for a minute with the heater running. I'm unsettled by how close I came to making a serious gaffe. As I'm trying to regain my composure, my phone trills with a text from Mitchell, asking me to swing by the pharmacy on my way home and pick up his blood pressure medication. "Yes, Mitchell," I say out loud, my tone brittle and sarcastic. My brief interlude of independence has come to an end, and now it's time to return to my domestic duties.

I drive back into town and pull into the Walgreens. I park and go inside instead of using the pharmacy drive-thru, figuring I might as well stock up on paper products while I'm here. I pick up Mitch's prescription, then fill a shopping cart with paper towels, Kleenex and toilet paper.

In the parking lot, as I'm loading the goods into the back of my Civic, an older model sedan pulls into the handicap space next to mine, and Edith Scanlon eases herself out of the vehicle. "Speak of the devil," I mutter under my breath. The wicked witch herself, in the flesh.

I haven't seen Edith in a long time, and I'm startled by how unwell she looks. Her face is sallow and her back is stooped, as though she doesn't have the strength her hold herself upright. I still dislike her, but she's an old woman now, so I should at least give her the courtesy of a polite greeting. "Hello, Edith," I call to her. "How are you?" Edith raises her head as she passes by, and the instant she recognizes me, her blank expression turns venomous. I take a quick step back, repelled by the intense hatred in her eyes.

The sound of boots crunching on ice nearby causes me to turn my head, and I see my church friend Carrie Walters approaching with a pharmacy bag in her gloved hand. "Debra!" she exclaims. "How've you been? My husband said he saw you at the shooting range earlier today. I didn't know you'd taken up a new hobby." I tell her I'm doing fine. "I'd love to chat," Carrie says, "but I've got to run. Call me later, so we can catch up!"

Turning back to the items in my shopping cart, I see Edith Scanlon is still standing a few feet from me, her dark eyes boring into me from beneath her heavy brow. "Guns are dangerous," she says in a menacing whisper. "You'd better be careful or you might hurt someone else."

My mouth drops open and I freeze with a jumbo package of Charmin in my hands. I hear Edith's slow footsteps receding, but I remain rooted to my spot, staring into space, wondering what she meant. Surely not—*No.* She couldn't possibly be referring to the accident, not when so much time has passed. It's ancient history that was laid to rest over twenty years ago. The woman must be off her rocker, driven into senility by a lifetime spent with that horrible husband of hers.

Looking over my shoulder to make sure Edith is gone, I stuff the last of my purchases into the car and slam the hatchback closed. My pulse is racing. *Damned Edith.* Why can't she mind her own business, and leave me alone? There's no need for her to go stirring up the past, when there's nothing anyone can do about it anymore.

I get in my car and head home, blind to the traffic around me. Edith's words are haunting me, and I know I'm not going to be able to sleep tonight. I don't need this kind of stress, not when things are finally beginning to turn around for my family. If Edith doesn't keep her mouth shut, I may be forced to do something.

22

Laci

I've been searching all over the place for my messenger bag, and when I arrive at City Tech for my classes this morning, I finally realize I must have forgotten it at the Batemans' house when Rudy and I went over there for dinner on Friday night. Debra had offered to hem an old skirt for me, so I'd stuffed it into my bag to bring it with me, then left the bag behind in the sewing room upstairs. Now I'm in desperate need of it, because the bag contains a textbook I have to use for an assignment that's due in two days.

Going all the way out to Centerport to retrieve my bag is going to be a huge time suck, on top of all the other stuff that's stressing me out. It's only the first week of school, but I've already got tons of homework to do; plus, my aunt is laid up because she slipped and fell on the ice the other day and injured her knee, so all the errands and housework have fallen to me.

But worse than anything, I'm worried to death about Jayden. Tiff called and told me the charges against him are more serious than she was expecting because a gun was involved, and the case may be transferred from Family Court to Criminal Court. I can't sleep at night for worrying, but I have to keep my anxiety to myself. I haven't told Rudy anything yet, and I'm not sure when I'm going to. Even though I'm certain Jayden is innocent, what's Rudy going to think when I tell him it was my brother who got arrested? I'll have to explain the whole story about Jayden's involvement with that sleazeball Dion, which will reflect badly on me. When my boyfriend hears about the sort of people I used to live among, he'll probably want to run the other way.

We're both at City Tech today, but Rudy's classes are in a different wing than mine. I call him to let him know I've figured out where my missing bag is, and ask if he can give me a ride over to the house to get it this evening. He's currently in the shop, and there's machinery whirring and banging in the background. "I wish I could," he shouts over the noise, "but my boss needs me to work tonight, to help organize a big shipment of parts that's being delivered today. If you drop me off at the warehouse around five, you can borrow my car. Mitchell will be getting ready to go to work by then, but I'm sure Debra will be glad to see you."

Rudy has to stay late at school to work on a project, so I take the bus home by myself that afternoon. I spend an hour doing homework, then prepare an early supper and carry a plate in to my aunt, who's camped out on the living room couch watching a rerun of Law & Order, with her swollen leg propped on a pillow. I'm relieved to get out of there when Rudy comes to pick me up at 4:45. When I get in the car, he kisses me on the cheek like he always does, but his manner seems almost tentative, as though he's unsure of himself—most likely because I've been so distracted these past several days, and haven't been as affectionate toward him as I normally am. To make him feel better, I lean over and kiss him firmly on the lips. "You're a lifesaver, Rudy. Thanks for doing this."

After dropping him off at the warehouse, I'm not in any hurry to get to the Batemans' house. Even though Mitchell was perfectly cordial the last time I was over there, I still feel uncomfortable around him, so I'd rather not arrive until after he's left for work. I stop at the grocery store to pick up a few items for my aunt, then take my time driving out to Centerport.

When I turn onto Crestview Drive, Mitchell's truck is still in the driveway, so I keep going past the house. As I'm cautiously coming around the loop a second time, I slow to a crawl when I see Mitchell hurrying out of the garage. His truck lights up, then backs swiftly down the driveway and roars off.

I wait till he's out of sight before proceeding to the house. As I'm walking up the driveway, I notice one of the overhead garage doors is still open—Mitchell must have been running late and forgot to close it. I go into the garage and knock on the door that leads into the mudroom. There's no answer, so I open the door and call out, "Debra? Are you home?" It's a dumb question since her car's right there in the garage; but I don't want to barge into the house without warning, since I forgot to call first and tell her I was coming.

I step into the mudroom. The floor is cluttered with shoes and boots, and an assortment of winter coats are hanging from hooks on the wall. The door to the kitchen is ajar, so I poke my head in and listen for a second. I can faintly hear Debra's voice coming from the direction of her office—she must be on the phone. I don't want to startle her, so I decide to wait until she finishes her conversation before I call out to her again, to let her know I'm here.

Cocoa trots into the kitchen and I bend down to scratch her behind the ears. While I'm waiting, I glance around the room, looking for my bag, but I don't see it anywhere. In the office, Debra continues her phone conversation. I hear her mention the police, which grabs my attention. Stepping quietly, I move down the hall toward the office, and stop a few feet short of the open door, where she can't see me.

"Do you remember Gary Scanlon, who we went to school with?" Debra says. "He's the detective on the case. The boy they arrested is only fourteen, so the police aren't supposed to release his name, but since Gary knows Mitch personally, he bent the rules for us. He says the kid lives in that scuzzy low-income housing project behind us. His name is Jayden Wright."

Hearing my brother's name coming out of Debra's mouth hits me like a blow to my gut. It's only a matter of time before she makes the connection between Jayden and me, and tells Rudy. I hold my breath as she goes on. "Gary stopped by last week and showed me a photo of the boy, to see if I recognized him. I told him it was definitely the same kid I saw standing on my patio back in August, when he broke into the house."

My mouth drops open in disbelief. There's a pause, then Debra continues: "I absolutely agree with you, Denise. The boy's father is apparently a deadbeat alcoholic who's taken no responsibility whatsoever for his son, and the mother isn't much better. Those people in Woodland Homes are nothing but trashy welfare scum, and their children are growing up to be savages. I mean, a fourteen-year-old breaking into a house and stealing a gun—I can hardly believe it, at such a young age! I hope this boy Jayden gets the maximum punishment for what he did. In the meantime, they need to keep him locked up, so he can't terrorize anyone else. There was a court hearing this afternoon, to determine how the case is going to be handled. Gary promised to call this evening, to let me know what the judge decided."

I ball my fists, and it's all I can do to stop myself from bursting into the room and screaming at her. I'll be the first to admit my father's a deadbeat, but making a blanket statement about the residents of Woodland Homes being welfare scum is going too far. And maximum punishment? Jayden's a *child*, for godsakes! It's not his fault he got dragged into this. The blame should be placed squarely on Dion, for using Jayden, then discarding him; and on my father and Tiff, for being self-centered idiots who've completely disregarded their responsibility as parents.

But my anger at all of them is nothing compared to the burning rage I'm feeling toward Debra right now. It's impossible that she saw Jayden on her patio that night because *he wasn't there*. The fucking bitch lied to the police, and pinned the crime on my defenseless brother. But why would she do that? Doesn't she want them to find the person who really did it, so she doesn't have to worry anymore?

I stand there trembling with fury. It sounds like Debra's winding up her conversation, so I tiptoe back down the hall to the kitchen. I hear her say goodbye, and a moment later, she comes out of the office. Her hand flies to her chest when she sees me in the kitchen. "Laci! My goodness, I didn't hear you come in!"

"I–I'm sorry, I didn't mean to scare you," I stammer, trying hard to act natural. "The garage door was open. I called out to you, but I guess you didn't hear me, so I let myself in."

"That's all right. I was on the phone with my sister." Debra lowers her hand. "Is Rudy with you?"

"No, he's working tonight."

Debra keeps looking at me as though she's waiting for me to explain why I'm here, but then she figures it out. "Oh, your bag! I meant to call you when I saw you'd forgotten it the other night, but there was so much going on, it slipped my mind. Wait a second, I'll go get it for you." She disappears upstairs, then comes back down and hands me my messenger bag. "I'm sorry, I haven't had time to get to your skirt yet. Maybe next week, when I'm not so busy."

I'm so angry, I'm having trouble looking her in the eye. As if I give a darn about my skirt, when my little brother's freedom is at stake! I can feel Debra's gaze on me, so I make myself look up. "That's okay, it can wait." I want to say something scathing that will show my utter disdain for her, but once I get started, I'm afraid I won't be able to control my mouth. This isn't the right time or place for me to confront her, anyway. Jayden's neck is on the line, and I don't dare do anything that might backfire on him.

Debra looks puzzled. "How did you get here, anyway?" I don't have the chance to answer because her phone starts ringing from down the hall. "You'll have to excuse me," she says, patting the air between us in apology. "I'm expecting an important call." She gives me a dismissive wave, then hurries back to her office and closes the door behind her.

There's no way I'm going to stand here waiting for her to get off the phone again. I'm about to leave, but then I hesitate, wishing there was some way to show her how disgusted I am. I could leave her a note, telling her what I overheard, and how it made me feel. It would be much easier for me to admit in writing that Jayden is my brother, rather than the awkwardness of telling Debra to her face, or holding my breath until she finds out on her own.

In search of a pen and paper, I rummage through the kitchen drawers. Silverware, utensils, kitchen towels, random odds and ends—but nothing to write with. The last drawer is the one beside the stove. I pull it open and see a stack of colorful potholders, but it feels like there's something hard underneath. Pushing them aside, I see the dull gleam of metal.

Debra has a *gun?* No freaking way. That's completely out of character for her. But it's got to be hers, judging by the size of it. It's much too small for Mitchell's big hands, but it looks just right for Debra's. I'm no stranger to handguns, having grown up in a dicey neighborhood. My mom had a snub-nosed revolver that she taught me how to use, and when I lived with my dad, he always slept with his .38 Special beside his bed.

Fury seizes me. What if Debra had shot Jayden when she saw him in the backyard? Without stopping to think, I shove my hand into the drawer and grab the gun. I don't know what I'm going to do with it, but I do know that I don't want to leave it in Debra's hands. With the gun clutched in my hand, I stop for a second to listen, but she's still blabbing away on the phone. Lifting the flap on my messenger bag, I drop the gun into it, then hook the strap over my head and shoulder. Pausing only long enough to give Cocoa a swift farewell pat on the head, I hustle outside.

The first thing I do when I'm in the car is call Tiff. She doesn't pick up, which isn't much of a surprise. After Jayden's arrest, she made a big show of being a concerned parent, but since then, she's slipped back into her usual negligent ways, and has been unreachable. I try my dad next, but he doesn't pick up either, which is just as well, because he's useless.

I drive back to Rudy's, crying and fuming the entire way. I'm furious with Debra, but also with myself—first, for not doing anything when I knew Jayden was at risk, and secondly, for falling for Debra's act. She's had me totally fooled this whole time, with her virtuous knitting and sewing, and her bullshit talk about forgiveness and redemption. I thought she was a kind and gentle person, but beneath her churchy, homey facade, she's nothing but a merciless suburban bitch.

I'm bitterly disappointed, too. Debra and I were growing close, and she was starting to feel like the mother I never had. I worked hard at persuading Rudy to make up with his stepparents because I was yearning to become part of a family, but now my hopes have been dashed by Debra's privileged arrogance. She thinks she's so high and mighty, with her demands that Jayden be locked up and severely punished. How could she be so cruel, when she doesn't even know him? He's a good kid who made a mistake, just like tons of other teenagers have.

A looming traffic light turns from yellow to red, and I stomp on the brakes. My messenger bag slides off the slippery velour passenger's seat and lands on the floor, and Debra's gun falls out. I reach down and shove it back in. She has no idea what it's like to be brought up the way Jayden and I were—alone and unloved, with incompetent parents who can't hold it together. The light changes to green and I continue on my way, wiping my wet cheeks with the palms of my hands.

It's too early to pick up Rudy, so I go to his apartment to wait for him to get done with work. Fudgie's sprawled on the couch, watching TV and texting with his girlfriend. I must look pretty bad because he puts his phone down and asks me what's wrong. I drop my bag and coat on a kitchen chair and slump onto the futon. "You don't want to know."

Fudgie regards me soberly. "Something happen to Rudy's car?"

"The car's fine." I scrape my fingers through my hair, avoiding his concerned gaze. "Did you know the police arrested someone for breaking into the Batemans' house?"

"Yeah, Rudy told me. Said it was some teenager that did it."

This infuriates me all over again. "They arrested a *kid*, Fudgie! An innocent fourteen-year-old boy."

He looks at me in surprise. "An innocent kid? How do you know about it?"

Oh my God, I can't talk about this. I scrunch my hair in my hands and make a screeching sound through my clenched teeth.

Fudgie comes over and sits beside me. "Shit, Lace, what happened? Do you know this kid or something?"

I push my hair out of my face. "When I went over to the Batemans' house tonight, I overheard Rudy's stepmother talking about it on the phone. The police told her the kid's name, even though they're not supposed to." I hesitate for a second, gathering my courage. "It turns out, it was my half-brother, Jayden."

Fudgie's eyes grow wide. "*Shiiiit.* Your little brother. Man, that sucks."

"The thing is, Jayden didn't do it! He's in Stonebrook, and they arranged a video call, so I got to talk to him. He said this thug in Woodland Homes pressured him into getting involved on the side, but it wasn't him who broke into the house." I'm crying again, but I talk right through my tears. "The worst of it is that Debra was the one who falsely identified him. The police showed her a picture and she said it was him, even though she never saw him. She was *gloating,* can you believe it? She's actually happy she helped put a boy in jail."

I'm energized by my anger. "My brother lives in Woodland Homes with our dad. Do you want to know what Debra thinks about that? She *despises* the people who live there. She thinks they're all scum, and she has no qualms about putting one of them in jail, even if it's the wrong person. You probably don't know this, but I used to live there myself, before I moved in with my aunt. It really hurt to hear her talking like that."

Fudgie shakes his head in sympathy. "What're you gonna say to Rudy?"

My shoulders sag. "I don't know. I'm ashamed to tell him my brother was involved. Things have been warming up lately between him and his stepparents, so I'm worried he'll be mad, because this is going to set everything back. Debra and Mitchell will think I'm a scumbag by association, and won't want me to come over anymore. If you knew what a screwed up family I come from, you'd probably think so, too."

"Nah," Fudgie says. "Rudy won't be mad. He loses his cool sometimes, but not about stuff like this. You can't help what some thug put your little brother up to, Lace."

I check the time on my phone. "I've got to go pick him up soon. Will you be here when I get back? I might need you for moral support."

Fudgie gazes up at the ceiling. "Yeah, no. I think I'd better go over to Sabrina's instead, and let you guys work this out. Trust me, Rudy won't hold it against you. He'll be more pissed at his stepmother, for lying about it."

"Maybe," I say, worriedly chewing my lip. "I hope you're right."

23

Rudy

The warehouse where I work is noisy and drafty. I spend my evening shift unloading pallets of air conditioning parts, scanning them into inventory, and stacking them on the long rows of metal shelves. It's dull work that doesn't require much concentration, which is good because I have a lot on my mind.

I'm worried Laci's feelings about me have changed. She hasn't been texting as much, and she was very quiet the night Debra had us over for dinner. Instead of being her usual bubbly, talkative self, she left the bulk of the conversation up to me, which definitely isn't my jam. Afterward, she asked me to drop her off at her aunt's instead of coming over to my place. I was majorly bummed because Fudgie was out for the night, so we could've had some serious hookup time.

At 9:00, I call goodnight to my boss in his office, then go to the break room to clock out and get my coat. The other employees have left already. I walk outside, and feel a thrill of pleasure when I see the LeBaron in a nearby parking space, and Laci sitting behind the wheel. Her coming to pick me up makes it feel like we're still a real couple.

When she sees me, she gets out of the car. I'm expecting her to come give me a hug, but instead, she walks around to the passenger's side and gets in without a word.

"Is everything okay?" I ask as I drive out of the lot. I'm getting the same tight feeling in my chest as I did when she hid that mysterious text message from me the other day.

"I'm fine," she says, even though I can tell she obviously isn't. "We'll talk about it when we get home."

At the apartment, she follows me inside, still not speaking. As I'm pulling my gloves and coat off, Fudgie comes out of the bedroom with a backpack on his shoulder, and says his girlfriend's coming to pick him up to spend the night. "Later," he calls, and the door thumps closed behind him.

Laci beckons me over to the couch. "Rudy. We need to talk."

Obviously. I hope I haven't done anything wrong. I'm still getting used to this girlfriend/boyfriend thing, and I often feel like I'm off balance, trying to figure out how I'm supposed to act. I kick off my wet boots, then go and sit down next to Laci, and clasp my hands between my knees. "What's the matter?"

Her face is somber. "I'm not sure how to tell you this," she says, nervously twisting her fingers together. "It's about that teenager the police arrested for breaking into your stepparents' house."

"Yeah? What about him?"

She lets out a long sigh and hangs her head. "He's my brother, Rudy. It was Jayden."

I go blank. "Wait, what? Your brother?"

"They found a gun on him when he was arrested. They think he stole it from the house."

It takes a couple seconds for this to sink in, then my mood does a sharp one-eighty. *Woohoo!* I'm totally off the hook now. This is awesome, stupendous news!

But then I notice how upset Laci is. Her cheeks are flushed and she's blinking back tears. I compose myself and hold my arms out to her. "Aw, baby. Don't cry."

She presses her face into my neck. "I'm so sorry, Rudy! Since before Christmas, I had this bad feeling that Jayden was in some kind of trouble, but I didn't pay enough attention. I feel like such a jerk for letting him down, and not doing anything to prevent this."

I pat her back, waiting for her to calm down. I've got to get the whole story out of her, to make sure I'm truly in the clear. I gently peel her off me. "So, how did this happen? Are you sure it's your brother they arrested?"

"Yes, I'm sure! But that's beside the point, you haven't let me finish. Jayden didn't do it, Rudy! He never broke into the house or stole the gun. It was someone else."

Uh oh... "How do you know? If the police arrested him, he must've—"

"I know because I had a Zoom call with him from jail. He looked in my eyes and told me he didn't do it."

My insides twist into a knot. I'm reluctant to ask, but I need to know if anyone suspects me. "Who do you think did it, then?" I ask carefully, trying to conceal my fear.

"I think it was this bad guy named Dion, who lives in Woodland Homes."

It suddenly clicks in my head: Jayden was the kid on the street corner, the one playing lookout for Dion's gang of hoods. My blood turns cold. If the police go after Dion, I'll be royally screwed. My leg starts jumping in a nervous rhythm. I can't let on that I know him, because it'll freak Laci out that I associated with a thug. I'm unable to string a sentence together, so I repeat his name: "Dion?"

"Yeah," Laci says. "I don't know him personally, but I've heard he's a badass. He used Jayden to scope out the house so he could rob it himself, and then he set Jayden up to take the fall."

The fucker! Dion was supposed to be partnering with me, not cutting me out of the money.

"That's not the worst of it, though."

Oh great, I think. *There's more?*

"This is the worst part." Laci twists her fingers again, and her expression morphs rapidly from anguish to anger. "The reason Jayden's still in jail is because Debra identified him as the person who broke into her house."

My body's probably going *WTF?* right now because my fear instantly evaporates, and relief rushes through me again. If Debra believes she saw a fourteen-year-old boy on the other side of her shattered slider, I'm golden. End of story, nothing to see here, folks.

Laci jabs my arm. "Did you hear me, Rudy? Your stepmother lied to the police!"

I've gotta keep my ass covered. "She didn't *lie*," I say. "She just told them what she saw. Or thought she saw."

Laci draws herself up like her head's going to launch through the ceiling. "Are you not *listening* to me, Rudy? What part of this don't you understand? Jayden wasn't even there, but Debra purposely gave the police a false eyewitness account saying he was. She's a *liar*, Rudy!"

The word "purposely" hits me like an electric shock. I consider the implications for a few moments, and the conclusion I reach stuns me. My stepmother saw me that night, and now she's trying to cover for me. The clarity of it takes my breath away. *Debra wants to protect me.*

Laci's nose is running, so I get up and grab a handful of toilet paper from the bathroom, then hurry back to her. She dabs at her face, then crushes the wad of tissue into a tight ball. "You should've heard the awful things she said about Jayden, Rudy! She thinks they should keep him locked up forever, like he's an animal or something." Her lower lip trembles and the tears begin to flow again. "She called him all kinds of terrible names, and she made Woodland Homes sound like the worst ghetto. I wonder what she'd have to say if she knew I used to live there, too."

I can't stand to see my girlfriend hurting like this, but in a flash of insight, I realize it might be useful to keep her outrage directed at my stepmother, so she doesn't start asking questions and become suspicious of me. It'll buy me some time, and give Laci something to chew on while I sort everything out in my head. I take her hands in mine. "You're right, this is all Debra's fault. She's always been a self-righteous priss. Don't let it get to you, she's an ignorant hypocrite who doesn't understand anything outside of her own little world."

Laci pulls her hands away. "If they'd only let Jayden out of jail, he could come live with me! I'm eighteen, that's old enough to raise a sibling by myself. I'll be working full time once I finish school, so I'll be able to support him. I could make sure he stays away from the evil friends he's made, and force him go to counseling, or whatever it is that they require for kids like him."

I gape at her in amazement. She's got to be the most caring, selfless, generous person on this earth. I think back to Christmas day—the smug look on Mitchell's face when he told us the police had made an arrest, and Debra's sanctimonious blather about her belief in redemption. What a crock. All those two care about is themselves, and how they can safeguard their tidy, boring suburban existence. They're oblivious to people like Laci, who's had to struggle with hardship and poverty her whole life, and poor, neglected Jayden, who's got no one to look out for him but his big sister.

I'm facing a major conflict here. If I keep quiet about what I did, Laci's little brother stays in jail. But if I admit what I did, I'll land myself in the clink, and blow up my relationship with my girlfriend in the process. Laci won't want to keep dating a criminal, and her opinion of me will be damaged beyond repair.

I get up and begin pacing—five steps to the kitchen, five back to the couch, five more to the kitchen. I'm gripping my head between my forearms like it's going to explode. Laci's gaze follows me, her eyes red and teary. If I tell her the truth, she'll dump me in a heartbeat. I don't deserve someone as good as she is, but I can't afford to lose her.

Laci goes off on another tearful tirade, and I half-listen as my thoughts churn. As she pointed out, Jayden's just a kid, alone and scared in juvie, so it's highly likely he's already told the police it was Dion who gave him the gun. When the police get hold of Dion, he'll rat me out in a hot second, to save his own neck. Which means I need to find him as quick I can—like right now, tonight—and warn him that the cops will be coming after him soon. And at the same time, I need to somehow convince him to keep my name out of it. I'm sure he'll be willing to help me, since I'll be doing him a favor by tipping him off.

I feel good about my plan of action. It won't completely absolve Jayden, but at least he might only end up being charged with trespassing, instead of illegal possession and burglary. Most importantly, it will keep my butt out of jail, and salvage things with Laci.

I return to the couch and stand over my sniffling girlfriend. "Listen, Laci. I know you're really upset about this, but I think you'd better go home now."

She looks up at me in disbelief. "You want me to *leave?*"

I grasp her hands and try to haul her to her feet, which takes some effort because she's resisting me. I've got a plausible lie at the ready: "I'm gonna go confront Debra about what she's done."

Laci jumps up, and I stumble backward. "I'm going with you!"

"No!" I hold her at arm's length. "You can't."

"Why in the world not, Rudy? I've got way more reason to be mad at her than you do."

"Because," I say, floundering for a reason. "Because she's my stepmother, so I should be the one to speak to her. You don't need to go with me, after all you've been through tonight. You should go home and get some rest, and let me handle this."

Laci sinks back down to the couch and rubs her forehead with both hands. "I was so angry a minute ago, but now I just feel—drained, I guess. I don't know what I'd even say to her." She sighs heavily. "Okay, I suppose you're right. It'll be better if you go by yourself."

Wanting to keep the momentum going, I pull her back to her feet, grab her coat and help her into it. She stops with one arm in the sleeve and grabs my wrist with her other hand. "Rudy, I was so worried you'd hate me because of my brother being involved in this. Are you sure you're not mad at me?"

"Of course, I'm not mad!" I take her arm and steer her toward the door. "Come on, I'll drive you home." I snatch up my coat, stuff my feet into my unlaced boots, and keep her moving, down the back steps to the car.

"Wait!" A look of panic flits across Laci's face as she pulls loose from me and runs back inside to grab her messenger bag.

24

Rudy

It's insane of me to be driving alone into a place like Woodland Homes at 10:00 at night, but if don't get to Dion before the police do, I'm dead meat. I cruise the quiet streets, keeping my eyes peeled for the black Monte Carlo. The curtains are drawn on most of the apartment windows, and the streetlights cast eerie splashes of light on the snowbanks. Even though it's freezing out, there's a knot of people in dark clothing huddled beneath a leafless tree on the same corner I stopped at the last time.

The LeBaron blends right in with the neighborhood, so I reduce my speed and scan my surroundings. The parking lot of the building opposite me is shrouded in shadows because the streetlight is out. Squinting into the darkness, I spot Dion's car parked at the end of the row, and see lights on in a ground floor apartment. I pull into the vacant space next to the Monte, get out and climb over the snowbank, then stride purposefully toward the front entrance of the building, as though I have every right to be here.

The entryway is dim and cluttered with bicycles and baby strollers, and bulging garbage bags are piled beneath an open staircase leading to the second floor. There are four apartments on the ground floor, and loud hip hop music is playing behind the door marked 1A, the unit where I saw the lights on. I take a deep breath and knock. The peephole goes dark, then the door swings open. It's Trey, and he looks supremely annoyed. He rubs one large hand on his bulky thigh as though he's warming it up, and stares at me from beneath his hooded eyes. "You got a lotta fuckin' nerve comin' here, boy," he says.

I feel a jolt of alarm, but keep my cool. Me, Trey and Dion go way back, after all. We're old friends, I've got nothing to fear. "I'm looking for your cousin. Is he around?"

Trey props a muscled forearm on the door frame and gapes at me like I've grown an extra head. "No, he ain't. Police come this afternoon and haul his ass off."

Oh shit. Over Trey's shoulder, I see two other dudes lounging on the couch with their eyes glued to me and their hands hidden in their waistbands. My educated guess is that they've got guns concealed inside their voluminous sweatpants, so I'd better not do anything to piss them off. I take a step back, holding my hands up. "Sorry to bother you, I was just—I wanted to tell him—"

Trey's hand darts out and grabs me by the front of my coat. He jerks me inside the apartment and kicks the door closed, then slams me up against it. Behind him, the two dudes are on their feet, regarding me with glee. I try to speak but nothing comes out but a high-pitched, girlish whine from the back of my throat. Trey gets in my face, gripping me by the collar. "The kid squealed."

For some idiotic reason, I play dumb. "Wh-what kid? Who're you talking about?"

"You damn well know who I'm talkin' about," Trey growls. He tightens his grip, making it hard for me to breathe. "The kid they busted for stealin' the Glock."

"It wasn't mine!" I gasp. Trey loosens his hold slightly, allowing me to speak more easily. "It belonged to a friend, like I told you. I was doing him a favor by selling it for him. I came here to ask Dion not to tell anyone where it came from, so I don't get in trouble."

A slow smile spreads across Trey's face. "We know where that piece come from, dumbass. We been in your house, remember?"

Fuck, fuck, fuck. I rack my brain, scrambling for something, anything, that might get me out of this jam, but Trey isn't finished yet. "And guess what else, boy?" he says. "Dion don't give a shit what happens to you, cuz he knows you ain't loyal. Not like Jayden was. Kid tried his best to keep quiet, but it's tough when you young and they puttin' the pressure on hard." He slams me against the door one more time, then lets go.

I slump to the floor, not daring to move, but Trey appears to be done roughing me up. I relax a bit and try to catch my breath. Trey crosses his arms across his broad chest and eyes me with a smug expression that reminds me of Mitchell. I'm incensed by the disrespectful way I'm being treated, when I came here in a gesture of goodwill and friendship. Judging by his flimsy grip on the basic rules of grammar, Trey doesn't have a whole lot of brain power in that Neanderthal skull of his. I stand up and shrug my rumpled coat back into place. I know I should keep my damn mouth shut, but I'm so mad, I can't resist. I raise my chin defiantly. "You're a stupid motherfucker."

BAM. Trey's fist connects with my left eye socket and I crumple to the floor. Bells clang and sparks explode in my head. I sense the two other dudes closing in, feel rough hands hauling me to my feet for another round. One of the guys wrenches my arms behind my back while the other one slams more punches into my nose. Next thing, my body goes spinning into the cluttered entryway, where I crash into a kid's bike and land in a heap on the dirty floor. The apartment door slams, followed by hoots of laughter. The music blares louder, a heavy bass line that pounds painfully inside my battered skull.

It takes several minutes for me to recover enough to grab hold of one of the strollers and drag myself to my feet. I slowly swivel my head from left to right, making sure there aren't any more malicious gangsters coming to beat the rest of the crap out of me. I hear someone coming down the stairs from the second level. The footsteps pause and there's a sharp gasp, followed by the sound of a door slamming and a bolt turning. The four apartment doors on the ground floor remain closed.

I stagger outside. My car is dusted with snow but I don't have the strength to brush off the windows. I get in and crank the engine. My face is throbbing and blood drips down the front of my coat. I turn on the wipers and throw it in reverse without looking. *Everybody get the hell out of my way.* Tires squealing, I leave the parking lot and blow through the stop sign, careless of anything that might be in my path, then speed out of Woodland Homes and haul ass back to the safety of the west side.

•   •   •   •   •

Since Fudgie's at his girlfriend's for the night, I can patch myself up without getting badgered with questions. I go into the bathroom, switch on the light over the sink, and take a look in the mirror. My left eye is swollen shut, the area surrounding it a vicious red. My nose and chin are covered with blood, and my entire face is puffed up like a water balloon. It was beyond stupid of me to diss Trey like that, but I couldn't help myself. I run cold water into the sink and ruin a couple of Fudgie's hand towels washing the blood away. Touching my injuries makes my head reel and my stomach lurch. I brace myself over the toilet and throw up.

When I'm done retching, I sink to the floor and cradle my throbbing skull in my hands. I don't know what to do next. Dion's in jail, and the cops will be coming for me next. I should hide out someplace until this all blows over, but there's nowhere else for me to go.

•   •   •   •   •

Fudgie's still not back when I wake up late the next morning, which allows me to sulk on the futon in peace. I don't need him seeing the ugly evidence of my disgrace, demanding to know how it happened. My roommate is a kind soul, but his compassion goes only so far when there's an excess of stupidity involved. I hunker down beneath the covers, determined to keep my face hidden if he happens to walk in.

I check my phone, and see that Laci's been texting me since early this morning. We've both got classes to go to, but that's not happening for me today. I skim through the messages—she wants to know how my confrontation with Debra went last night. *Yeah, right,* I think bitterly. Heroic Rudy, standing up to his evil stepmother. I feel bad for deceiving Laci, but that's a conversation for another day. I delete the texts, turn my notifications off, and shove the phone beneath my pillow.

A half hour later, I'm sprawled out on the futon with a bag of frozen mixed vegetables on my face when there's a knock at the apartment door. I lunge for the remote and mute the TV so whoever it is will think no one's here, but a second later, the door bursts open and Laci barges in. She starts talking as she pulls her coat off, and stomps into the living room without removing her boots. "Rudy! I've been calling and texting you all morning. Didn't you see my messages? I'm dying to hear what Debra had to say when you went over there last night." She walks around the couch to where she can see my face, and her hands fly to her mouth. "Oh my gosh, Rudy! What happened to you?"

"Nothing," I mutter, shifting my blanket to conceal the worst of the swelling.

"What do you mean, nothing?" Laci leans over me and reaches for the mixed veg. "Let me see." She wrenches the bag from my hand and grimaces. "Ew, that looks really bad." The plastic bag is slick with blood, and the veggies are beginning to defrost. "Here, let me make you an ice pack." She goes to the kitchen and digs an ice cube tray out of the freezer, cracks a handful of cubes into a damp towel, and brings it over to me. "Hold this on your eye for fifteen minutes, and tell me what the heck happened. I'm guessing Mitchell was there, and you guys got in a fight?"

I gingerly apply the ice pack to my swollen eye. "No, it wasn't anything like that."

Laci nudges my hips over so she can sit facing me on the edge of the futon. "Then what was it? C'mon Rudy, you're scaring me! You've got to tell me how you got hurt so bad."

There's no avoiding it, she's going to hound me until she squeezes the story out. I've got to give her something, but not everything—only enough to satisfy her curiosity and divert her from the truth, and quell her fears about what happened to me. I readjust the ice pack with a sigh. "I didn't go to my stepparents' house last night, after all. I went to look for somebody I thought might be able to help with Jayden's case instead."

Laci frowns. "How would you know someone like that?"

"It's a guy I used to play with, when we were kids. You wouldn't know him, he's a lot older than you."

"Where did you go looking for him?"

I hesitate. "In Woodland Homes."

"*Woodland Homes?* You never told me you knew anyone who lives there!" Laci fixes a suspicious eye on me. "What's his name?"

"I'd rather not say."

"Oh my *God*, Rudy! He's not a friend of Dion's, is he?"

"Um," I say. "Maybe."

"Holy crap!" She punches my leg. "Dion's bad news, Rudy! Seriously bad news. How on earth did you get mixed up with people like that?"

"I told you, we used to hang out when we were kids. It was his cousin Trey who I saw last night. I thought he might know something that could help Jayden, since he knows everybody in the Homes."

The color rises in Laci's face. "There's a gang operating in Woodland Homes, and Dion and his cousin are the ringleaders of it, you dummy! Asking them for help was the last thing you should've done." Her eyes narrow. "Something's not adding up here, Rudy. Why did you think someone like Dion would care what happens to my little brother?" She sits back and folds her arms. "I don't think you're telling me the whole story. There's more to this than what you're saying."

I have to own up to at least part of the truth, or Laci's going to lose her patience with me. Averting my eyes like a coward, I mumble, "There is more to it. It wasn't Dion who stole Mitchell's gun."

"Then who did?"

"I did. Jayden didn't have anything to do with it."

Laci gawks at me. "I don't understand. Are you just saying that to cover for Dion and Trey, or something? Because if you are—"

"No, I'm not trying to cover for anyone! I'm telling you God's honest truth, Laci. I stole the gun the day I moved out of the house, then sold it to Dion."

"You stole a gun and sold it to a *criminal?*" Laci raises her eyes to the ceiling in bewilderment. "This is insane. Please tell me you're kidding."

"Wait a minute, let me finish. When you told me you suspected Dion was the person behind the break-in, I thought it might help Jayden if I went to talk to him, and found out what really happened. But it turns out, Dion's been arrested too, and his cousin thinks it's my fault somehow. That's how I got beat up."

Laci shows no reaction, so I press on. "I know it was wrong of me to steal from my stepfather, and selling the gun on the street was risky and foolish. The only thing I'll say in my defense is that I was under tremendous strain at the time. I was this close to being flat-out broke."

Jumping to her feet, Laci glares at me. "I don't care to hear your excuses, Rudy! Why didn't you admit to this last night, when I told you about Jayden?"

"Because I was afraid of losing you." I give it all I've got to make myself sound as humble and contrite as possible. "I'm a terrible person, I know it. But if you'd let me explain—"

"There's no excuse for what you did, Rudy!" Laci shoots back. "No possible excuse at all."

I throw the ice pack aside and push myself up to a sitting position. "Just listen to me, Laci. Please. I know there's no excuse for what I've done, but there's another thing I never told you, because I was too ashamed to admit it."

She raises her eyebrows and jabs a fist into her hip. "Is there, now? And what might *that* be?"

I've got to regain her sympathy or I'm going to lose her forever—which means I have to tell her everything. Well, *almost* everything. "Remember how I told you I moved out because Mitchell and I weren't getting along?"

"Yeah? So?"

"Well, that wasn't quite the whole story. See, the truth is—" I pause to swallow my pride. "I didn't move out on my own volition. They evicted me."

Laci's eyes go huge. "They *evicted* you from your own house? Like, legally?"

"Yes. They took me to court and everything. I had to testify before this arrogant judge who was prejudiced against me, and he forced me to comply with the eviction order. It was totally humiliating."

Laci stares at me a moment, then her expression softens. "Oh, Rudy. I had no idea. You should have told me."

I've got to keep this sympathy train rolling. "They gave me like two days to pack up my stuff and find someplace else to live. Mitchell started making threats, saying he was gonna throw me out with his bare hands, and would have me arrested if I didn't leave on time. If it wasn't for Fudgie, I would've ended up on the street." I'm talking out my ass, but that doesn't matter, as long as Laci takes my side. I hang my head in shame. "I should've told you a long time ago, but I was too embarrassed. I thought you'd think I was a loser." I rub my eyes to make it look like I'm fighting tears. "I stole the gun in a moment of anger. I'm trying hard to be a better person now, and it's all because of you." I reach for Laci's hand, bring it to my lips and kiss it. "Please don't hold my past mistakes against me."

Laci melts a little more, but a second later, she withdraws her hand and her anger flashes again like lightning. "This isn't about *you*, Rudy! My little brother's future is in jeopardy, and you don't seem to care!"

My injured eye burns like it's on fire, and nausea roils my gut. I deserve to feel pain, to suffer for what I've done. I'm a terrible person with no moral compass, completely lacking in backbone. What I'm doing isn't right. I can't allow Jayden to take the fall for me. If I do, I'll never be able to live with myself.

I swing my feet to the floor and stand up to face Laci. My head's spinning, but that doesn't stop me from telling her the whole truth. It takes less than ten seconds for me to explain that I was the person who broke into my stepparents' house—not Jayden, or Dion, or anyone else.

"That's ridiculous!" Laci says. "You would never break into anyone's house. Why are you saying this, Rudy? What are you trying to prove?"

"Let me explain, then maybe you'll understand. I was pissed off at Mitchell, and I needed money real bad. I was planning to steal a couple more guns and some other stuff from the basement, but Mitchell changed the locks. I didn't go there intending to do anything destructive, but when I couldn't get into the house, I sort of went berserk. I took a shovel and broke the glass on the sliding door. Then Debra came home, and I ran away."

Laci stares at me with her mouth hanging open. I've lost her, I'm sure of it. "You probably hate me now," I say, "and I don't blame you one bit if you do. I'm sorry I kept this from you for so long, and I'll totally understand if you don't want to see me anymore."

"Oh my freaking God, Rudy!" Laci is trembling and her eyes are flitting all over the place, instead of looking at me. "Debra didn't see you?"

I shake my head uncertainly. "No. Maybe. She might have, I don't know for sure."

Laci takes a few ragged breaths, her chest heaving. "Jayden went to jail because of what you did. That is unbelievable." Her fury flares up again, and she turns the full force of it on me. "How could you *do* this, Rudy? You committed a violent, criminal act, then hid your guilt from everyone. What you did is the most despicable, unethical thing I've ever heard!"

Tears stream down her face. "I was falling in love with you, Rudy! For the first time in my life, I thought I'd met someone I could trust and rely on. I thought you had my back, but now you've gone and ruined everything. I can't believe I was so wrong about you!" She buries her face in her hands and sobs.

Her words tear at my heart. "Laci, please believe me. I never, ever meant to hurt you." I reach my hand out to her. "That's the last thing I'd ever do. Things just spiraled out of control."

She pulls away and spits more angry words. "Don't touch me! You have no idea how badly I wanted to be part of a normal family, and then I find out you're all vicious, hateful liars. What a fool I was!" She grabs her things and marches to the door, then turns back to me. "Don't call me anymore, Rudy. I mean it, we're through. And don't think for one second that you're going to get away with what you've done."

25

Laci

Fudgie's car keys are sitting on the little table by the door, and I palm them as I walk out. It's an impulsive move, prompted by my intense anger and disappointment, and an almost crippling sense of betrayal. I've got no boyfriend, no parents of any kind, and a kid brother who's stuck in jail. It's me against the world.

The Nissan is parked in its usual spot behind the house, blanketed with snow. I pull my mittens on and scrape at the windows until they're clear enough for me to see out, then jump in. I've only driven a stick shift once before, about two years ago when my father got it into his head to give me a driving lesson. As I'm struggling to turn the car around in the narrow driveway, I cast a glance toward the house, half hoping I'll see Rudy at the window, waving and pleading for me to come back. There's no sign of movement behind the venetian blinds, and the door to the apartment remains closed. I ram the car into gear and take off.

I haven't felt so lost since my mother died. There's a weight in the center of my chest that's making it difficult to breathe, but my heart is thudding crazily against my ribs, like it's trying to fight back. *Damn you, Rudy. Damn you for getting my hopes up, then snatching them out from under me.*

I'm sorry for what happened to him, losing his mother when he was so young and all, and not having a father in his life. I know from personal experience how painful that is, and I can only imagine how rejected he felt when Mitchell evicted him. If somebody pulled a shitty trick like that on me, I'd hate them, too.

But my first loyalty has to be to my brother. If Rudy is allowed to get away with his dirty little secret, Jayden will get screwed, and I won't stand for that. I've got to fight for him as hard as I can, because he might be all I have left.

The sky is a heavy gray and the houses on Rudy's street have that forlorn post-Christmas look, with strings of lights sagging from the eves because it's too cold for anyone to go out and take them down. The roads on the west side don't get plowed very well because of the residents' flagrant disregard for the odd-even parking regulations, so the car skids and slides every which way, and makes a grinding sound every time I change gears. I turn onto Avery Avenue where the going is smoother, and slow down for the traffic light where it intersects with busy Genesee Street.

A truck speeds past, clearly exceeding the speed limit, and a cop car on the opposite side of the road whoops its siren and takes off in pursuit. The light turns green, but I don't move. *The police*, I think. *I could turn Rudy in.* A horn honks, startling me. I ease my foot off the clutch and the engine stalls. The horn blares more insistently. Trying again, I manage to get through the intersection and make a right, the car bucking and grinding through the gears. I drive two more blocks and turn into the parking lot of an auto parts store. Taking my phone out, I google the number for the Centerport Police, and tell the woman who answers that I need to talk to someone about a recent burglary. "I have new information. I know who did it."

She asks me which burglary I'm referring to, then puts me on hold. A moment later, she comes back on the line and says I'll need to speak with a Detective Scanlon. "He's not available at the moment, but he should be returning around four o'clock. Can you come in then?" I tell her I can, and give her my name and number.

I end the call with a grim sense of satisfaction. It feels good to be taking action, even though my former boyfriend is the target. I'm hurting badly and I don't know how I'm ever going to get over this breakup. Rudy has proven himself to be a sneak and a liar, just like that phony Debra. They're both going to get exactly what they deserve.

26

Rudy

After Laci goes storming out, there's nothing for me to do but go back to bed and nurse my wounds. The ice pack she made for me is melting, leaving an obscene wet mark on the sheets. I shuffle to the kitchen with the soggy towel, and assemble another one with the handful of ice cubes remaining in the freezer.

I try to keep my mind off what's happened by watching a replay of a Formula One race that took place in some Middle Eastern country yesterday. I'm having trouble focusing on the TV. I can't see out of my swollen left eye, but it isn't my injuries bothering me so much as the yawning ache in my heart. It's been only a few minutes since my girlfriend chewed me out, then dumped me, but I miss her already.

I take two of Fudgie's Extra Strength Tylenols for the headache that's been building all morning, then turn my notifications back on, in case Laci calls to say she's sorry and wants me back. I'm dozing off when a call comes in from my Uncle Gene. "THAT YOU, RUDY?" he shouts. The man always shouts, even if the person he's speaking to is standing two feet away. "UNCLE GENE HERE."

I put the call on speaker because it hurts too much to hold the phone next to my head, and turn the volume way down. "Hello, Uncle Gene." He's actually my great uncle, since he's my grandmother's brother, but he doesn't like to be called that because it makes him feel old. "How are you?"

"I'm calling about your grandmother." His speech is slightly slurred, on account of the stroke. "She fell and busted something yesterday, and they operated on her this morning. I can't go up to the hospital to visit because I'm homebound now, as you're aware. We can't leave her on her own in that place, what with her having the Old Timers and all. She needs a family member at her side, and it looks like you're it. You have the car now, so I thought you could run on up there and sit with her awhile."

I hold the phone poised in my hand, fervently wishing I could pitch it across the room and make this all go away. Unfortunately, my uncle is correct—there's no one else to call on my mother's stunted side of the family. Once Nan and Gene are gone, I'll be the only one left. I heave a big sigh. "All right, Uncle Gene, I'll go. She's at University Hospital?"

"Yes indeed, right next door to that old folks home where she's been living. They roll 'em in one door and ship 'em out the other, like an assembly line. I'm telling you, I think they ought to—"

"Right, Uncle Gene. I got it." I can't listen to his geriatric ranting. "I'm on my way now."

I heave myself off the futon and change into a clean shirt. The front of my coat is splotchy with bloodstains from last night, so I rinse it off as best as I can in the bathroom sink. The blue material has turned a sickly purple where I bled on it. I pop another Tylenol for good measure, drink half a glass of water, and go outside. There's a blank spot on the driveway where Fudgie's car should be. I thought his girlfriend picked him up last night, but maybe not. Either that, or he came back for his car when I was asleep earlier this morning, and slipped away again without me hearing him.

•   •   •   •   •

Up at the hospital, I find a spot in the parking garage, then follow the covered walkway over to the main building. I'm glad it's the middle of the day, so I don't have to worry about running into Mitchell. I show my ID and get my visitor's pass at the security desk, then traverse a maze of corridors and elevators until I find Nan's room. An RN at the nurse's station stops me before I go in, likely due to the scary condition of my face. After confirming I'm the grandson of Nancy Garber, the nurse pulls me aside and gives me the rundown: late last night at Autumn Meadows, Nan got out of bed and went for an unsupervised stroll that ended in another resident's room, where she tripped and fell, sustaining a fracture to her right femoral neck. In other words, she broke her hip.

Despite the extra Tylenol I took, I've got a whopper of a headache revving up, and I have to make an effort to follow what the nurse is saying. I don't know what a femoral neck is, but I'll take her word for it. "The surgeon repaired the fracture with internal fixation," the nurse says, "which means your grandmother now has a pin in her hip. She'll stay in the hospital for another three or four days, then we'll transfer her to a rehab facility for physical therapy. You should also be aware that she's been extremely disoriented and agitated. In patients her age, that's a common after-effect of the surgical anesthesia, in addition to her underlying dementia. We've currently got her on one-to-one monitoring, as a safeguard against her getting up and hurting herself." The nurse looks at her watch. "She's due for her next dose of medication now. Give it a few minutes to take effect, then you can go in and see her."

I wander down the hall and stand looking out the window by the elevator for a while. It's the 3 p.m. shift change, so hospital personnel are coming and going in a steady stream, the elevator doors quietly whooshing open and closed. Each time the bell dings, I turn my head away so no one can see how awful I look. After what I hope is an adequate amount of time for Nan's medication to kick in, I walk down to her room and cautiously poke my head inside.

The aide who's been assigned to monitor Nan looks alarmed when she sees my face. I explain that I'm a family member, and tell her it's all right with me if she wants to go take a break while I'm here. Before leaving the room, she extends the privacy curtain for me, to block some of the noise and bustle from the hallway. I pull the chair closer to the bed and turn it around to face Nan. I was worried my bruises might scare her, or prevent her from recognizing me, but it turns out there's no cause for concern because she's fast asleep. Her skin is pale and her cheeks are sunken. A machine next to her bed emits a steady beeping, and a tube in her arm is hooked up to a bag of fluids hanging on an IV pole.

I sit down and take her hand in mine. It's warm and soft, like a grandmother's hand is supposed to be. We sit quietly like that for quite some time. I'm battered and weary, and the achy, empty place in my heart is gaping wider. Nan sleeps on with her mouth partially open, breathing in a slow and peaceful rhythm. I'm glad she can't see my injuries, and that there's no need for me to explain anything. It's enough for us to simply be together, quietly recovering from our respective injuries.

I zone in and out, until a light tap at the door rouses me. I'm slumped over in my chair, and quickly straighten myself up and call to the person to come in. I'm expecting it to be the nurse on her rounds, or the aide returning from her break, but it's neither of them. Beneath the hem of the privacy curtain, I see a pair of sensible old lady boots approaching. A gnarled hand brushes the curtain aside, and there's Edith Scanlon staring at me.

27

Laci

I leave my messenger bag in the car, because I have enough sense not to bring a gun into a police station. The place is small and surprisingly shabby. In the overheated reception area, I tell the uniformed woman behind the glass partition that I have a 4:00 appointment. She speaks briefly to someone on the phone, then buzzes me into another room where a cluster of desks are crowded together, each of them equipped with a computer and a landline phone. A broad-shouldered man with a puffy 80s hairdo strides across the room and introduces himself as Detective Scanlon.

It's exciting to meet with a real live police detective, and I feel like I'm starring in a TV show as Scanlon leads me over to a desk in the corner. He offers me a chair, then seats himself behind the jumble of papers on his desk. He threads his long fingers together over his slight paunch and looks at me expectantly. "I understand you would like to make a report pertaining to the burglary at the Bateman residence."

I fold my hands in my lap as well, trying to project an air of maturity and trustworthiness. "Yes, I do. You arrested the wrong person."

Scanlon tilts his chair back. "Would you care to elaborate, please?"

I lean forward, meeting his steady gaze. "It was Rudy Hodgens who broke into the house. He's the Batemans' stepson. He stole a gun from them, too."

Scanlon doesn't blink. "What is your connection to the parties involved in this matter, Miss Wright?"

"Rudy's my boyfriend." I get a sudden catch in my throat. "I mean, he *was* my boyfriend. We recently broke up."

"How recently?"

I look away and shift my feet uncomfortably. "About an hour ago."

"An hour ago." Scanlon's eyebrow twitches. "May I ask why the two of you broke up?"

The officers seated at the surrounding desks appear to be immersed in their work, but one of them, a woman, raises her head slightly and sends a sideways glance in my direction. I hold my head high when I reply. "Because of what he did. He's a bad person."

Scanlon rocks his chair a few times before asking his next question. "So, you're saying it was you who broke up with him? Are you sure it wasn't the other way around, miss?"

What does he think I am, some overwrought hussy going postal over her boyfriend's rejection? "No, it wasn't the other way around!" I snap. "Rudy did a terrible thing, and I refuse to be associated with someone like that anymore." Scanlon is giving me an odd, closed-mouth smile, as though he doesn't believe me, so I raise my voice. "He *told* me he did it. He literally admitted he committed a crime. Aren't you going to do anything about it?"

Scanlon ignores my outburst. "How old are you, Miss Wright?"

"Eighteen."

"And where do you live?"

I tell him my address on Charles Street. "It's my aunt's place. I've been living there for about a year."

"And before that?"

I suddenly get where this is going. "Before that, I lived with my father." I hesitate, then say, "in Woodland Homes."

"Woodland Homes. I see." Scanlon straightens up his chair and places his hands flat on the desk. "Are you aware that Mrs. Bateman has already provided us with eyewitness testimony in complete contradiction to the story you've just told me, and that she has positively identified the perpetrator, whom we have in custody?"

I grip the arms of my chair. My palms are sweating. "What she told you isn't true! She saw Rudy when it happened, but she wants to pin everything on my brother because—"

Scanlon interrupts. "Your brother?"

"Yeah, they arrested my brother for it, but he told me he didn't do it. He's only fourteen, so he—"

Scanlon thrusts a palm at me, and I stop in mid-sentence. "Do you know what I think?" he says. I don't say anything, but I'm pretty sure I do. "I think your boyfriend jilted you, and you thought that presenting a fabricated story to the police would be a clever way to exact revenge upon him."

My jaw drops. "But, that's not—"

Scanlon slaps his hand on the desk. "That's enough, Miss Wright. There's no reason to dig yourself in any further. I was young once myself, so I understand what motivated you, but making a false statement to a police officer is a crime. Consider yourself fortunate that you didn't submit anything in writing before speaking with me." He rises from his chair and motions for me to get up. I follow him in an excruciating walk of shame past the cluster of officers at their desks. In the reception area, Scanlon gives me a curt dismissal, and returns to his lair.

I stand on the neatly snowblown sidewalk a moment, thankful for the cold air in my lungs, and to not have a roomful of judgy cop eyes on me anymore. My phone dings with an incoming text; I take it out and see a message from Fudgie: *Do u know where my car is?*

Shoot. I was in such a state when I left the apartment, I didn't think to text him and ask if it was okay if I took his car. So now I've committed Grand Theft Auto, along with allegedly lying to a police officer. I'm getting myself into some deep shit, when I'm not even the one who's done anything wrong.

The car is parked at the end of the visitors row. I get into the freezing cold vehicle and sit there staring at my phone, my thumbs hovering over the keyboard. I'm not thinking about what I'm going to say to Fudgie, though. Instead, I'm replaying the events of the last twenty-four hours—overhearing Debra on the phone, Rudy's shocking confession, our horrible argument. My thoughts spin round and round in a blur, like a playground whirlybird packed with screaming schoolkids. Detective Scanlon's words resound in my head: *Mrs. Bateman—eyewitness testimony—perpetrator in custody.*

The lying bitch! Everything that's gone wrong in my life keeps circling back to Debra. Indignation builds inside me, and rapidly turns to outrage. All the things I care about have been taken from me, and it's Debra Bateman who's to blame. Without responding to Fudgie's text, I stuff my phone back into my pocket and turn the key in the ignition. The engine sputters and stalls twice, but catches on the third try. As I wait for it to warm up, I reach for my messenger bag on the seat beside me, and unbuckle the flap. Sliding my hand inside, I curl my fingers around the cold steel of Debra's gun.

28

Rudy

Edith stares at my mangled face for a second, then looks over at Nan in the bed. "Your uncle called me. He said Nancy fell and hurt herself."

I'm groggy from my brief nap, and annoyed by her intrusion. "Hello to you too, Mrs. Scanlon."

She stares back at me. "What happened to you?"

"I had an accident," I mumble. "I'm fine."

Edith *humphs* and gives me an accusing look. "You don't look fine to me." She turns her eyes back to Nan, and her expression mellows. "What did she injure?" she asks quietly.

"Her hip. The nurse gave her something for pain, so she's been asleep for a while."

When I was little, Debra warned me to stay away from the Scanlons' house, especially on Halloween. Merv was the type of person you wouldn't be surprised to hear had put straight pins in the candy bars he handed out to the neighborhood kids, and his wife was equally unfriendly and intimidating. It was always a mystery to me, how my kind, gentle grandmother could be friends with a hag like Edith. Nan explained to me one time that they used to be best buddies who went to the same Catholic grammar and high schools together, so I guess the early bond between them carried over into their adulthood.

Edith's abrasive manner is grating on me, but if there's one thing I can give my stepmother credit for, it's teaching me good manners. I rise from my chair. "Would you like to sit here, Mrs. Scanlon?"

"No, no," she says, waving me away. "I'll sit over there." The odor of mothballs follows her as she goes to the chair by the window. She sits with her pocketbook in her lap, gripping it with both hands, and speaks without looking at me. "The nurse wouldn't tell me anything because I'm not a family member."

She shifts her eyes across the bed to me, expecting an explanation. There's no reason not to fill her in, so I explain how Nan fell at Autumn Meadows, and is now recovering from surgery.

"The poor dear." Edith reaches out to pat Nan's arm, which is resting on top of the covers. "She's suffered so much. It's been hard on her, losing your grampa and coping with the memory loss."

Tell me about it. A minute or two passes without either of us speaking. Nan snores on, unaware of the beeping machine next to her bed, and the periodic inflation of the blood pressure cuff on her arm. I'm not particularly enjoying sitting here with my unpleasant former next-door neighbor, but I'm not sure if it would be right for me to leave, either. Edith looks so frail and glum in her frumpy brown coat and boots, hanging onto her pocketbook like it contains her last dollar. It can't have been a joyride for her, I suppose, living under the thumb of her curmudgeonly husband all these years. She might appreciate me staying and keeping her company.

Another awkward minute passes, then Edith speaks up. "I always felt sorry for you Rudy, being raised by that woman."

I assume "that woman" refers to Debra. I'm aware the two of them have never liked each other, and they've had a rocky time of it as neighbors, but I'm puzzled as to why Edith would bring up my stepmother at a moment like this. "Why did you feel sorry for me," I say, "when you never came over to the house, or even talked to us?"

Edith keeps her eyes fixed on the hump of Nan's body beneath the gray hospital blanket. "It wasn't your fault, of course. You were only a child, you had no say in who he chose to marry."

"You mean Mitchell?"

"Yes." A faraway expression clouds Edith's face. "I understand why he fell for her. After Ann Marie died, he needed someone to help him take care of you, and Debra was dead set on filling the empty space in his bed. I knew she wouldn't be satisfied till he'd made her his wife."

I'm following now. Mitchell was never willing to talk to me about my mother's death, but Nan was, once I grew old enough to handle that kind of conversation. Having lost her daughter in a senseless accident, Nan understood the toll that grief can take on a person. After my father disappeared and I became a virtual orphan, Nan was the only person I could share my fears with. She listened to me without judgment as I struggled to make sense of the unusual circumstances that were tearing my life apart.

I grew up knowing my mother had died in a car accident, but that was about it. Nan knew I was anxious to learn more, to somehow make sense of my loss, so when I was a teenager, she told me the details: at the age of twenty-two, while driving home from work one snowy night, my beautiful, spirited mother—Nan's beloved only child—lost control of her car on a slippery road, crashed into a tree and was instantly killed.

Edith continues talking. "Of all the girls I supervised at the restaurant, your mother was my favorite. It was partly because she was Nan's daughter, but mostly because she reminded me so much of my Wendy—so full of light and laughter, always up to some sort of mischief."

I remember hearing something a long time ago, about the Scanlons having a daughter who died when she was a teenager. Now that I'm thinking about, I vaguely recall she might have been killed in a drunk driving accident. No wonder then, that Edith turned into such a miserable person.

Clicking her pocketbook open, Edith fishes out a handkerchief and dabs at her eyes. When she's done, she crumples the handkerchief in her fist. "The weather was awful," she says, shaking her head. "She finished her shift, but she didn't want to drive home yet because of the snow squalls."

I'm confused for a second, then realize with a start that she's flown back in time, to the night my mother died. I'm beginning to wonder if this woman isn't a little bit cuckoo.

"Mitchell was away at his Army Reserve training that weekend, and you were spending the night with your grandparents." Edith casts a sad glance toward Nan, then goes on. "Debra still had tables to wait on, so Ann Marie went into the bar by herself and ordered a drink. We were busy that night, despite the snowstorm. There was a basketball game on TV, and the bar was packed with people who'd come to watch it. I tried to keep an eye on how much she was drinking, but it was difficult to keep track when I had so many other things to do. They were short-handed in the kitchen, so I was running all over the place, trying to keep things moving.

"When it got toward closing time, the crowd in the bar thinned out to where I had a clear view of her. She was still sitting on the same barstool, and I could see she was drunk. I called Debra over, and told her to take Ann Marie's car keys away. 'Don't take no for an answer,' I said. 'You've got to make sure she gives them to you.' Once the keys were safely in my hands, I was going to give her some coffee, then drive her home myself.

"I watched from across the room, to make sure Debra did what I told her. There was loud music playing in the bar, and Ann Marie was joking and laughing with a couple of young men she'd met. When Debra went over, Ann Marie gave her the brush-off at first. She swung her legs around on that stool and turned her back, and went right on chatting with those boys.

"Debra kept at her though, just as I'd asked. It took a while, but when she held her hand out for the keys, Ann Marie finally handed them over." A shadow crosses Edith's face. "But then they started arguing, and I saw—" Her voice catches, and she struggles to compose herself. "I saw Debra give her the keys back. She slid them along the bar, and Ann Marie grabbed them. I was about to march right over there and order her to give those keys to me, but then someone came running up, hollering that something had caught on fire in the kitchen. By the time I came back out, Ann Marie wasn't in the bar anymore. I questioned Debra, but she only shrugged and said she'd probably gone to the bathroom. I checked the ladies' room but she wasn't there, so I ran out back to look for her car." Edith covers her mouth and chokes back a sob. "I was too late. She was gone."

I'm too stunned to speak. I've never had even the slightest inkling that there was an issue between my mother and my stepmother. Over the years, Debra had mentioned once or twice that they grew up on the same street, so I always assumed they were friends. It never crossed my mind for one second that she might have been involved in my mother's death.

The nausea I've been battling all day swirls and sloshes. I reach for the cup of water on Nan's bedside table, and take a gulp to try and settle my stomach.

"The accident was on the local TV news the next morning," Edith goes on. "I was devastated, but I still had to go to work, because there was no one available to fill in for me. When Debra clocked in for her shift that afternoon, I cornered her. She was acting funny and she refused to talk to me, and that's when I knew she'd done it on purpose. She was jealous, you see. She wanted Mitchell for herself, but she couldn't have him because he belonged to someone else." Edith fixes her eyes on me. "The way I see it, Debra killed Ann Marie the same as if she'd murdered her with her own two hands, and she deserves to roast in hell for what she did."

Edith ceases speaking and we sit in silence for a full minute, until the hospital sounds begin to seep back into my consciousness. My phone buzzes with an incoming text message; I see it's from Fudgie and ignore it. In the bed, my grandmother stirs and her eyelids flicker open. She regards me confusedly for a moment, then closes her eyes and drifts off again. I'm grateful for the medication the nurse gave her, because it has mercifully prevented her from comprehending any of her friend's tragic story.

An intense feeling of disgust washes over me as the ugly truth sinks into my brain. My stepmother was responsible for my mother's death. It was Debra who killed her—not a snowstorm, or a car wreck, or too much alcohol. Timid, dutiful, pious Debra Bateman is a murderer.

"Why didn't you tell anybody?" I ask Edith. "Debra let my mother leave the restaurant, when she knew she was too drunk to drive. She should've been held responsible somehow."

Edith won't look at me. "It wasn't that simple," she says, staring into her lap. "I was the restaurant manager, so the responsibility fell on me. I should have told the bartender not to serve her anymore, and taken her keys away myself. I didn't say anything because I was scared. At the time, the police were cracking down on drunk driving in the city, and the downtown bars were in danger of being held liable for serving customers who were already intoxicated. I was afraid of getting in trouble with the law, and losing my job."

"So, Debra got away with it," I say bitterly. "Unbelievable." I look at Nan. Her lips quiver slightly as she exhales a slow, relaxed breath. "Did my grandmother know what really happened?"

Edith flinches. "I think she suspected Debra had a hand in it, but there was no way she could prove anything. We never talked about it, but I know she carried the pain with her for years, the same as I did after I lost my daughter. No matter what you do, there's no way to escape that kind of sorrow. It seeps into every corner of your life, and never lets go."

She dabs at her eyes again, then puts her handkerchief into her pocketbook and snaps it closed. "Mitchell was a good man until Debra got her claws into him. I know all about the eviction, you know. I'm sure it was all her doing. She's a manipulative woman who always gets her way in the end."

Edith stands up and hooks her pocketbook over her forearm, and finally looks at me. Her eyes are red and watery, but her gaze is steady. "I'm sorry for what happened to you, Rudy. I'll go to my grave wishing I'd done something to make things turn out differently." She gives Nan's hand a lingering squeeze, sends a sharp nod in my direction, and walks out.

29

Laci

I'm waiting for the car to warm up when my phone dings with another incoming text. It's Fudgie again: *Call me when u get this.*

Now I feel guilty. He probably needs his car to get to work, and he's panicking because he has no clue where it's disappeared to. I tap the Call button, and he immediately picks up. "Hey, Lace. Sabrina dropped me off at home a while ago, and my car's gone. I tried texting Rudy to see if he knows where it is, but he didn't reply. You didn't borrow it for some reason, did you?"

"Um, actually, yeah, I did. I had to go to the police station to report something, and I didn't have time to ask you. I'm really sorry. I'll bring it back right now."

"You're at the police station? Why? What happened?"

I don't want to get into the details. If one of those cops comes out and finds me still sitting here after the scene I made inside, I'll be totally embarrassed. "I'll tell you when I see you. I'll be there soon."

The car stalls three more times as I make my way home. When I get to the apartment, Fudgie meets me on the back step, looking frazzled. He holds the storm door open for me, beckoning wildly. "There's blood all over the bathroom, and Rudy isn't answering my texts! Come in and tell me what the hell's going on."

After the stress of trying to get the car home in one piece, I've worked myself into a frenzy. "It's Rudy!" I sputter the moment we're inside. "He did it! He did everything. I went down to the station and told the police, but they wouldn't listen to me." I grip the strap of my messenger bag in both hands. "Fucking Debra was behind it all!"

"Whoa, whoa, whoa, slow down." Fudgie leads me to a kitchen chair, then pulls another one over and sits facing me. "Start from the beginning. What did Rudy do, and why did you have to go to the police?"

I explain everything, from Rudy getting evicted, to the break-in, to Trey beating him up.

"*Rudy* broke into their house?" Fudgie says when I've finished my tirade. He scratches the back of his head. "I knew about the eviction, but he never told me any of the other stuff. I can't believe it. He's not the kinda guy who'd do that sorta thing."

"He admitted to all of it, Fudgie! He told me himself, every single guilty detail. I was upset, so I went to the police to tell them, but the detective I talked to didn't believe me because he thinks I'm a jilted woman out for revenge."

Fudgie screws his face up. "Jilted? Whaddaya mean?"

"After Rudy confessed what he did, I told him it was over between us. I couldn't possibly stay with him after the awful things he did."

Fudgie's mass of frizzy hair bounces as he nods in agreement. "You right about that."

"The trouble is, the cop assumed it was the other way around—that Rudy broke up with me, and I'm trying to get back at him because of it."

Fudgie regards me carefully. "You're not fixin' to do something crazy, are ya, Lace? Cuz if—"

I jump up from my chair. "Fuck, Fudgie!" I don't normally throw many f-bombs, but I'm under duress. "I'm furious with Rudy, and really, really disappointed in him, but it's Debra who I'm the most pissed at. I've gotta go find her, and make her face up to what she's done to my brother. She's a goddamn liar and she's not going to get away with it!"

"You better not go there," Fudgie warns me. "You'll be asking for trouble."

I realize I still have his car keys clutched in my hand. Fudgie's legs are crippled, so he won't be able to catch me if I bolt outside. If the car won't start, I'll head to the bus stop. It'll take me a lot longer to get out to Centerport by bus, but Mitchell should be gone by the time I get to the house, which will make what I intend to do a whole lot easier, without him there to defend his wife.

I make a run for the door, but Fudgie chases after me and catches hold of my coat when I slip and fall in the icy driveway. "Wait, Laci! Let the police sort it out, that's the best way."

"The *police?*" I yank myself free from him and get up. "The longer I wait for them to piece this together, the longer Jayden sits in jail." The injustice of it all suddenly overwhelms me, and I burst into tears. "It isn't *fair*, Fudgie! It's just not fair." My messenger bag slips off my shoulder and falls to the ground, and I crumple into a heap beside it.

Fudgie sees I'm coming unhinged. He takes the keys from my limp hand and pulls on my arm. "C'mon back inside and we'll talk about it."

"Talk about it? What's there to talk about?" I scowl at him through my tears. "If you won't drive me to the Batemans' house, I'll find some other way to get out there."

He looks at me skeptically. "Like how?"

It's the afternoon rush hour, so the bus will be packed. "I'll take an Uber, I guess."

"Uh huh. You got the app?"

Of course I don't. I've never ordered an Uber before, don't have any idea how it works. I get to my feet and brush the snow from my knees. "Please Fudgie, can't you just drive me? All I want to do is talk to Debra, and make her understand how much damage she's done. I'm only going to ask her to tell the truth, to save my brother. I promise I won't do anything stupid."

Fudgie regards me for a long moment, then heaves a resigned sigh. "Okay, I'll take you. You're way too upset to go alone." I try to hug him but he fends me off. He picks up my bag and holds it out to me, and I snatch it from his hands.

I feel a little more in control as I slide into the passenger's seat and buckle my seatbelt. "I really appreciate you doing this for me, Fudgie. When Debra hears what I have to say, she'll have no choice but to make things right for Jayden."

"Hope so," he replies. "I'd hate for this to be a wasted trip."

It's slow going because there's a lot of late afternoon traffic going in and out of the various strip malls that line Genesee Street. Butterflies swirl in my stomach. I'm eager to get on with it, so I urge Fudgie to hurry, but he continues noodling along at a sedate, law-abiding pace. At least the temperamental car is performing better with him in the driver's seat.

The traffic eases up when we get out to Centerport. Fudgie puts his left blinker on, then waits for a large gap in the oncoming traffic before turning into Spruce Tree Knolls. I'm humming with eagerness to wreak my vengeance. It's past five now, and Crestview Drive is dark. The lights are on at the Batemans', and Mitchell's truck is gone. "You'd better park down the street," I tell Fudgie, "so your car won't be in anyone's way." He obligingly continues around the bend, then pulls over. I strap my messenger bag to my chest and open my door.

"You want me to go in with you?" Fudgie asks.

"No, it'll be better if I go by myself. This is personal, I need to talk to her alone."

"Okay, I'll wait right here. Call me if you need me."

My heart thumps against my ribs as I pick my way up the slippery driveway. The garage doors are closed, so I can't sneak in through the kitchen, like I did the last time. I could go around to the slider in back and see if it's unlocked, but that means floundering through snowdrifts, freezing my tatas off. I figure my best bet is to go right up to the front door and ring the bell. When Debra sees it's me, I'm sure she'll invite me in. We'll make fake friendly small talk for a few minutes, then I'll put her on the spot, and drag the truth out of her.

I climb the front steps and press the doorbell. Footsteps approach, then the inner door swings open and Debra appears. Her exclamation is muffled by the plexiglass storm door. "Laci!" She swings the door open for me. "What a nice surprise. Please come in."

30

Rudy

After Edith Scanlon walks out of the hospital room, I have to sit for a few minutes to try and absorb everything. It's insane, what she just told me. Jealousy, revenge, and a deep, dark secret—it's like an episode from a television reality show.

The nurse comes in to check on Nan, so I get ready to leave. My grandmother snoozes on, insensible to the painful drama her old friend Edith has resurrected from the past. I'm in shock, and filled with deep sorrow like I've never felt before. It's going to take a while for me to sort out my feelings, and figure out what I'm going to do with this newfound information.

As I walk out to the parking garage, I fight the urge to call Laci. She's the only person I know who'll understand how confused and hurt I am right now, but I know she won't talk to me. If I dial her number, I'm certain she'll reject the call, or worse yet, she'll answer and give me another well-deserved ass-chewing, then hang up on me.

I pay the parking fee and exit the garage, but instead of leaving the hospital grounds, I pull over to the side of the road. There's nothing for me at home. Fudgie might be there to commiserate with, but the prospect of confessing to him all the things I've done wrong is too depressing to face. There's no one else for me to turn to for sympathy, and loneliness settles over me like a suffocating blanket. Yesterday, I had everything in the world going for me, but today, I'm back to being a loser. I'm the pathetic version of Rudy Hodgens that I was six months ago, when I was forced to stand before the judge, having my failings thrown in my face.

I have no idea what Laci's going to do, now that she's aware of the crimes I committed. She warned me I wouldn't get away with what I've done, which means she's probably angry enough to tell the police. I can't afford a lawyer to defend myself from the inevitable charges, so I might as well shut this whole mess down and give up. I could drive to the police station right now, and turn myself in.

It's getting dark out and it's spitting snow. I sit hunched over the steering wheel, drumming my fingers and thinking hard. Turning myself in means I'm giving up the chance to confront Debra about the part she played in my mother's death, and I can't let that happen. I need some level of justice from this, even if it's only personal; so, before I talk to the police, I've got to go see my stepmother first. She needs to know that her secret's been exposed, and pretty soon, the whole world's going to find out what a depraved person she really is.

I straighten up and put the car back into Drive. It's fifteen minutes from here to Centerport, ten if I take the back roads and put the pedal down. I could care less if I get a speeding ticket along the way. All I want to do is tell Debra what I think of her. After that, I don't care what happens to me.

31

Laci

Debra shivers as she looks past me to the sleety snowfall that's studding the front stoop. "My goodness, the weather out there looks awful! What brought you out on a night like this?"

I step inside, hugging my bag to my side. I don't want to give away my intentions yet, so I force a polite smile. "I was in the neighborhood, so I thought I'd stop by real quick and say hi."

Debra's eyebrows twitch. "I didn't know you were acquainted with anyone else around here."

I'm tempted to dive right into it with a sharp response, but I'd rather draw this out, because it'll be much more effective and satisfying that way. Instead of offering an explanation, I just stand there looking at her. "Anyway," Debra says, to fill the awkward pause, "I'm glad you stopped."

We're standing in the foyer and there's a cold draft blowing through the storm door. I wish Debra would show some manners, and invite me to sit down and stay awhile. Not that I'm going to, of course. When I don't respond to her comment, she offers to take my coat. I tell her no thanks, I'm chilly and I'd prefer to keep it on.

"Well, then," she says, and glances down at my wet boots. After hesitating a second, I bend down and pull them off, because she might think it was odd if I refused to remove them. It'll be easy enough to slip them back on before I leave, since she won't be running after me.

"Why don't we go into the kitchen," Debra says, "and I'll make you a hot cup of tea, to warm you up."

"That would be lovely." I follow her to the kitchen and take a seat at the round table. The vertical blinds are drawn across the sliding door, and the room is neat and tidy. I watch Debra bustle about, putting the kettle on and gathering cups and spoons. While I'm waiting, I slip my hands beneath the table and unbuckle the flap on my bag.

The kettle whistles. Debra fills two cups with boiling water and hands one to me on a saucer. I'm enjoying being waited on. I take my time, dunking my tea bag and stirring in a spoonful of sugar. Across from me, Debra smiles and adds milk to hers. I raise my cup to my lips, pinky out like a lady, and blow on the tea to cool it. I take a tentative sip, then blow some more, relishing my power to control the pace of the events that are about to unfold.

At last, I'm ready to speak. I set my cup on the saucer with sharp *clink*. "You were wondering who else I'm acquainted with in the neighborhood?"

Debra tilts her head to one side. She obviously can't conceive of a lowly person like me being friends with anyone in a swanky development like Spruce Tree Knolls. "Do you know someone who lives on our street?" she asks.

"Not on your street, but nearby. My father and my little brother live over there—" I gesture toward the backyard, "—in Woodland Homes." I sit back in my chair and let that nugget sink in.

"Oh!" Debra's eyes grow wide. "I didn't—"

I lean across the table. "Or I should say, my brother *used to* live there, until he went to jail for burglarizing someone's home."

Debra's jaw drops. After a few seconds, she recovers herself, and her face grows hard. "Do you mean to tell me," she says slowly, "that your brother is Jayden Wright, the boy who broke into my house?"

I stand up and plant my hands on the table, my eyes boring into Debra's. My voice rises to a shout. "Jayden didn't do it, and you know it!"

Debra jumps to her feet as well, her chair legs scraping the floor. "Yes, he did! I saw him standing outside. I gave his description to the police, and they went to that filthy housing project and arrested him!"

"*You lied*," I scream. "You didn't tell them who you really saw!"

Debra's phone is sitting on the counter nearby. She grabs it and taps frantically at the screen, and a second later, Mitchell's voice comes on speaker. "Hey, Deb. Everything all right?"

"*Mitchell!* You need to come home *right now*. It's an *emergency!*" Debra throws the phone down and comes at me, screeching like a maniac, and I dodge out of the way.

I'm not afraid of her, but I can't let her get too close before I'm in position. We circle the table, eyeing each other warily. I take a couple of steps toward her, and inch my right hand toward my bag.

She backs away, keeping the table between us. Her eyes are wild with fright. *Good*, I think. I take another, more aggressive step toward her. She scrambles away and pulls a chair in front of her, like a shield. "You were too embarrassed to tell us where you came from, weren't you?" she yells. "I'd be ashamed too, if I was a piece of trash like you! It's no wonder your brother's a criminal, growing up with deadbeat parents in a place like that."

"You know it wasn't him you saw that night!" I shout back. I slide my hand beneath the flap of my bag. "You made up a story, to cover up the truth!"

"That's preposterous! You're not making any sense. You need to get out of my house, right now!"

She's definitely losing it, and I'm enjoying every moment of her downfall. I smile sweetly, and tell her I'm not going anywhere. In another second, she's going to get what's coming to her, and I can't wait to see her reaction when I make my move. My hand is inside my bag now. I curl my fingers around the gun, feel the cold metal against my palm.

Then Rudy bursts into the kitchen.

32

Fudgie

I get cold waiting in the car for Laci, so I restart the engine and turn up the heater, but keep my lights off so I won't draw attention to myself. If any of these Centerport suburbanites spot a dude like me loitering on their street after dark, they might get suspicious and call the cops.

I'd rather not be here at all, if you want to know the truth. I'm well aware of Rudy's issues with his stepparents, and I totally get why Laci's steamed up at them now, too. I hate conflict and I'd rather stay out of their hot mess, but Laci was acting so whacked, I couldn't let her come out here by herself. I hope she gets what she's after from Debra, but I'm not holding my breath. I'm glad I was able to talk her down, at least. Maybe that'll keep things from getting out of hand when she gets up in Debra's grill.

I shoot another text to Rudy, asking where he's at, but he still doesn't reply. I wonder how bad he got hurt last night. Not so bad that he couldn't walk away, I guess. It was pretty ballsy of him to go out to the Homes by himself. Or stupid. You wouldn't catch me going there at night, that I can tell you. Least he could've done was clean up after himself in the bathroom, instead of leaving a gross bloody mess for me to find.

I'm getting bored sitting here. I scroll through TikTok on my phone, but it's a bunch of random people complaining about their first world problems. After a while, I need to take a leak. I turn the car off and pull my hat down over my ears before opening my door. It's cold as balls out, and I'm tempted to go right here where I'm standing, but a flash of headlights at the far end of Crestview stops me. Instead, I walk down the street a ways, my sneakers sliding on patches of black ice that I can't see. I step behind a row of snow-covered bushes and take care of things, out of sight of the house.

I go back to my car, trying not to slip and fall on my butt, and notice a vehicle parked in the Batemans' driveway. When I get closer, I see that it's Rudy's LeBaron, and there's Rudy himself, hustling up the front steps. I'd call out to him, but from the way he's moving, it looks like he's on a mission, and I don't want to interfere. As I'm watching him, I can faintly hear the sound of people arguing inside the house. Rudy hesitates on the stoop for a second, then pulls the storm door open and goes inside. *Oh man*, I think. Dude has no idea what he's walking into. Gonna be a shit show.

33

Rudy

My righteous anger propels me out to Centerport in record time, without getting pulled over for speeding. There's very little traffic this far out on Genesee Street, so I swerve into the turn for Spruce Tree Knolls without slowing down, and go barreling up Crestview Drive. As I turn into my stepparents' driveway, the car skids on the ice and my headlights reflect off a vehicle down the street near the Scanlons' property. It's a bad place to park because it's right on the curve. I get out of my car, walk a few steps down the driveway, and squint into the darkness. I see a cracked windshield and a cockeyed front bumper, and realize it's Fudgie's Nissan.

What is he doing here? I don't want to make a scene in front of my roommate who, for some inexplicable reason, is currently inside the house with my stepmother. Fudgie's put up with a ton of my bullshit over the past year, and it doesn't seem right to drag him in any deeper. A chill dude like him shouldn't be burdened with the ugly things I'm about to expose.

But then again, I think, why shouldn't Fudgie, and everyone else in this town, know the truth about how my mother died? Debra's evil deed shouldn't be kept a secret any longer. I stride up the walkway toward the house, then pause on the front steps when I hear raised voices coming from inside. The glass on the storm door is fogged over, but the inner door is open. More shouting, louder now. Two voices, both female. One of them is definitely Debra, but the other one is... *Laci?*

The shouting swells into violent argument. I yank the storm door open, rush inside and follow the noise to the kitchen.

Debra and Laci are screaming hysterically at each other. If it wasn't for the kitchen table between them, they'd be clawing at each other's throats. "Hey!" I shout, waving my arms. "*Hey!*"

Debra freezes, her face flushed with anger and fear, and Laci's head whips around. When she sees me, she quickly raises both hands, as if she's surrendering to me. I ask what's going on, but don't dare get any closer because Laci looks like she wants to chew my head off. She stares at me a second, then drops her hands and turns back to Debra. "*He didn't do it,*" Laci snarls, like I'm not even there. "Why do you keep insisting he did, when you know it isn't true?"

"Then who was it?" Debra screams back. "Some other sleazy relative of yours from the projects?"

Okay, now I know what this is about. Laci's eyes blaze and I brace myself. *Here it comes.* She opens her mouth to speak, but before she can say anything, I hear the storm door bang, and Mitchell comes flying into the room.

34

Mitchell

I was in the middle of a routine security sweep of the hospital basement when I got the panicked phone call from Debra. She sounded frightened out of her mind, and disconnected before I could ask what was going on, which scared the heck out of me. I immediately contacted my supervisor and told him there was an emergency at home. He's generally a jerk to me, but the man's got a wife and kids of his own at home, so he gave me the okay to clock out.

I race home, and I'm surprised to see Rudy's car parked smack in the middle of the driveway. I've never trusted the little rat, and the sight of his vehicle worries me even more. I leave my truck in the street and sprint up to the house. The front door's wide open, and I can hear people screaming. I run inside and swiftly scan the scene.

Rudy's standing by the refrigerator with his arms dangling uselessly at his sides. His face is cut and swollen like he's been on the wrong side of a fight, but the bruises are a light purplish color, which means he didn't get them tonight. He's apparently not the threat here, but Debra and Rudy's fat girlfriend are squared off on opposite sides of the kitchen table, looking like they want to strangle each other.

I rush to Debra's side and ask if she's okay. She indicates Laci with a sharp toss of her head. "She came barging in here, accusing me of lying to the police. You need to get her out of here, Mitchell!"

Laci sputters something in return, but I silence her with a raised hand. "Hold on, you'll get your chance." I turn back to Debra. "What does she think you lied to the police about?"

"She says that boy Jayden Wright wasn't the one who broke into our house, and I told her that's ridiculous, because I saw him with my own eyes!"

Laci steps out from behind the table, and I throw my arm up. "Stay where you are!"

"But she's lying!" Her face contorts with rage, but she remains where she is.

Debra's eyes flick back and forth between us. "Jayden's her brother, Mitchell! She's trying to protect him. It won't work though, because we've got the video proof from our cameras."

"Not of him breaking in, you don't." Laci's entire body radiates hatred. "And your so-called eyewitness description doesn't count for anything, because I know for a fact that it wasn't him."

In my line of work, I've been trained to give people the benefit of the doubt until all the facts are in. But I've also learned how to read body language, and something doesn't sit right with me when I look at my wife. "All right, Laci," I say. "If your brother didn't do it, then who did?"

She draws herself up and looks me straight in the eye. "It was Rudy."

"*What!*" Debra gasps. She looks shocked, but quickly fires back. "That's an outright lie! How dare you say such a ludicrous thing!"

I notice Laci glance over at Rudy, who's standing in the corner like a dunce. Her face turns stony as she responds to Debra's outburst. "You know perfectly well that it's true, Debra! Rudy stole the gun from the basement the day he moved out, then came back a week later and broke into your house." She points at the sliding door. "You saw him plain as day, right there on your patio, but you chose to cover up for him, and now my little brother's paying the price."

Debra's eyes jerk from Laci to me. I stare back at her for a moment, then at Rudy, who's trying to hide behind the refrigerator. He hasn't uttered a word since I got here. There's something about him that reeks guilt, and I cross the room in two rapid strides. I grab him by the front of his bloodstained coat. "Is this true, Rudy? Was it really you?"

He winces and shrinks from my grip, his neck and chin disappearing into his jacket. "Yeah," he mumbles. "It was me."

"*You son of a bitch.*" I slam him against the side of the fridge. The impact causes the freezer door to pop open, and a box of frozen waffles falls out. I make a fist and draw my right arm back, ready to whale the living daylights out of him.

"Mitchell, don't!" Debra pulls on my arm as Rudy cowers in my grip. "Please, Mitchell!" she begs. "You haven't heard the whole story."

I'm mad as bloody hell for what Rudy's done to my property, and for every wrong he's ever committed against me. I'd like to choke the breath out of him, but I don't want to land myself behind bars. I release him and he sags to the floor.

Rudy doesn't look like he plans to get up again, so I take a step back and survey the room. Debra is hunched over in a kitchen chair and crying, and Laci has retreated to the corner behind the kitchen table. I tower over my wife with my hands on my hips. "Let's hear it, then. What's the whole story?"

Debra wipes her tearstained cheeks and draws a shuddery breath. When she looks up at me, there's shame written all over her face. "What Laci said is true. I saw Rudy on the patio after he shattered the door. I didn't want to believe it, though. I knew he'd go to jail if I turned him in, and I couldn't bear to do that to him, not after—" She breaks off in a sob.

I have no patience for her drama. "Not after what? C'mon, Debra, spit it out!"

She can barely speak through all her sobbing and hiccupping. "I've already ruined his life by—by—"

"By *what?*"

Rudy speaks up from the floor. "By killing my mother."

We all turn to stare at him. Several stunned seconds tick by before I can speak. "What do you mean, she killed your mother?" I say quietly.

"Ann Marie died in a one-car accident. There was no one else involved."

"Yes, there was."

"Who?"

"Debra."

The color drains from my wife's face. In the corner behind the table, Laci's mouth is agape. "How?" I ask in a strangled voice. "How is that even possible?"

35

Rudy

I raise my aching head and struggle to my feet. My knees feel like they're going to buckle, and I have to lean against the refrigerator to keep from sliding back down to the floor. "Mrs. Scanlon told me. I went up to the hospital to see my grandmother today, and she was there. She told me she saw what Debra did the night my mother died."

"I didn't do anything!" Debra leaps from her chair. "Edith Scanlon's a crazy old woman who doesn't know what she's talking about!"

A surge of adrenaline gives me the strength I need to keep myself upright, and finish what I came here for. "Edith's a little odd, but she isn't crazy. She told me what happened that night." Sweat breaks out on my forehead and the room starts to spin. "I need to sit down," I gasp, and stumble across the room to a chair. I put my head between my knees, breathing heavily until the dizzy spell passes.

I close my eyes to shut it all out for one last second, then open them and look at Mitchell. "The weather was bad, so instead of going home after her shift ended, my mom stayed in the bar. She had too much to drink, so Edith told Debra to take the car keys away from her, and was going to drive her home herself." I turn to Debra, who has backed herself up to the counter by the stove. "You took the keys away like Edith told you to, but when she wasn't looking, you gave them back."

Mitchell inhales sharply and stares at his wife. Debra clenches her fists and stamps her foot with each word: "*That's—not—true.* Edith always hated me, for no good reason. She'd say anything to get me in trouble. She's so senile, she probably thinks it's still the 1980s. You can't listen to anything she says!"

I'm not done yet. I look at Mitchell again, and my voice drops to a whisper. "My mom got in her car and drove away, and Debra did nothing to stop her."

"*I'm not going to listen to these lies!*" Debra claps her fists over her ears and starts screaming like she's losing her mind.

Mitchell grabs her by the forearms and gives her a vigorous shake. "Stop it, Debra! Calm down!" The manhandling only makes her squirm and scream louder. While the two of them are grappling with each other, I notice out of the corner of my eye that Laci is creeping out from behind the kitchen table. She's got her messenger bag in one hand, and she's reaching into it with the other. Some sort of instinct trips an alarm in my head. I call a warning to Mitchell, but he can't hear me over Debra's screaming. Laci throws the bag aside, and there's a gun in her hand.

36

Laci

When Rudy blurted out Debra's ugly little secret, I wasn't the least bit surprised to hear what a horrible thing she'd done to his mother. The woman doesn't blink an eye at sacrificing other people to serve her own selfish motives. I'll have to thank Rudy someday, for doing the heavy lifting for me. I already despised Debra for being a liar, and now I'm doubly justified in seeking my revenge against her for being a cold-hearted killer. I'll be doing the world a service by taking her out of it.

I'm going to murder the bitch, and while I'm at it, I might as well take Mitchell down too, for the hand he played in this. He's the one who installed the security cameras, then backed up his wife's false accusations, which landed Jayden in jail. I know I'll get away with it because no one will suspect me of premeditated murder when big, bad Mitchell's in the room. I'll claim he attacked me, so I had to shoot him in self-defense, and Debra got in the way. Plus, it's her gun, not mine, which will bolster my case. I'll tell the police I was in fear for my life. I was searching for something to defend myself with, and found the gun by chance in the kitchen drawer. I could take Rudy down as well, but I might have to give him a pass, for what he's already suffered in his life. I think the fact that his mother was basically murdered by his future stepmother outweighs all the other stuff he's done.

At the moment, Mitchell is focused on Debra, trying to get her to calm down and shut up, but Rudy sees what I'm doing. He hollers a warning, but Mitchell doesn't hear him because of his wife's screeching.

Rudy holds his hands up in a mute plea to me, and starts backing away. I keep moving toward Debra, my eyes on the prize.

Debra shuts up long enough to draw a breath, and the next thing I hear is Rudy screaming *"Laci's got a gun!"*

Debra goes limp in Mitchell's arms. He lets her fall to the floor, and pivots to face me. "Easy does it," he says, holding his hands open at chest level, the same way Rudy just did. His voice is low and steady. "Take it easy, Laci. You don't want to do this."

He's wrong about that. Dead wrong. I raise the gun in my right hand, aim it at Mitchell's heart, and hook my finger around the trigger. He takes a cautious step closer, speaking in a low, soothing tone. "Give me the gun, Laci. You don't want anybody to get hurt."

Oh, but I do want someone to get hurt. So hurt that they die a slow, painful death. I know Mitchell's a security guard who's probably trained in martial arts, so I've got to be careful he doesn't get close enough to overpower me. *"Get back,"* I scream at him. *"Don't come near me."*

I don't see it coming. Mitchell's hand closes around my wrist and he wrenches my arm down. There's a snapping sound and a hot flash up my arm, and the gun is in his hand. I double over in pain, gasping for breath and clutching my wrist.

37

Rudy

Laci's wrist is broken. Mitchell swiftly unloads the gun and shoves it into his back pocket. There's so much insanity going on here, I don't dare move or open my mouth. Laci's on her knees, crying and gasping for breath, and Mitchell is barking at someone on the phone, probably a 911 operator. Debra seems to have recovered from her deranged outburst, and is pawing through the drawer beside the stove.

Fear jolts me—*she's looking for a knife to attack us with.* But the knives are in their usual place, in the wooden block on the counter. Debra grows more possessed, flinging potholders onto the floor. When she doesn't find what she's looking for, she runs out of the room.

Mitchell ends his call and puts his phone in his pocket. I know from all the television shows I've watched that you're not supposed to hang up on 911 until the cops arrive, but I guess that doesn't apply here, because Mitchell's got the situation under control. He sighs heavily and runs his hands through his hair. "You okay, Rudy?"

I don't respond because Debra has returned. She's standing in the kitchen doorway, holding a gun. It's a lot bigger than the one Laci had. My heart lurches. I'm too petrified to call another warning to Mitchell, but it doesn't matter because he's already zeroed in on it.

Debra's hair is in disarray and her eyes are out of focus. She grips the gun in both hands, and looks like she knows what she's doing. I notice Mitchell is being more cautious with her than he was with Laci, since Debra's had firearms training. He keeps his distance this time, but speaks to her in the same soothing voice. "Put the gun down, Deb, so no one gets hurt."

His words don't seem to register because her wild eyes are fixed on me. "I never wanted you, Rudy," she says in a voice that sounds like a stranger's. "I never liked your slutty mother, and the last thing I wanted to do was raise someone else's brat."

Her words hit me like a sucker punch. "Then why did you marry me?" Mitchell says sharply. "You knew Rudy and I were a package deal."

Debra glares. "Because you needed someone to replace his mother, and I needed a husband." She lets out a harsh laugh. "It was that simple. Problem solved for both of us."

"You don't need to hurt anyone, Deb," Mitchell says, returning to his practiced, soothing tone. "It's over and done with. We don't need to rehash it."

Debra's voice rises to a screech. "Yes, we *do!* I've held this secret long enough, I won't have it weighing on my conscience anymore!" She turns back to me, and she looks like she's come unglued. "It was more than I could bear sometimes, having Ann Marie's son in my house. You were a daily reminder of my guilt. It ate and ate at me, till I couldn't stand it anymore. Kicking you out was the only way I could escape it."

I have to speak up. My mouth has gone bone dry, and I have a hard time getting the words out. "But it was Mitchell who had me evicted, not you. He was the one who went to a lawyer, and dragged me into court."

"No, it wasn't." Mitchell is addressing me now. "I was at my wit's end with you Rudy, but I wouldn't have gone through with it if Debra hadn't agreed to it. You might not believe me, but she was the one who insisted on going ahead." He turns back to his wife, and his face is heavy with regret. "All it would've taken was one word from you," he says softly, "and I would have called the whole thing off."

"*Liar, liar, liar!*" Debra waves the gun around like a lunatic, pointing it first at Mitchell, then me, and then at Laci, who's cowering on her knees. Mitchell makes another attempt to calm her, but she screams at him to shut up. "I can't take anymore!" she shrieks. "Every one of you needs to die, then I'm putting this gun to my head and shooting myself!"

From the front of the house, I hear the storm door open, and relief floods over me. *The police are here!* They're going to swarm into the kitchen and stop this massacre from happening. Debra will drop the gun, and they'll take her away in handcuffs. They'll come back for me soon enough, but at least I'll be alive. I brace myself for their entrance, waiting for the shouted "POLICE!" and a wave of blue filling the room, but it doesn't happen. Instead of the cops, it's Fudgie.

38

Rudy

Fudgie doesn't notice that Debra's got a gun. As he enters the kitchen, his eyes are on Laci, who's curled herself into a blubbering ball on the floor. He rushes over and drops down beside her, and places a gentle hand on her shoulder. "What happened, Lace? Are you hurt?" When she doesn't answer, he lifts his head to look around at the rest of us, and there's Debra, poking the gun's muzzle in his face. Fudgie goes still, his eyes wide with alarm.

"Stand up," Debra orders. "Back away from her." Fudgie's head swivels left, then right, looking from me to Mitchell. Mitchell gives a slight nod, telling him to comply. Fudgie gets to his feet, holds his hands up and takes a few steps backwards.

Debra shifts her stance and scowls down at Laci." You're first." Laci lets out a long, high-pitched whine and squeezes her eyes tight shut. I want to protect her, but I'm too much of a coward to move. Debra sticks her foot out and prods Laci in the side with her toe. "This is what you get, for being a no-good piece of trash." I shy away, ducking my head behind my raised forearms. My vision shrinks to a tunnel. I can't breathe and my heart's going to explode. *Where the hell are the police?*

"Deb," Mitchell pleads. "Don't do it."

Debra pivots to face him. "Center of mass," she says, aiming at Mitchell's torso. "I can't miss at this range." Her smile is cold and merciless. "Good thing you made me take that Basic Pistol class."

Laci has stopped crying. While Debra is distracted by Mitchell, she slowly uncurls from her fetal position and rotates herself onto her hands and knees. I watch her, holding my breath. Maybe she'll be able to slip away unnoticed. Laci casts a swift glance at Debra, then drops her head and takes a tentative crawling step toward the door. One step. Two. The third step catches Debra's eye and her head snaps back to Laci. Swinging her arms around, she screams *"Stop!"* and aims the gun at Laci's head.

It happens so fast, it doesn't seem real. Fudgie lunges. A gunshot blows my hearing out. Mitchell tackles Debra, sending the gun spinning across the kitchen floor. Someone's screaming, but the sound is oddly muffled. There's a lot of blood. It pools on the tiles beneath Laci's head and seeps into the grout lines. She's lying face down with Fudgie sprawled on top of her, one of his skinny legs twisted at an unnatural angle.

I need to help Laci. I force myself to move. I drop to my knees and put my hand on my Fudgie's back. "It's over, Fudge. It's okay now." He doesn't move. I grab his shoulder and shake him. *Why isn't he getting up?* Using both hands, I roll him toward me, off Laci and onto the floor. He's covered in blood from his chin to his chest. He's dead.

I feel like I'm swimming underwater and can't draw a breath. I don't have the strength to raise my arms and reach over Fudgie's body to Laci. There's so much blood in her hair, I'm certain she's dead, too. The bullet must have sliced through Fudgie's neck and struck her in the head.

Across the kitchen, Mitchell's holding tight to Debra, her arms pinned behind her back. She's stopped screaming and hangs like a wet towel in his grip, her face ashen and her breath coming in shuddering gasps. I look at Mitchell and our eyes lock for a second. And then— *finally*—a voice bellows "POLICE" and a swarm of uniformed officers flood into the kitchen with their weapons drawn.

39

Rudy

The cops swoop in and a team of paramedics pushes in behind them. The first medic squats beside Fudgie and presses her gloved fingers to the side of his neck, then puts her stethoscope on and places the end of it on his chest. After a moment, she shakes her head, then turns to help her partner assess Laci. Working together, they dress the wound on the side of Laci's head, and insert an intravenous line. Underneath the smears of blood, Laci's face is sickly pale, and her breathing is shallow and rapid. I'm astonished she's alive.

Debra is handcuffed and taken outside. The police question Mitchell, and secure both guns. I'm sitting at the kitchen table with my head in my hands, trying to stay out of the way. An officer comes over to speak to me. I can tell by the movement of his lips that he's asking if I'm okay, but I can't hear him because my ears are ringing so bad. The paramedics load Laci onto a gurney and wheel her out to the waiting ambulance. A pair of officers escort me and Mitchell to their squad cars, so they can take us to the station for further questioning. As we're leaving, the Medical Examiner's vehicle pulls up and backs into the driveway.

40

Mitchell

I served in Iraq during the Global War on Terror, and was discharged with the rank of Specialist a few months after Saddam Hussein was captured in his spider hole in the desert. My infantry unit sustained a number of fatal incidents with IEDs. I don't ever talk about it, even to my wife. I'm the kind of guy that would rather keep his personal demons to himself, and let the past stay in the past.

After we got engaged, Debra started complaining that I was often moody, and accused me of being "emotionally detached." In her opinion, those faults, along with my stubborn distrust of people, were a direct result of my time in the service. I suppose she was right. Although I'd never been diagnosed, my armchair psychologist wife was convinced I was suffering from a mild case of PTSD.

I never did anything about it, though. I went to work every day and got the job done, same as everybody else. Sure, I was irritable at times. I had a five-year-old boy on my hands, and he wasn't even my biological son. As for me being emotionally detached—what man wouldn't be, after his beautiful young wife gets killed in a car wreck? I'd been in love with Ann Marie since my senior year of high school. Losing her nearly did me in.

It felt like a blessing when Debra came into my life. She eased my sorrow, and took poor, lonely Rudy under her wing. But a few months into our too-soon marriage, I came to the uncomfortable realization that our relationship was hollow. What Debra said on the night she shot

Fudgie was the plain, honest truth—we used each other to fill our respective needs. She thought she needed a man to take care of her, and I needed her to care for Rudy. Love had nothing to do with it.

I genuinely wanted to be the best father to Rudy that I possibly could, but it was a challenge when my wife seemed determined to undermine me. Debra sabotaged every effort I made to teach Rudy to be a responsible person. To our friends and neighbors in Centerport, she was a paragon of generosity and community service; but meanwhile, she was setting Rudy up for failure with her excessive coddling and endless excuses. She turned a blind eye to his unacceptable behavior, and refused to impose consequences when he crossed the line.

I asserted my authority as far as I could, but it eventually boiled down to a domestic power struggle—I was a lowly shift worker, subject to the whims of a supervisor who disliked me, while Debra worked from home, where she was queen of the realm. She'd probably say that's not true, it was the other way around—and sometimes, it was. I can be brusque and pushy, and I usually get my way on the bigger issues; but when it came to Rudy, I always went along with Debra's wishes, in order to keep the peace.

You're probably wondering why I stayed with her. Mostly out of duty, I guess. Loyalty was also a factor, along with a sense of responsibility. Rudy's real father had skipped town, leaving him flapping in the breeze. It wasn't right for a kid to grow up like that, and he needed a mother's love to make up for it. At the time, Debra was the only option I had.

The gun that Debra shot Fudgie with was mine, of course. I should have been more vigilant that night, and prevented her from slipping up to the bedroom and taking it from my nightstand. But the scene was chaotic, and things were happening faster than I could react. I know that's not an acceptable excuse, and my error in judgment is going to torment me for the rest of my days.

41

Rudy

When we're finished answering questions and giving our statements at the police station, Mitchell and I are allowed to leave. Officer Tobin drives us back to the house so we can retrieve our vehicles. Despite the frigid temperature, we stand at the foot of the driveway, discussing what to do next. Mitchell needs to talk to Debra's family, and I'll have to get in touch with Fudgie's grandparents at some point. I have no clue who to contact about Laci, so I'm leaving that up to the police and the hospital's emergency department.

Mitchell stands with his hands shoved in his pockets, looking up at the house. His head is bare and the wind's got his hair standing on end, giving him a shocked appearance. He can't stay here tonight because it's a designated crime scene, and I have no desire to return to my apartment without Fudgie. It's well after midnight, so we decide the easiest thing to do is get a room at a nearby Holiday Inn Express, and deal with things in the morning.

At the hotel, neither of us is ready for sleep. It feels strange to be in the room together, so we go down to the lobby and get instant coffees from a machine, then sit in the empty breakfast room. We sip our drinks and exchange barely a word. Debra's in custody, Laci's in the hospital, Fudgie is dead. There isn't much else we could possibly want to discuss.

Except for one thing. Mitchell wants to hear more of what Edith Scanlon had to say about the night my mother died. "Tell me everything," he says. "Don't leave anything out."

When I've finished telling him the entire story, I feel like I'm going to be sick to my stomach. I stagger into the restroom off the lobby, rush to the nearest stall and hurl into the toilet. I haven't eaten all day so there isn't much that comes up, but my stomach won't stop heaving. When the nausea finally passes, I sit back on my heels, rest my head against the partition, and close my eyes. I'm totally spent.

I hear someone enter the restroom, and recognize Mitchell's step. I'm in a handicap stall because it was the closest one to the door. In my rush to get to the toilet, I didn't turn the latch, so the stall door is ajar. Mitchell pushes it open with one hand and looks down at me on the floor. "Are you all right?"

I nod wearily. He extends a hand, and I allow him to help me to my feet. I go over to the sink to wash my hands and rinse my mouth out, then lean on the counter and stare at my damaged face in the mirror.

Mitchell comes and stands beside me. "No one told the police what she did?" he asks quietly.

I shake my head. "Edith was afraid of getting in trouble, and no one else knew what happened."

Mitchell nods. He looks shell-shocked by the horrible events of the night, and the secrets that have been revealed. If he's anything at all like me, the ugly details of my mother's death have cut him pretty deep. I'm surprised to realize I'm feeling a little sympathy for him. He stares at me in the mirror, and I stare back. We almost look like father and son.

After a minute, Mitchell places a hand on my shoulder and steers me back out to the lobby. The night clerk is seated behind the front desk, listening to music through his ear buds and tapping on his keyboard. He glances up at us for a moment, then returns to his work.

42

Rudy

The bullet that killed Fudgie took a chunk out of the back of Laci's skull, and she had to have surgery to repair it. After the operation, she was in the ICU overnight, then got transferred to a regular floor. I've been up to visit her every day since. The first day, she wasn't aware of my presence because she was asleep the whole time, except for when the nurse came in to do neuro checks, and made me step out of the room. I wasn't sure if I wanted Laci to know I was there anyway, because my presence might upset her too much.

The second day, a woman named Tiff showed up at the same time I did. She stopped me in the hallway after overhearing me ask about Laci at the nurse's station. "You must be her boyfriend Rudy," she said. "Her father told me she had surgery, so I thought I'd better come see her, since I doubt he'll even bother." After thinking about it for a minute, I put it together that Tiff was Jayden's mother. Being around her made me very nervous and uncomfortable. I got away as fast as I could, but not before she insisted on giving me her phone number, so we could keep in touch.

Today is the third day. Laci is awake when I poke my head into her room. She looks surprised to see me, but she doesn't frown or wave me away or anything, so I go on in. I googled *recovery from brain surgery* last night, so I'd have some idea of what she's going through. The article I read mentioned slurred speech and difficulty walking, and a thing they call "brain fog," which includes memory issues, confusion, and clouded thinking. *Kind of like Nan*, I thought. *I can handle this.*

I pull a chair up to the bed, but not too close, in case she doesn't want me near. The head of her bed is raised, and she's staring at me like she's trying hard to remember something. After a moment, she says "Hello, Rudy," but slurs the R so it comes out sounding like a W. When she does that, I can't help scooting my chair a little closer and reaching for her hand. She lets me hold it, but the serious expression on her face doesn't change, and a minute later, she slides her hand out from beneath mine.

It's something, anyway. A sign that maybe she doesn't hate me as much as I had feared. I sit with her for another ten minutes, without either of us talking. Her eyelids start to droop, but then she opens them wide, looks at me, and says, "Is Fudgie okay?"

I don't know how to break the news to her that he's dead. I could pat her hand and tell her he's fine, and wait till she's recovered some more before I tell her the truth. But it would be one more brick in the wall of lies I've already built between her and me, and I'm through with that. Taking her hand again, I choke the words out. "I'm sorry, Laci." I can't bring myself to say *he's dead*, but I know she's caught my meaning because her eyes well up.

Someone comes to take her for an x-ray, so I have to leave. I say goodbye and tell her I love her, and I feel her gaze following me as I walk out. I've decided not to visit anymore, unless she reaches out to me first. I don't know if she'll ever be able to forgive me for what I've done, but at least she knows I still care about her.

•   •   •   •   •

A week after her surgery, Laci is transferred to a rehab facility. I get the news in a lengthy voicemail from Tiff, who doesn't seem to know that Laci and I have broken up. I also learn that Jayden's been released from juvenile detention, and the charges against him have been dropped for lack of evidence. He's living with his mother and stepsisters in a rental house on a street near his school, and he's doing okay after his ordeal.

The relief I feel is huge, and the oppressive weight that's been dragging on my conscience lightens up a bit.

Jayden's release gives me the courage to pay Laci another visit. Her speech is much clearer than before, and there's a walker at her bedside, which she says she'll need to use until her strength and balance improve. I give her a bouquet of pink carnations, which brings a glimmer of a smile to her face. I start to apologize for everything all over again, but she holds her hand up, shushing me. "Not yet, Rudy. It's too much. I need some time to think first." I tell her I understand, and I'm here if she needs me. She nods tiredly and closes her eyes, which I interpret as a sign for me to leave.

•   •   •   •   •

I take over the lease on Fudgie's apartment, and help his grandparents when they come to pack up his things. I wait a week before moving my futon into the bedroom. It feels weird to be sleeping in there at first, because it's Fudgie's old room, but after a few days, it starts to feel normal. I continue going to my classes at City Tech, and keep working at the warehouse after school and on the weekends. I try to stay busy because that's the only way I can keep the guilt and the flashbacks at bay. I'm living in a constant state of paranoia, waiting for the police to show up at my door, and place me under arrest for the stolen gun and the break-in. But the weeks pass, and no one comes.

•   •   •   •   •

One rainy Saturday afternoon in mid-March, Mitchell calls and asks if I'll meet him for a beer at Tully's. It's more of an order than an invitation, so I beat back my anxiety and tell him I'll be there in fifteen minutes.

I see him standing at the bar when I walk in. He apparently changed his mind about the beer because he's got a Coke in his hand, which is all right with me. I order one as well, and we go over to a table by the window. His face is drawn and his clothes are hanging loose on him, as though he's lost weight. "How've you been?" he asks, and I tell him I'm fine.

I can see he's checking out my face, but trying not to be obvious about it. When we stayed at the hotel on the night of the shooting, I ended up telling him the whole Trey story over breakfast the next morning, since my injuries were so obvious, and I couldn't avoid saying something. The cuts have healed and there's only a trace of yellow remaining on my left cheekbone. Pretty soon, there'll be nothing left.

I talk about my classes, then Mitchell talks about his job at the hospital. His supervisor is moving out of state, so he's applying for the vacant position. I tell him that's great, and wish him good luck.

The conversation stalls, and we both stare out the window at the rain-slicked cars in the parking lot. "How is Laci doing?" Mitchell says after a while. Like Tiff, he isn't aware that we've broken up, either. Thinking about Laci tears open the barely-healed hole in my heart, but discussing my love life with my stepfather is the last thing I'd ever do. "She's doing well," I say. "Going to physical therapy and stuff. They expect her to make a full recovery."

Mitchell nods. "Glad to hear it."

I don't want to bring it up, but I feel like I have to ask. "How is Debra?"

Mitchell's jaw goes tight and he taps his fingers on the table. "She was hospitalized briefly for a psychological evaluation, then there was a hearing, at which they determined she's competent to stand trial for homicide."

I'd heard about it on the news, but didn't care to follow the story too closely. Fudgie's gone, and there's nothing the law can do to bring him back. Debra can end her days in jail, for all I care.

I notice Mitchell has barely touched his Coke. He sets his glass aside and squares his shoulders, like he's getting ready to say something important. I tense up, waiting. If he's going to bring the hammer down on me, now's the time to let me know.

"You heard they let that kid go?" he says.

I clasp my hands beneath the table. "Yeah, I heard."

Mitchell's looking intently at the TV screen above the bar, instead of at me. "The detective told me there wasn't enough evidence to nail him for the break-in. They could've charged him with trespassing since they had the video from our cameras, but they let him go because the kid informed on another guy, the one who planted the stolen gun on him. Turned out, the guy used the gun to commit an armed robbery, so the kid's testimony helped put him away."

I don't know how to respond. I clutch my hands tighter, waiting for him to go on. Mitchell keeps staring up at the TV. "Not enough evidence," he repeats.

He has every right to turn me in for what I've done, but his manner's so cryptic, I can't tell what he's decided. "Does—does that mean—" I stammer. "Are you—?"

Mitchell drags his eyes back to me and slowly shakes his head. "No, Rudy. I'm not going to pursue it. We've both been through too much already. I don't see what good it would do to drag it all up again."

We switch the subject to basketball, and discuss the March Madness brackets that have just come out. A waitress stops by our table, and Mitchell asks her for two more Cokes and a large order of Buffalo wings for us to split. For the rest of the afternoon, we eat wings and watch basketball, and when the check comes, Mitchell picks it up.

ACKNOWLEDGMENTS

Thank you to the staff at Black Rose Writing for once again allowing me the honor and privilege of bringing another novel to my loyal readers. I'm also grateful for my fellow authors at BRW, whose generous camaraderie and excellent advice have helped me find my way through the world of writing and publishing. Looking forward to many more AuthorFests in beautiful San Antonio! Special thanks go to my dedicated and insightful editor, Rowan Humphries, and to my topnotch beta readers—Ralph Uttaro, Ted Obourn and Brendan Humphries. Your feedback has been invaluable and your ongoing support is much appreciated.

ABOUT THE AUTHOR

Regina Buttner was raised in beautiful upstate New York where she spent many happy years exploring the small towns and scenic hiking trails of the Adirondack mountain region. She recently traded the snowy northern winters for the tropical breezes of the Sunshine State where her favorite pastimes are kayaking among the mangroves, strolling the gorgeous beaches, and teaching tricks to her crafty little corgi, Pekoe. Connect with her on her website: www.reginabuttner.com.

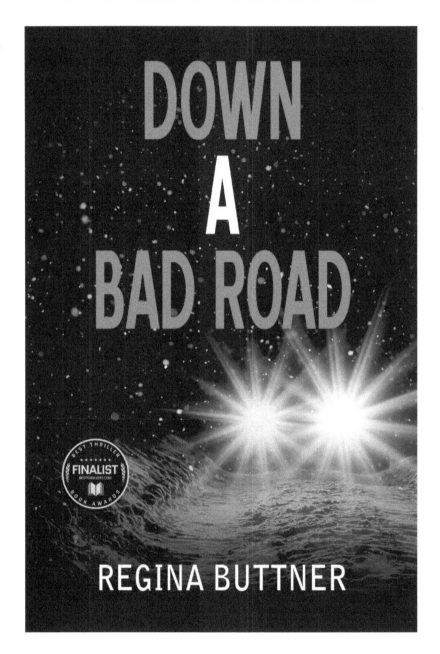

NOTE FROM REGINA BUTTNER

Word-of-mouth is crucial for any author to succeed. If you enjoyed *The Revenge Paradox*, please leave a review online—anywhere you are able. Even if it's just a sentence or two. It would make all the difference and would be very much appreciated.

Thanks!
Regina Buttner

We hope you enjoyed reading this title from:

www.blackrosewriting.com

Subscribe to our mailing list – *The Rosevine* – and receive **FREE** books, daily deals, and stay current with news about upcoming releases and our hottest authors.
Scan the QR code below to sign up.

Already a subscriber? Please accept a sincere thank you for being a fan of Black Rose Writing authors.

View other Black Rose Writing titles at www.blackrosewriting.com/books and use promo code **PRINT** to receive a **20% discount** when purchasing.

Printed in the USA
CPSIA information can be obtained
at www.ICGtesting.com
JSHW020820150624
64643JS00011B/7

9 781685 134969